Willowkeep

OTHER BOOKS AND AUDIO BOOKS

BY JULIE DAINES

A Blind Eye

Unraveled

Eleanor and the Iron King

Willowkeep

A REGENCY ROMANCE

JULIE DAINES

Covenant Communications, Inc.

Cover image © *Lee Avison* / Arcangel Images

Published by Covenant Communications, Inc.
American Fork, Utah

This is a work of fiction. The characters, names, incidents, places, and dialogue are either products of the author's imagination, and are not to be construed as real, or are used fictitiously.

Printed in the United States of America
First Printing: June 2016

22 21 20 19 18 17 16 10 9 8 7 6 5 4 3 2 1

ISBN 978-1-52440-040-8

For John

Our own Captain America, Luke Skywalker, Hulk, Peeta Mellark, Jean Valjean, Spider-Man, Batman, Phantom of the Opera, and so much more.

CHAPTER ONE

"Twelve thousand a year?" Charlotte stared at the letter in her hands. So much money could never be hers. "That's obscene. Can it be right?"

Mr. Sutton nodded, his furry hair swaying to and fro. Between the bushy gray tangle atop his head and the long spray of beard, his eyes and large red nose were all what set him apart from a sheepdog.

"I assure you, Miss Darby, that is the amount." The solicitor removed another paper from his case and put it on her lap. "From Willowkeep, the estate in Kent." He tapped his finger on the document as if somehow that made it more believable.

"How can this be? I didn't even know the man." Until this morning, she'd had no idea he'd existed at all. 'Twas far too much to take in before noon.

"He was your mother's brother. Your uncle," Mr. Sutton explained again. He frowned at her as though her disbelief made her unfit to inherit. But he was the one who'd shown up with no warning, flashing his papers and his fancy case. Who could blame her for being flustered?

It wasn't that the words didn't make sense. She had wits enough for this. Charlotte's difficulty lay in the impossibleness of the situation. When she went to bed last night, she was Charlotte Darby, daughter of a shipping merchant, penniless and forgotten. This morning, a stranger had rapped on her door, and now she was an heiress. Her mother—God rest her soul—had never bothered to mention this generous uncle. Generous and dead.

Charlotte's little sister snatched the paper from her hands.

"Susie, no!" Charlotte lunged for the page as Susie threw it at the fireplace. It fluttered to the ground, missing the hearth by a good three feet. "Susie, you mustn't burn these. They are very important."

Mr. Sutton retrieved the document and proceeded to smooth it on his lap. He scowled at Susie. "Perhaps you should call for the nurse. It may be easier to finish our business without . . . the child."

As far as Charlotte was concerned, her business *was* the child.

"I'd love to, Mr. Sutton, but as you can see, I've run low on blunt. I can no longer afford a nurse."

The older man's brows came together in a jumble of gray fuzz. No doubt he thought what everyone thought: the girl ought to be locked away in some kind of asylum. Charlotte would die first. Susie was her sister. And family did not abandon family. Not anymore.

Charlotte had tried often enough to get work as an abigail or scullery maid—or, worse, a laborer down at the fishing docks with the rest of the rabble. None would hire her with a slow-witted child in tow.

Susie was nearly eight, though she looked more like four. Old enough for a regular child to find work of her own, getting her finger snipped off cleaning the mules up at the cotton mills. Susie could never work, nor could she be left home alone. But taking her out was worst of all—the stares, the whispers, the stones.

Mr. Sutton cleared his throat and went on. "Prior to your uncle's death, he altered his last will and testament, bequeathing to you the estate, inclusive with all its holdings, lands, and tenants, and with full and legal rights to all income accumulated therewith. Those are the facts." He shuffled his papers into an orderly stack. "His only stipulation is that you leave Kingston upon Hull and return to Willowkeep."

How could she return to a place she'd never been? Her mother had lived there. Grown up there, according to the sheepdog. Perhaps that was what he meant by *return*. Return to the family estate.

She had little enough left tying her to Hull. Naught but the graves in the city cemetery, for the church would have none of her mother or brothers buried within its holy grounds.

Strange and sudden as this news had come, it was a blessing from heaven. More than a blessing. A miracle, to be sure. Because of her uncle, she had a house. Not just a house, an estate. Worth more money than Charlotte could fathom.

Charlotte had made her last twenty pounds stretch for nigh on two years. She'd dismissed the last of the servants and cared for her sister on her own. She'd purchased foods discarded by the grocers. Three months ago she'd sold her mother's china—at least what was left of it that wasn't broken.

Any day she expected the landlord to appear and toss them out, forcing them to make a home shivering their bones under the bridge.

Now she'd never have to worry about money again. Her dear uncle's death—God rest his soul—couldn't have come at a better time.

"'Course I accept. Thank you, sir."

The man grunted. "Don't thank me. This was not of my choosing. If you must thank anyone, thank your uncle."

She would. Every blessed day for the rest of her life. Only one problem. "What was his name again?"

"Kelton. Walter Kelton."

That was her mother's name—Louisa Kelton—before marrying her father. Her mother had never spoken of her family or her life before she married Thomas Darby. Never.

"Mr. Sutton," Charlotte said. "Why me? Has he no children of his own?"

The solicitor shook his head. "None." He tucked his papers away in his case and pulled it closed. "I have taken the liberty of arranging transportation for you. Tomorrow week, the steward will come to collect you and the child. He will accompany you into Kent and help you get settled. Your"—he glanced round the room with a crinkled nose—"belongings will be brought by coach."

He stood. "I will leave you now. If you have questions, I suggest you take them up with the steward, Mr. Morland."

Charlotte hurried to her feet and dipped the man a quick curtsey.

He huffed as he turned and walked out the door. Through the window, Mr. Sutton's yellow post chaise pulled away, clattering down the street.

Susie's hand slipped into hers. Charlotte looked down at her sister's large blue eyes and smiled as she hadn't done in a very long time. She grasped Susie about the middle and swung her round and round in tight circles.

"We're saved, little sister. We are saved."

CHAPTER TWO

Henry Morland had no time for this. His duties as steward did not include traveling for two days to the north country to collect a spinster and her orphaned sister. Then two more days to get home. It was a waste of resources. They could have taken a servant with them and been perfectly fine on the public coach.

But Mr. Sutton had threatened Henry's job. Not that Mr. Sutton had authority to terminate his position. No, that privilege now belonged to Miss Charlotte Darby, a woman none of them had ever heard of. So Henry had obliged, and he would be civil and generous and servile no matter how unpleasant the journey. In any case, this Miss Darby couldn't be worse than the old scarecrow Mr. Kelton had left behind.

The coach rolled along, following the River Humber as it approached the city of Kingston upon Hull—a fast-growing shipping port of the north. The landscape outside Henry's window turned from farmland to houses to merchant shops.

Then the docks appeared, lining the River Hull where it fed into the Humber. Boats packed the river so tightly one could almost cross it leaping deck to deck. Most of the vessels were small fishing boats, but a few frigates and a brigantine were anchored out in the harbor. His father would have loved to see this.

Henry had stopped off in London on his way north to visit Henry Morland Senior at the Marshalsea. His father's health was quickly failing. The old man wouldn't survive in debtor's prison much longer. Henry paid the warden the prison rent for his father's keep, plus extra for a doctor, but unless he could pay off his father's debts soon, it would be too late.

Coachman Jim brought the carriage to a stop in front of a modest townhome backed up against some warehouses and the docks. A small stack of luggage waited outside the door on the cobblestone road. At least she was punctual.

Jim opened the carriage door, and Henry stepped out, taking a moment to stretch his legs. He breathed in the air, heavy with the stench of rancid animal fat. Not the finest location in town to live, though he had no doubt it was not the worst. He tapped on the front door.

The door opened, and a small child with the bluest eyes he'd ever seen stared up at him.

"Hello," Henry said. "I'm looking for Miss Charlotte Darby and her sister."

More staring.

"Are you Susan Darby?"

The girl blinked once but did not give up her staring match.

The eyes that were at first charming now unsettled Henry. "Can you take me to Miss Darby, please? It's time to go."

The girl's lip quivered exactly once before she burst out in a wail that would likely summon the fire brigade. Henry knelt in front of her, desperate to make her stop. "I'm sorry." He patted the child on her head. It only made the wailing louder.

Henry had little experience with children, but there was something off about this girl. The look in her eyes, the slightly odd placement of her ears. Her head perhaps the tiniest bit too large for her body. Even the way she walked. She must be five or six, but she seemed much younger.

A patter of footsteps sounded on the floor above. He followed their progress across the ceiling, down what must be a rear staircase, and then a young woman came running full speed from a back room.

"Susie, what's all this?" She scowled at Henry but not before he glimpsed that she had the same enchanting blue eyes as the younger girl. They must be sisters. Which meant they were likely his cargo.

"I'm so sorry. I didn't mean to frighten her." He stood and bowed. "I'm Henry Morland, from Willowkeep. I'm here to escort you and your sister home. I presume you are Miss Charlotte Darby?"

"I am," she said over the din of the crying. She pulled a handkerchief from her sleeve and used it on the girl's nose, then lifted the child onto her hip and whispered into her ear. The crying diminished to hiccoughing breaths, though the girl still clung to her sister with a formidable grip.

She gestured for Henry to step inside. "And this here's Susie. She's none too happy over leaving her home. She don't like change. And she don't like strangers." Miss Darby turned so her body completely shielded her younger sister.

Henry might as well have been a cutthroat for all the welcome in her eyes. Even so, he could hardly look away.

She was no spinster, that much was clear. She couldn't be more than nineteen or twenty. Dark strands of hair fell out of the knot on the back of her head, wisping and floating around her face. Her eyelashes were dark too, creating a fascinating frame around her eyes.

"Sir?" she asked.

"Yes." He straightened his coat. "Let me apologize again for unsettling your sister."

"You seem awfully young to be a steward. After the sheepdog from London, I expected someone . . . different."

The sheepdog? She must mean Mr. Sutton. If she'd dropped Henry in the same category as Sutton, Henry was not making a good impression.

"Yes, well. My father was the steward before me. He retired seven years ago." He'd say no more on that subject. It would only further lower her opinion of him. "Mr. Kelton offered the job to me even though I was only twenty at the time." Apparently neither he nor Miss Darby had fallen within the expectations of the other. "The carriage is ready whenever you are, Miss Darby."

She turned and glanced around the barren room. Henry did the same. A threadbare sofa and a chair leaking stuffing stood like weathered statues in a ruined monastery. The wallpaper peeled in strips of faded blue and gray, while a few brighter squares revealed where pictures had once hung. An odd collection of fist-sized stones was piled next to the door.

"I was just upstairs, looking at everything empty," she said. "I've never lived anywhere but here." She hefted Susan higher up on her hip. The child appeared all too grown to be carried like an infant. She laid her head on Miss Darby's shoulder.

"Gaw, it's hard to leave this place." And for the first time, she smiled at him, but there was a sadness to her. "There's nothing for it. We haven't a sixpence to scratch with, so we're very grateful of your generous offer."

Henry choked. Where did she learn to talk like that? Down at the docks, no doubt. "Miss Darby, I'm only the steward. I assure you I had nothing to do with it."

She let the child slide to the floor, though the girl still held fast to Miss Darby's leg.

"The baggage I saw outside, that is all you're bringing with you?"

She nodded. "I sold most everything I could that would fetch a price." She shook her reticule, and some coins clinked together. "Got nearly five quid." She wagged her eyebrows, clearly pleased with her earnings.

In her new life, that was a trifle. "You do understand that you are now one of the richest young ladies in the country, do you not? You didn't need to trouble yourself with selling belongings. If you need five pounds, it is yours to command."

She blinked at him, looking exactly like her sister when she'd first answered the door. "It's hard to imagine, though, isn't it? And I couldn't let these things go to waste. I s'pose it'll take awhile to feel real."

Understandably so. Especially if she'd lived her whole life in this small home. Henry knew very little about Miss Darby and her family. Just that her parents and his former employer were estranged for years, until on his deathbed, when Mr. Kelton astonished everyone with the last-minute adjustment to his will.

"I've just got one last box upstairs, and I'm ready to go."

"Would you like me to fetch it for you?" he asked.

"No, no. Won't be but a flash." She pried Susan's hands off her legs and hurried back the way she'd come.

The little girl stood in the center of the room. He'd already brought her to tears once, and being left alone with her again didn't seem entirely wise. Susan sniffled, her face twisting into a woeful expression.

"Hello, there." He smiled at her, his best and friendliest grin.

Her frown deepened.

"I'm Henry. What's your name?" He already knew, of course, but could think of nothing better to say. His only goal was to not mention the word *leaving*. That and keep her wails from going off.

Her bottom lip quivered, jutting from her mouth. He was failing. What did children like? Sweets? He had none. Toys? No. Stories? Again, nothing. "Do you like horses?"

The girl's face brightened.

"Horses?" he said again. He'd never been good at tête-à-tête; still, he hadn't expected his greatest challenge would come from a child.

Little Susan walked toward him, a slow and ungainly gait. She lifted her arms, reaching for him.

Good heavens. Did she expect him to pick her up? Was it even his place to do so? What would Miss Darby say when she returned and he was holding her sister?

The girl's face crumpled, her lower lip creeping out into the familiar frown.

"Bother." He lifted Susan into his arms. "Now what?"

The child opened her mouth and paused until at last a faint word escaped. "Powpy." It was the first time she'd spoken.

She'd seemed interested in the horses, and that sounded a bit like *pony*. So he carried her out into the street toward the four poorly matched animals pulling the Kelton family carriage.

"Just going to show the little one the horses, Jim," he said to the coachman.

Jim grinned at Henry. "If it keeps her from howlin' again." He climbed down from the bench and took hold of the lead horse's straps, keeping the beast steady. This had been by far the worst set of horses they'd picked up along the journey, but at least they were gentle.

Henry ran his hand along the animal's neck. "See, he's a nice fellow."

Susan smiled.

"Do you want to pet him?" He took the girl's hand and showed her how to stroke the horse's neck. "Only down, see. Down and off. Down and off."

He released her hand, and she continued, just like he'd shown her.

"Well done."

Little Susan's brows wrinkled in concentration as she continued stroking the horse.

"Susie?" Miss Darby called from inside.

Henry dared not turn away lest the child burst into tears. "Out here."

Miss Darby stepped outside, carrying what looked like a small jewelry case tucked under her arm. She stopped midstep and gaped openmouthed at Henry.

He shrugged. "I hope you don't mind. She wanted to see the horses."

Susan turned her head and smiled at Miss Darby. The small girl's face transformed into something almost as lovely as the returning smile she got from her older sister. Miss Darby's blue eyes lit up, and some hidden floodgate of devotion opened in them as she walked over and caressed her sister's hand.

Henry had never seen anything like it. Not from his mother; she'd died years ago, and Henry hardly remembered her. Certainly not from his father, who reserved most of his affection for whatever bottle was within reach. His sister came closest. Jane was very dear to him, and he to her. But such an outpouring of tenderness from a single glance had never been directed at him.

"We're ready now." Miss Darby's eyes turned to Henry, and the moment was gone. "Sorry to keep you waiting." She smiled at him, a mere trifle compared to the look she'd bestowed on her sister. Then her finger went to her mouth, and she chewed on her nail.

"I don't think you understand that I am in your employ," Henry said. "It is my job to wait for you, and as you can see"—he nodded toward the child stroking the horse's neck—"I've made the most of it." He set Susan down and opened the carriage door. "Shall we put that behind with the trunks?" Henry asked, pointing to her case.

She gripped it tighter. "No." She lifted the lid of the rosewood box, revealing a matching set of sapphire earrings and an enormous single sapphire necklace. The sun caught the jewels, reflecting pale blue lights onto her face. "These were my mother's. All I've got left of her."

"They're stunning."

They must have come from Louisa's parents. A coming-out gift or some such thing. They suited Miss Darby perfectly, the setting simple yet elegant, displaying the sapphires for the lovely jewels they were. No distractions. She could have sold them and lived comfortably for the next ten years.

"Most certainly they should ride with us." Henry stowed them beneath the seat. When he turned back, she had a letter in her hands.

"Would it be too much trouble to drop this off at my father's warehouse?"

"Not if that is your wish."

"It's just 'round the corner, quayside along the river. Burton Shipping."

Henry glanced at Jim, and the coachman nodded.

He offered a hand to Miss Darby, and she took it, holding tight as she stepped up and into the carriage. Henry lifted Susan in behind her.

Miss Darby had taken the rear-facing seat. It seemed it was going to take some time for her to come to terms with her new situation. A mercy, then, that all the neighbors in Kent were in town for the Season.

"You sit here." Henry pointed to the front-facing bench upholstered in blue-striped velvet.

"I don't want to take your seat."

Henry laughed. "This is your carriage. They are all your seats. Besides, a gentleman would never make a lady ride backwards." Not that he was a gentleman. As her steward, he had no claim to any seat.

Miss Darby considered for a moment, then stood and switched sides, taking her sister too. She looked very sheepish as Henry sat across from her.

Though he sat facing reverse, the scenery was already infinitely improved from when he'd come up from Kent. Of course, also as her steward, he should not be noticing such things.

The carriage lurched forward and clacked across the cobblestones as Jim took it to the end of the lane and turned it. Henry motioned toward the ships out in the Humber. "Are any of those your father's ships?"

Miss Darby nodded. "Yes. That one there, the frigate in the dry dock. Or it was, until it were commandeered by His Majesty's Royal Navy to fight the French. It's being fitted up with cannons as we speak."

Henry watched the flurry of men scrambling around the dock.

She scooted onto the edge of her seat. "And there, look there. A greenlander—a whaling cat. Looks like they caught one. Those barrels there are filled with blubber. Ever seen a whale, Mr. Morland?"

He shook his head. "No, I can't say that I have." Henry peered out the window at the whaling ship. "Where is it?"

She laughed. "They don't bring them in, only rarely. They cut 'em up still floating in the ice. I've seen a few, when father were here and he'd take me down. Great black beasts with eyes near big as my whole body. You've never seen nothing like it."

He didn't doubt that for a moment. The only whale he'd ever seen was a drawing in a children's alphabet book.

"One time they pulled in a shark, big as a smack, it was, with teeth like a thousand knife points. And when they cut it open, can you guess?" She sat on the edge of her seat.

"No, I cannot."

"The head of an African slave." She nodded solemnly. "I saw it with my own eyes." She leaned back. "They said the shark must've swum up from the southern waters. Lost its way or something. Mad Milly said it were cursed for eating the head of a person and that's why it ended up in the cold water of the North Sea."

Henry had never heard such a tale. "Well, that is quite something." It came to Henry that this girl's life had been vastly different from his own.

The coach stopped in front of a large, redbrick building with a sign over the door. *Burton Shipping.* Under the thin coat of paint, Henry made out the words *Darby and Burton.* After Miss Darby's father had died, Burton must have changed the name.

Jim opened the door and lowered the step.

"Would you like me to take it in?" Henry asked.

She shook her head. "No. Best I do this myself." But she didn't move. She just stared at her letter.

Henry leaned forward enough to see it was addressed to Mr. Thomas Darby. Her father, who had passed away. At least that was what Sutton had said. But if her father was dead, why the letter? "Shall I accompany you?" Henry offered.

She smiled. "Yes. I would like that very much."

Henry stepped out and handed Miss Darby down. He reached for her sister, but Miss Darby stopped him.

"It's best if she don't come out."

If that was her wish. As long as leaving her alone in the carriage wouldn't result in another fit.

"Jim, eyes on the little one, eh?" Henry closed the carriage door. "We'll be right back."

Miss Darby took a deep breath, straightening tall, and, with surprising dignity, walked into the warehouse.

The room inside was filled with every object imaginable. Barrels labeled *Whale Oil*, coils of ropes, bolts of cotton and wool, crates of whale-bone combs—anything that could or would be shipped.

A tall, lean man came forward. "Miss Darby." He had narrow-set eyes and a thin mouth, so when he grinned, his lips vanished.

"Mr. Burton." She dipped her head.

"Word is yer moving out."

"Yes." She held out her letter. "I would like to leave this here . . . for my father . . . in case. He won't know where to find me."

The man's grin broadened, and his eyes flicked to Henry, then back to Miss Darby. "He ain't comin' back. He's gone, an' we both know it."

She looked down at her worn halfboots.

Burton took the letter from her. "Hear yer swimming in lard now. Rich as Croesus, they say. How 'bout that."

Henry didn't at all care for the steely glint in Burton's eye. He stepped forward. "Mr. Burton. Pleasure to meet you. I'm Henry Morland, steward for the estate in question."

"In question?" He turned his attention on Henry.

"Yes. It seems there is a stepson with a claim. Set to inherit. Entailed to a male heir. A bunch of legal jumble."

Mr. Burton frowned.

"It's all a bit of a mess. Miss Darby will be lucky if she gets anything."

"But I—" Miss Darby started to protest.

"Our coach is waiting, though most likely it will be a pointless trip." He rolled his eyes at him as if this weasely merchant was the one person in the world who could understand the inconveniences of having one's time unnecessarily wasted. He put his hand on Miss Darby's elbow and turned her toward the door.

"Mr. Burton." Miss Darby curtseyed quickly as Henry gave her a nudge to exit.

"Mr. Burton." Henry bowed and hurried them both away.

Outside, Miss Darby looked up at him, her eyes full of questions.

Henry opened the carriage door. "Inside."

Susan had her face pressed against the opposite window, watching the cargo ships loading and unloading.

When the carriage door closed, Miss Darby gave Henry a panicked look. "I thought it was to be mine. I told the landlord to find a new tenant. If it's entailed away, we'll be on the street."

Henry smiled. "I do hope you'll forgive me, but I didn't like the look in that man's eyes. Perhaps it's best he doesn't know that the daughter of his former business partner has recently come into money. Don't you agree?"

A smile slowly spread across her face, her blue eyes radiant inside their ring of dark lashes. "Shamming it. To throw him off. You are a cunning man, Mr. Morland."

Henry settled back into his seat as the carriage jolted across the cobblestones again. "At your service, my lady." Though a lady wouldn't be caught dead using such cant.

She laughed, and little Susan laughed too, clearly having no idea why. As the dock grew distant, little Susan stood, turned, and plopped herself down right next to Henry.

Miss Darby leaned toward the window, following the road without looking back. She withdrew the handkerchief from her sleeve and twisted it in her hands. She was leaving her old world behind, her new world far beyond her imagining. Only natural she should feel it keenly.

Susan tugged on her sister's hand. Miss Darby turned from the window and stashed her handkerchief back into her sleeve, then opened her reticule. Out came a piece of arrowroot. She handed it to Susan, and the child settled onto the bench, chewing on the plant.

The two girls' features were astonishingly similar. Henry had never seen a picture of Miss Darby's mother—Louisa Kelton—he assumed they'd all been removed after she'd run off with Thomas Darby. Mr. Walter Kelton, Louisa's twin brother, had hazel eyes, so perhaps Miss Darby's brilliant blue eyes came from her father, along with her dark hair.

And what of this Thomas Darby? If he wasn't dead, where had he disappeared to? Miss Darby must have some kind of hope that he might be alive since she left a letter for him. Burton seemed quite sure of the opposite.

If only Henry could have gotten her away before the people of Hull learned of her inheritance. Burton would not be the last man interested in her new wealth. He hated to think what some desperate dockworker might do to get his fingers on her money.

Which brought up a new question. It was not really his business, but as steward, it would be good to know in case some scheming rogue showed up claiming more than he ought. "I hope we have not torn you away from too many beaus."

She snorted. "Not hardly."

He pressed further. "None of the sailors managed to catch your eye?"

"I won't never marry," she announced.

Quite a bold statement. She must be teasing. "Never?"

"Never," she repeated with great earnestness. "I can't."

Henry stared at her, trying not to imagine the worst. She kept her gaze out the window. He could not question her further and still maintain even a sliver of propriety.

At last she gave him a playful grin. "They're not much for looking at, sailors. If you ask me, they've all got shifty eyes." She considered for a moment. "Besides, I always get the feeling they prefer the convenients to a respectable lass." She nodded in the direction of a rather shady part of town.

Henry could not get Miss Darby away from the docks fast enough.

CHAPTER THREE

Charlotte hadn't a notion what drew Susie to Mr. Morland. She'd never seen her sister take to another man like she had to him. Usually people treated her like chaff—the parts that got thrown out like refuse. Susie had sat beside him nearly all day yesterday and the day before.

They'd had to stop for the night twice, once in Grantham and once in Royston. Mr. Morland said the trip should take two days, but because of Susie, it was taking three. This morning Susie again wanted a seat by Mr. Morland. He didn't seem to mind, though Charlotte wasn't convinced he loved it neither.

"I want to thank you again for all your help with little Susie." Charlotte whispered so as not to wake her sister, whose head lay planted on Mr. Morland's lap.

"My pleasure." He had a kind face, and handsome—with brown eyes that matched his brown hair.

Charlotte smoothed her hair back into her topknot. She'd put it up barely an hour ago, and already pieces of it were everywhere. She must seem a ragamop to Mr. Morland, with his fine clothes and fine ways. All his staring at her only made her more uncomfortable.

"Not everyone is so tolerant of such a child."

"I wonder," Mr. Morland said. "If you don't mind my asking, what exactly is wrong with Susan? Was she simply born . . . ?"

"Sackless? Shanny-pated? Dicked in the knob?"

"That's not what I was going to say." Mr. Morland's voice was stern, but he rather looked about to laugh. "Nor should you, mind."

Charlotte had spent most of her life trying to keep Susie hidden from the world. She lifted her sister's hand, so smooth and warm. Her face like an angel while she slept.

"Aye, she were born this way."

He looked down at Susie, asleep with her face pressed up on his fancy breeches. "I'm sorry. That must have been a trying time for your family."

He had no idea. 'Twas what drove her mother to the river and her father to the sea. "Yes, sir."

"I'm surprised she's not . . . that you . . ."

He didn't need to finish his thought. Charlotte knew exactly what he was going to say: that she'd kept such a child at home. Most would have sent her to an asylum—or let her wander into the bay. She was sick through to her soul of people treating Susie like an abomination.

Charlotte pulled the sleeping girl off Mr. Morland's lap and onto her own side of the carriage. "She's not some used-up piece of horseflesh to be sent to the gluer at the first sign a trouble. She's my sister. I'd be alone in this world without her. Family does not abandon family."

Mr. Morland's face went slack. "Miss Darby, I do beg your pardon. In no way did I mean to imply that your sister is without worth."

Charlotte smoothed her sister's hair, pulling her close.

"And certainly I'm not suggesting you abandon her."

Thus far Mr. Morland had been a complete gentleman, 'specially when compared to Mr. Sutton and most of the population of Hull. Charlotte had good reasons for keeping her sister hidden.

Susie whimpered as she looked up at Charlotte, then over at her former seat beside the steward.

Mr. Morland reached out and placed his hand on Charlotte's, his eyes fixed on hers. "I've only known Susan for two days, and already I'm better for it. It was not my intent to disparage her or you."

Mr. Morland's fingers gave Charlotte's a little squeeze. His hand was soft. No calluses and burns where rigging lines had ripped through. No scars from a slip of the knife while gutting fish. He really was a gentleman. The most gentlemanlike man she'd ever met. He treated her with a respect she'd never known before. And here she went blowing off her top.

"It's all right," Charlotte said.

He nodded and leaned back, stretching out his legs. He was far too tall to fit in the carriage. Every time they stopped to change horses, he spent the first five minutes just shaking out his legs.

"Tell me about Willowkeep," Charlotte said.

"Gladly. The first thing you need to know is that you will not be the only person living there. You will have Mrs. Kelton to contend with."

"Mrs. Kelton?" Her grandmother perhaps? If Charlotte still had family living, that would be something. She was down to the dry bones when it came to relatives these days.

"She is your uncle Walter's second wife. No blood relation. She was to inherit until your uncle had a change of heart. The estate belonged to your grandfather, Giles Kelton—Walter and your mother's father. When Louisa married your father, Giles did not approve. She was disowned by the family. Completely cut off."

A low-born shipping merchant must have been a poor match for a Kelton of Willowkeep. So Louisa had been discarded. Deserted by family. Seemed Charlotte and her mother had more in common than she'd known.

"Walter and your mother were twins," Henry continued. "My father told me it never sat well with Walter that Louisa had been so utterly cast off. When Walter knew he was going to die, he changed his will and gave you everything."

Charlotte still couldn't believe how it had all come about. If her uncle had had guilt to mollify, he could have just left her some money; she didn't need the whole estate. There must have been some reason for him to change his will like that. Something more than regret about his forsaken sister.

"What about Mrs. Kelton?"

"He left her a goodly sum. She need not stay at Willowkeep if you do not wish it." He lifted his arm to make room for Susie, who'd deserted Charlotte again for his side of the carriage. "It will take her time to secure new lodgings, however. So you shall have to endure her company for at least a few months."

"Endure?" If Charlotte had an aunt—even a stepaunt—that was reason to rejoice.

Charlotte had spent the last hour singing to Susie in an attempt to make her stop running from window to window and treading on Mr. Morland's feet. Three days in a carriage had been quite an ordeal. Every time they'd stopped to change horses, Mr. Morland had had to coax Susie back into the coach with a cherry comfit. He'd picked up a whole bag of them at the very first stop outside of Hull.

With a lurch, the carriage turned off the main road, and Susie flopped onto the bench with a squeal.

"Here we are, then," Mr. Morland said. "This drive takes us to Willowkeep."

Charlotte peered out the window, but all she could see was field after field of vines growing up enormously high poles. "Is that beans? Whoever would want that many beans?"

"It is hops," Mr. Morland explained. "This is all Willowkeep land. These fields provide the estate a good portion of its income, along with numerous investments."

"Who lives in those?" Charlotte asked, pointing to the row of houses that looked like upside-down witch hats tipped in white.

"Those are the oasts, where the hops are dried. Come September, these fields will fill with hoppers who come from London for the harvest. Whole families of them."

Moving to the country was supposed to mean less people, not more. "And what am I s'posed to do with all of them?"

"You don't have to do anything with them. That's my job."

Seemed to Charlotte that Mr. Morland was a very busy man. Likely she'd not see much of him once they arrived. Which would be any moment now that they were on the final drive.

She looked out the window again, but a double row of tall oaks lined the lane and blocked her view. If only her hair would stay put. She tried to smooth it back into her knot, but without a complete repinning, it did no good.

"We're almost there, Susie." Gaw, the child was a disaster.

Charlotte tugged on Susie's frock and made an attempt to tidy her hair. Restraining her sister against her will was like herding cats. It simply could not be done.

After several minutes on the drive, Charlotte had still not caught sight of the house. "It's a bit of a ways, isn't it?"

Mr. Morland grinned at her. "A bit."

"And they know I'm coming, yes?"

"They know."

"All right, then." She straightened her bonnet again. "It's so hot here. I'm sweating through to my unmentionables." Charlotte flapped her arms to bring any sort of coolness to her body.

Mr. Morland passed her a handkerchief. "You're no longer in the north. The climate in Kent is mild in comparison. You'll get used to it."

They rounded another bend, and a huge stone edifice came into sight, bigger than any building she'd ever seen. The entire view of it couldn't fit in the window.

"What's that?" Charlotte asked.

Mr. Morland picked his top hat off the seat beside him and put it on his head. He looked like he'd just finished dressing, his cravat perhaps a little limp, but after Susie's climbing all over him, it was a lost cause. That and a small patch of drying spittle where she'd been sleeping before she'd woke up like the devil on fire.

"That's Willowkeep."

"That's—" There wasn't nothing thing like it in Hull. Leastways not the parts she'd been to. One time her father had taken her to York to see the minster. This place might have even been bigger than that. Such a thing could not possibly be hers. "You jest, right?"

He shook his head.

The carriage came to a stop. Out the window, a whole regiment of people had lined up. Maids in cotton aprons, footmen in polished suits and white wigs, and loads more. Charlotte didn't know who they could all be. In the archway of the door stood a woman, tall and angular, dressed in the finest of the fine. Silk and lace and velvet, all mourning black. Must be Mrs. Kelton, her uncle's second wife.

Charlotte leaned back, out of sight of the fleet. "I can't go out there. Look at me. Look at them. They're expecting something fine and elegant. Not this." She gestured at her worn dress and fraying bonnet.

The door opened, and a man lowered the coach step. He waited to hand her down.

She looked at Mr. Morland and shook her head. "I can't."

CHAPTER FOUR

"GIVE US A MOMENT, DANIELS," Henry said to the footman waiting for them.

The man moved to the side, out of view.

"I can't go out there. I'll look like a cod's head." Charlotte lifted her arms again, flapping like a chicken. "Why is it so blasted hot here? Not to mention what they're going to think about Susie."

Henry closed the carriage door. "Miss Darby, do please lower your arms." Society was going to eat her alive. "A lady does not speak of sweat. Especially not her own." Perhaps he should have prepared her better for the moment of arrival. She'd obviously had no way of comprehending the magnitude of her inheritance, even though he'd tried to describe it in full detail.

Charlotte rested her hands in her lap. Susan had climbed off the seat and now had her nose flattened against the window glass.

"These people know you have come from different circumstances." He nodded encouragingly. "They don't expect Caroline, Princess of Wales."

She stared at him, her blue eyes wild. Lud, she was beautiful.

"The staff is anxious to meet you, not because they care about your appearance but because they wonder about their new mistress. Is she kind? Will she be fair? Are their jobs secure? They care about their livelihood far more than your presentation."

He seemed to be getting through to her, so he went on. "Just show them your smile, and you will win their hearts in an instant."

"Do you think?" She tried again to tame her stray hairs, shoving them up and under her bonnet. They fell out immediately.

"I'm sure of it. Besides, it is in your blood. Your mother grew up at Willowkeep. You belong here."

"What about Susie? If they see that she can't . . . that she's different, they'll judge her. People always judge her." Her eyes were going wild again.

"I'll carry her. Straight up to the nursery. No one will be the wiser." Henry reached for the door latch. "Ready? We cannot stay here any longer without seeming untoward."

She nodded and clutched the jewelry box to her body. Henry lifted Susan onto his lap and pushed the door open.

Daniels appeared, lending a gloved hand to Miss Darby as she stepped down from the carriage. Henry hurried after her, keeping little Susan tight in his arms. Miss Darby seemed to be waiting for him. He couldn't walk with her; she was the mistress and he far below her station. The whole group stared at her in silence. The poor girl looked about to faint. Henry cast Old Tafford a pleading look.

The butler came forward, bowing low.

"Mr. Tafford," Henry said, "may I present Miss Charlotte Darby. Miss Darby, this is Jeremiah Tafford, the butler. And his wife, Mrs. Tafford. She keeps the house."

Mrs. Tafford curtseyed a few paces behind her husband.

"And this little thing is Miss Susan." Henry swiveled his shoulder around so they could get a peek at her face. The girl buried her nose in Henry's cravat. "She's had a difficult few days with all the travel. Perhaps Mrs. Tafford could show us to the nursery."

Henry knew every inch of Willowkeep, but he wanted Mrs. Tafford to be the first to see the child. He trusted her more than anyone else in the place. She would know best how to arrange for her needs.

First, though, they needed to get past Mrs. Kelton lurking in the entrance hall.

"Right this way, miss." Mrs. Tafford led Miss Darby along, pointing out a few of the servants lining the stairs to the front door. Miss Darby made brave work of it, nodding and flashing her magnificent eyes. Tentative smiles formed on many a servant's face, and more than once Henry had to administer his best steward's glare at the wandering eyes of the footmen. He made a silent note to dismiss immediately any man whose behavior toward Miss Darby became too familiar.

Miss Darby crossed the threshold and let out a sigh. She turned to say something to Henry, but as her mouth opened, she caught sight of Mrs. Kelton towering like a gargoyle chiseled from stone for the sole purpose of warding off evil. Though Mrs. Kelton smiled like honey, Henry had no doubt that in her mind, Miss Darby was the devil.

"You must be my dear niece Charlotte."

Miss Darby curtseyed. Henry stepped closer as the color drained from Miss Darby's face. If she went down, he'd be there to catch her—even with his arms full of little Susan.

"Welcome to Willowkeep. I hope you find yourself at home here," the gargoyle said. Lud, but she played her part well. "I trust your journey was pleasant."

"Very pleasant. Thank you, madam."

The old lady's nose was as high in the air as possible without actually scraping the lofty ceiling. "Come join me in the drawing room for some tea. I'm sure it will do you good."

Miss Darby's panicked eyes flashed at Henry.

A week ago, he would never have presumed to interfere in Mrs. Kelton's schemes. Now she was no longer in command. Miss Darby was. Using Susan as a shield, he leaned close and quietly whispered, "Your sister is very tired."

Miss Darby nodded and straightened. "Thank you, Lady Kelton. I don't mean to get your bristles up, but me and Susie are done to a cow's thumb from all the traveling. I must get her settled and resting." She dipped her head and turned away, following Mrs. Tafford up the grand staircase.

Mrs. Kelton looked as though she'd been slapped. Henry doubted she'd ever been spoken to in such a manner. No one would dare.

He trotted up the stairs, catching up to Miss Darby and Mrs. Tafford. They tunneled through the house until they reached the nursery—a block of rooms in the east wing.

"Oh, this is lovely," Miss Darby said, walking to the window and gazing out. The east wing overlooked sculptured gardens and a willow grove beyond—the root of the great house's name.

A modest case of books stood on one wall while shelves of toys filled another, most of it left over from Miss Darby's own mother and uncle, Louisa and Walter, since they were the last children to be raised here.

Mrs. Tafford opened a door revealing a bedchamber. "This will be for the little one."

Miss Darby walked through, running her hands across everything. A child's bed rested against one wall, covered by a canopy of cloth from the East Indies, with elephants and peacocks printed on it. In the corner by the window was a grand rocking chair. The wardrobe also had little animals painted on it. Even a fire burned in the fireplace. Mrs. Tafford had done well in organizing this room.

"It's lovely," Miss Darby said again. She looked quite pleased with the arrangement.

Mrs. Tafford crossed the little hallway and opened the door to a similar room but more modestly furnished. "And over here's the quarters for a nursemaid or a governess. Whichever you choose for the girl."

Miss Darby peeked in and then stepped back into the main room of the nursery. "It's bigger than my whole house."

Susan's soft snores found their way through Henry's cravat. "Miss Darby?"

She turned to him with a dazed stare.

"She's asleep. Shall I lay her in her bed?"

Miss Darby nodded. Henry laid her down, pulling a light blanket up over her shoulders. His cravat would never recover.

"Well, then," Henry said. "I shall leave you to get settled. Mrs. Tafford will show you to your room. Of course, you may have any room, as they are all yours."

Miss Darby's eyes flashed again with that wild edge. "But where are you going? What am I supposed to do? What about Mrs. Kelton? What if I can't find my way? What if—"

"Miss Darby."

Her mouth closed, and her hands strained as she clutched the rosewood case. She pushed a few strands of loose hair up into her bonnet, which she'd completely neglected to remove.

"You need not meet Mrs. Kelton until dinner if you keep to your rooms."

Miss Darby nodded. "Where are you going?"

He glanced at Mrs. Tafford as she busied herself with linens. Henry lowered his voice. "Home. I do not live here."

"No. Of course not."

Miss Darby backed toward the wall, her eyes darting about like a cornered fox.

"I live in Willow Grange. The estate's old cottage. It's but a quarter mile away. If you need me, send a servant, day or night, yes?"

She nodded again.

"Any woman who can keep herself and her little sister all alone in a place like Hull can surely manage Mrs. Kelton."

At last Miss Darby took a breath. She would be fine. Perhaps not immediately, but eventually. He took a few steps toward the door. He should tuck down to the servants' hall and put a stop to whatever gossip might be cooking about Miss Darby. The staff would no doubt be full of questions.

"Mr. Morland?" Miss Darby said louder than any words she'd uttered since arriving at Willowkeep.

Henry stopped and turned.

"I wondered if you might do us the honor of joining us for dinner this evening."

He almost laughed. Mrs. Tafford looked up at him, a glint in her eyes, even though the rest of her face was hidden behind a stack of sheets. "It would be my pleasure. Thank you." Then he added, "And what time would that be?"

She gave him a scowl and turned to Mrs. Tafford.

"That would be half seven, sir," Mrs. Tafford said.

Henry bowed to Miss Darby. He tugged on the chain and checked his watch. Nearly seven. That left him little time to go home and change. He'd have to postpone going below stairs till after dinner.

"Don't be late," Miss Darby said.

"I'm never late." He snapped his watch closed, tucking it back into his pocket, and hurried out the door.

Miss Darby seemed dead set against facing Mrs. Kelton without a second. Who wouldn't? The old scarecrow could be intimidating.

His feet skimmed down the servants' wooden staircase and out the back door. As soon as he was out of sight of the great house, he kicked into a run. Henry had been gone nearly a week. Leaving his sister home alone for such a length of time never sat easy, and now his homecoming would be cut short.

Henry reached the Grange and shoved the door open with his shoulder. "Jane?"

"In here," his sister called from the kitchen.

He hung his hat on the rack, then tugged at the knot in his neckcloth, creaking the floorboards as he followed the smell of stewed eels coming from the cookstove. Thank heavens he was dining out.

If he ever managed to come out of debt, he'd buy him and his sister back into the life they were meant to have. A cook, first of all. A housemaid or two. Until then, they got by.

Jane wiped her hands on her apron, then threw her arms around her brother. "Welcome home." She kissed his cheek. "How was your journey?"

Henry tore a piece from the loaf on the table. "Surprisingly pleasant."

"Why do you smile?" Jane tossed a bundle of green herbs into the cookpot.

"I'm simply glad to be home," Henry said.

"And?"

"And what?"

She threw an apple at him. He caught it easily.

"What about the new mistress of Willowkeep, of course? Is your position safe? Is she an ugly old spinster? We've all been dying of curiosity. You've got to give me something to take to the neighbors, else what's the point of having a brother up in the big house?"

"Well." He took a bite of the apple and chewed for a moment. "Miss Charlotte Darby is about your age. Her sister, Susan, is much younger. And I believe, at least for now, my job is secure." He took another mouthful of apple. "And that's all I've got time for. I'm summoned to the house for dinner, and I've got to change."

Jane's smile fell from her face. "But you've just arrived. And I've made your favorite."

His sister was tall and handsome, with brown hair the exact same color as his. She was a saint. However, when she finally did catch a man's eye, it would not be for her cooking.

"I'm sorry. But what can I do? She's more than a bit overwhelmed with her new circumstances. She dares not meet the scarecrow on her own." He tossed the apple core into the garbage, still starving but saving the remainder of his appetite for dinner.

Jane followed him into his room. "What is she like? I suppose she's full of airs now that she's the wealthiest lady in the county." Jane helped him shrug off his coat and waistcoat.

He pulled out his shirt pin and lifted his crumpled tunic over his shoulders. How could he describe Miss Darby? The manners she'd picked up from the docks. The way she'd flapped her arms to cool off. How fiercely she protected her sister.

He looked up to find Jane studying him carefully. "There's that smile again."

He shrugged. "She is unexpected. I don't believe she has any airs to speak of. She came from humble circumstances and has done a remarkable job caring for herself and her young sister. In fact, I think you might get on with her quite well."

Jane handed him a clean shirt. "You admire her."

There was much about Miss Darby to admire. He still didn't know her full history, but yes, despite her lack of upbringing, she had caught his sympathy. "I suppose in some ways I do. I suspect she has suffered much and yet still maintains an admirable spirit."

Jane watched him for a moment. "And father? Did you have time to see him?"

"Yes." He splashed some water on his face and dried it with a towel. "He sends his love."

"How does he fare?"

"Worse, I'm afraid. I gave the warden funds for a doctor, but I don't know what good it will do. That place is crawling with every kind of filth—and I believe the warden is the worst of them." He threw the towel onto his bed.

"Henry." She put a hand on his arm. "We will get him out."

If only he could believe that. His father had already been there beyond seven months. During winter past, he'd gone from whole and hale to nearly dying. He'd not survive another in prison.

Henry panned through his wardrobe to find a good pair of breeches that hadn't been drooled on by a small child. Jane located a clean neckcloth. "I'll just press this to freshen it up." She hurried off to the kitchen.

Henry checked his watch. No time for a quick shave, especially after his promise not to be late.

With his apparel in place, he joined Jane. She set the iron back on the stove, and he lifted his chin so she could loop the cloth around his neck and tie a simple yet elegant knot. Jane was excellent at cravats.

"Who needs a valet when they have a Jane? Your work would rival anyone's in London."

"Rather convenient since you can't afford a valet." She smoothed his lapels and brushed his shoulders. "Now go."

Henry tore off another piece of bread before tugging on the door. Peters should have fixed it by now, but still it stuck. He jerked harder, and it opened with a twang.

Henry walked in the back door of Willowkeep with exactly three minutes to spare. Perhaps he should have used the front door for a formal engagement. It had been so long since he'd been invited to the house for a meal. Considering the total dinner party would consist of the old scarecrow, Miss Darby, and himself, it likely made no difference which door he entered.

He strode briskly down the corridor toward the drawing room, where they would be assembling before going in to dinner.

"Mr. Morland," a female voice whispered from the parlor as he passed.

He turned with a start. "Miss Darby?"

She stepped into the hall. "I've been waiting for you."

"In the parlor? With no light?"

The poor girl was a stranger in her own home, afraid even to apply to her own servants for something as simple as a candle.

She dipped in a quick curtsey. "I didn't want to be alone in the drawing room with Mrs. Kelton. She must hate me."

For certain, Mrs. Kelton did not appreciate Miss Darby's new status. After the disclosure of the amended will, Mrs. Kelton had stayed shut up in her room for days. *Crying her eyes out,* according to her maid, Fleurette. Mrs. Kelton called her Fleurette, but everyone knew she was Betsy Taylor from Twitton. Henry doubted very much that Mrs. Kelton would ever forgive Miss Darby for subverting her.

"I daresay she will live. All is finished, and nothing Mrs. Kelton does will change it."

Miss Darby lowered her head. Henry stepped back, giving her time to turn over all he'd said. She too had made a quick change in her attire. Instead of the high-necked traveling frock, she wore a russet evening dress. Wool, and not that fine of wool. It would have been passable for a morning dress. The color did nothing for her fair complexion, nor her blue eyes, which now darted toward the entry with that wild look. She'd reset her hair, undoubtedly by herself, as strands were already working loose.

Was it his place to recommend a lady's maid? Surely not. She must know she should have one. Perhaps Jane would be able to find a girl to fill the position.

Henry motioned down the hall. "Shall we, then?"

Miss Darby took two steps before her finger went straight to her mouth.

Henry shook his head. "No nail biting. You will give yourself away."

She quickly put her hand behind her back. A pair of gloves was also in order.

He led her to the drawing room and pushed the door open. Mrs. Kelton was already inside, sitting in a stiff-backed windsor near the hearth.

She did not stand when the new mistress of Willowkeep entered the room.

CHAPTER FIVE

CHARLOTTE SMOOTHED HER SKIRT FRONT as she approached Mrs. Kelton. The woman was dressed to the hilt in an elegant black gown of glimmering silk. An enormous chain of diamonds sparkled round her neck. A bit much for a widow in mourning. Charlotte's fingers went to her own bare throat. Perhaps she should've worn her mother's jewels. She never guessed that a family dinner would call for such finery.

Not that Mrs. Kelton was family. She was her uncle's second wife and no real relation. Still, it was the closest thing she had to kin, save Susie.

Her sister was asleep for the night. A maid had been placed in the nursery to keep watch till Charlotte went up. The emptiness beside her seemed almost tangible, so long it had been since she'd had a meal without Susie next to her.

"Mrs. Kelton," Charlotte said with a curtsey.

"Dear Charlotte, please call me Aunt Nora. I'm glad to see you are recovered from your arduous journey." Mrs. Kelton took her hand and patted it. "You look . . . quite lovely tonight."

"Thank you, Aunt." How sweet the word tasted. Charlotte had never had an aunt before.

Aunt Nora nodded at Mr. Morland. "Thank you, Mr. Morland, for bringing her. You may go."

Mr. Morland bowed slightly.

"Oh, no." Charlotte pulled her hand away. "I've asked Mr. Morland to take dinner with us." At her aunt's scowl, she added, "'Tis the least we can do after he come all the way up to Hull to fetch me."

Mr. Morland gave Charlotte an approving smile—until her finger came up and slipped between her teeth. He shook his head the tiniest bit. Gaw. She would never remember. She forced her hands behind her back.

"Oh?" Mrs. Kelton said. "Odd to dine with the servants, but if that is your wish. After all, this is your home now." She sighed so loud Charlotte worried she'd have to send for the smelling salts.

With only her and her aunt in this great big place, what did it matter who ate with them? When Charlotte's mother was alive, they'd had all sorts over to their house for dinner. It had never mattered if they were deckhands or warehouse runners or the captain of Father's ship. And Mr. Morland was the most gentlemanly man she'd ever met. He could hardly be called a servant.

She tried again. "I wanted to thank you for having me here," she said to Aunt Nora. "It's very grand, and I'm much obliged."

"Do not thank me. It was my late husband's idea to give everything he owned to a complete stranger, I can assure you."

Charlotte stepped backward, bumping into a piece of furniture. Her arms flailed as she tried to maintain her balance but lost, landing on her backside in a soft chair near Aunt Nora. She was muddling everything.

"Mr. Kelton is greatly missed," Mr. Morland said. "He was always a generous man."

"It is I who should be thanking you," her aunt said to Charlotte, completely ignoring Mr. Morland and the fact that Charlotte had just toppled into a chair. "For not removing me from the premises."

"I would never," Charlotte said. How could she think such a thing? "We are family."

Her aunt smiled, but it looked a bit like she'd caught a whiff of rendered whale oil.

Mr. Tafford entered and announced dinner. At last. All Charlotte really wanted was to get some food into her belly and go to bed.

Mr. Morland offered his hand to Mrs. Kelton, but she wrinkled her nose. "I shall take myself in to dinner, thank you."

Mr. Morland extended his offer to Charlotte. She wasn't too proud to take his arm.

She glanced up at Mr. Morland. "Why do you laugh?" Charlotte asked him in a whisper.

"I'm not laughing," he said.

"Not out loud, perhaps. But your eyes are surely laughing." Charlotte slowed their pace so she could get her answer.

"Sorry. It's just, I haven't seen the old— Mrs. Kelton so flustered."

Charlotte came to a complete stop. "She despises me."

"Her whole life has changed," Mr. Morland said in a hushed voice. "Her future is uncertain. She is afraid, and that does not always make people wise."

He motioned for Charlotte to enter the dining room.

Charlotte hadn't meant to put Mrs. Kelton out of spirits. Really, it couldn't be that odd to— "Great conkers! Look at that table."

Her aunt gasped and covered her mouth with the back of her hand.

"Were it built to seat the entire parish?" Charlotte asked.

Mr. Morland pulled a chair out for her at one end while a footman did the same for her aunt at the other end. There had to be ten miles of gleaming mahogany between them. A place had been set for Mr. Morland near Charlotte's end. Probably Mrs. Tafford's doing.

"I assure you, dear niece, this is but an average-size table for a person of my—a person of your means."

A footman shook out a napkin and laid it in Charlotte's lap as another ladled thin soup into a shallow bowl.

"When my son arrives, you shall see how easily he can fill it with his vast number of acquaintances," Aunt Nora said. "Or he used to, before my dear husband passed."

"When might we expect to see Mr. Hardwick?" Mr. Morland asked.

Charlotte leaned forward and smelled her soup. It didn't look like much. This would never fill her. She dipped her spoon in, trying to be as delicate as Aunt Nora.

"Hurst is eager to meet the newest member of Willowkeep," Mrs. Kelton said. "He's leaving London early, before the close of the Season. I expect him here by the end of next week."

"This is delicious." Charlotte scooped another spoonful of soup. And another.

Mr. Morland nodded. "Cook is one of the best in the county."

Aunt Nora humphed when Charlotte lifted the bowl and tipped the remaining broth into her mouth. The footman cleared the bowls and brought out the next course: a roasted capon, creamed potatoes and ham, boiled carrots and parsnips, and some kind of cold salad with beets.

Each course brought something new and wondrous. If every meal was like this, how was Aunt Nora such a broomstick?

A footman set a honey almond tart in front of her. This had to be some kind of dream. She would have pinched herself to be sure, but she was too busy eating.

When Charlotte couldn't swallow another bite, she leaned back with a moan, rubbing her stomach. "Goodness. I've filled my corset near to bursting."

Aunt Nora choked, then pulled out her fan and wafted it about her face.

The footman laughed out loud, and Mr. Morland gave him a frown. "Watch yourself, Daniels."

The footman cleared his throat and looked straight ahead.

Aunt Nora pushed her chair back from the table. "Goodness me. I never." She muttered all kinds of astonishments as she rushed out of the room.

Mr. Morland pushed his chair back as well. "Shall we retire to the drawing room?"

"I didn't mean to offend her," Charlotte said. "'Twas a delicious meal. I only meant to compliment its finery."

Mr. Morland pulled out her chair as she stood. "A lady does not mention her . . . unmentionables in polite society. Or ever. Except, I suppose, to her personal maid."

"Right. Of course I knew of that." He must think her a complete heathen. "It's only been me and Susie for so long, I'm not used to thinking about polite society—or any kind of society." She pulled her finger from her lips and put her arm behind her back.

She followed Mr. Morland across the hall. He reached for the drawing room door, where she presumed Aunt Nora sat in her severe chair waiting for them.

Charlotte stopped him. "Must we? Is it improper of me if I don't want to withdraw and spend another hour in the company of that woman? She disapproves of me. She scowled at me through the whole meal."

Mr. Morland released the door handle. "I hadn't thought you'd noticed, so intent you were on your food."

"Well, I did look up occasionally."

He laughed out loud. "Miss Darby," he said. "You are entirely anomalous."

"What does that mean?"

His eyes sparked with some kind of mischief. "It means that you don't have to go into the drawing room if you don't wish to."

"Well, that's a blessed relief."

She didn't mean to be antymous—or whatever he'd said. She simply couldn't imagine passing the rest of the evening in her aunt's company. She had just spent three days trapped in a carriage, trying to keep a restless child under control. She was completely done in. "I really am exhausted."

"Of course. In that case, I'll bid you good night and make your apologies to Mrs. Kelton for you."

"Thank you, sir. You've been very kind."

He bowed to her, then pulled open the door to the drawing room. Charlotte leapt out of view, listening while Mr. Morland crossed the threshold.

"Mrs. Kelton. Miss Darby has informed me that she is very tired. She will not be joining you this evening."

Charlotte couldn't hear the reply. Would Mr. Morland stay with Mrs. Kelton? He couldn't be excited by the prospect. Mrs. Kelton had snubbed him before dinner, but she'd talked with him almost exclusively throughout the whole meal. Thank heavens he'd agreed to accompany them. If it'd been just her and Aunt Nora, it would've been an uncomfortable affair indeed.

Mr. Morland emerged from the drawing room, rolling his eyes. He stopped short when he saw her. He quickly closed the door. "Miss Darby. Still here? You haven't changed your mind, have you? I'm sure Mrs. Kelton will make room for you in there if you wish to join her."

"Goodness no. I just . . ." What? What did she want? She was dog tired. But being alone in her room was so . . . alone. She'd shared a chamber with Susie most of her life. She'd passed every night with the clacking of carriages and the clanging of ship's bells rattling through her window. Now she'd traded the smell of shipping docks and the cries of gulls for sculptured hedges and the chirping of garden birds whose calls she did not recognize.

Susie was asleep for the night. A maid had been placed in the nursery to keep watch till Charlotte went up. And when Mr. Morland left, she'd be lost in the giant house. Nothing more than a speck of dust in a world big as the universe. She didn't belong here. Not really.

"Miss Darby?"

She looked up at him.

"Perhaps, if you're not too fatigued, I might show you something."

"What is it?" Whatever he had in mind had to be better than Aunt Nora or alone in her room.

"Come with me. I want to show you how Willowkeep got its name."

"Yes, please." She followed him down the hall past the parlor, deeper into the belly of the house, until they emerged near a door leading to the outside.

He stopped and gestured at a room just to the right of the door. "This is my office."

"Is that so? And naturally Willowkeep were named after your workplace."

He grinned. "I merely point it out for your information. In case you need to find me." He pulled the back door open, and a splash of evening air flooded in. "We are going outside."

They stepped out onto a pebbled path. To the right, it led off through overtrimmed bushes, as if some gardener had gelded the rows of shrubs, which, if left to grow as nature intended, would have been quite handsome.

"This way," he pointed down a different path toward a wilder-looking area.

The lowering light cast long shadows, like fingers, across the way as the sun slipped down in the west, just resting on the horizon.

They crossed over a trail of moss-covered stepping stones set among the lavender and then came to a narrow river. A bend in its course created a sort of pond where three ancient willows stood like the towering masts of a shipwrecked galleon. Their long branches draped over the pool, dipping in just enough to test the waters.

Mr. Morland parted the branches for her, and there, in the bower of the largest tree, stood a wicker bench. She walked toward it, and he let the limbs fall back into place.

"This is lovely," Charlotte said, turning to take it all in. "It's like a secret hideaway, cut off from the whole world." The twilight cast the entire area into shadows of greens and blues. A gentle wind picked up, whispering through the branches and swirling round her as if welcoming her with its cooling breeze.

Mr. Morland sat on the bench, leaning back and stretching his legs. "I thought you might like it."

"Willowkeep," she said. "There's nothing like this up in Hull. Not that I've seen. Too cold, maybe. The wind can be fierce as it comes in from the North Sea." She bent over the pond, but it was too dark to see past the surface.

Mr. Morland appeared beside her, his feet making naer a sound on the soft grass.

Charlotte straightened. "And this is part of the estate?" It must be because Mr. Morland said it was the namesake.

He nodded. "All of it belongs to you now."

She turned in a circle, but the branches blocked her view. The lands of Willowkeep must go far beyond this spot. Far enough to include tenants, the fields of hops Mr. Morland had pointed out, and even the village of Kippingham. It was beautiful, but too much for one small girl from Hull. "I can't rightly believe it. I've never owned anything of my own before." She had one thing of value—her mother's jewels. "But it don't really feel like it's mine, do it? I mean, I'm a visitor here."

"Miss Darby." Mr. Morland handed her his handkerchief even though she was sure she hadn't shed a tear. "You've not been here above three hours. Give yourself some time."

Charlotte pulled the cloth in and out of her hands. "I don't even know what I'm s'posed to do. I can't manage a place like this. 'Specially while I've got Susie to mind."

"You are not expected to," Mr. Morland said. "That's why you've got me. And Mr. and Mrs. Tafford. And Cook. And gardeners. And chambermaids. And the lot. If the whole world collapsed tomorrow, this place would still keep running."

She balled the handkerchief into a lump, then wrung it like it had committed some horrible crime. "I must look like a fool to you," she whispered.

"Not at all," he said.

The water rippled and murmured as it rounded the bend. An egret called from somewhere downstream, raspy and hoarse. Not a gull, but at least she recognized it.

"What's through here?" Charlotte parted the curtain of draping branches and stepped into a second, smaller dome of green created by a separate willow tree. In the center, raised up on a pedestal, stood a statue of a lion. His face was worn and pitted like he'd had the pox. His mouth curved into a snarl. The mix of moss and bird droppings scattered across his mane gave him a pitiable look, not at all like the grand beast he was meant to be.

Mr. Morland came through the branches behind her.

"What's this?" Charlotte asked.

"You've found Henry's lion."

"Henry's lion?"

CHAPTER SIX

"YES." MR. MORLAND WALKED ROUND the beast. "Nearly three hundred years ago, this lion resided in the gardens of Hever Castle—where Anne Boleyn used to live before she married Henry VIII. Tradition has it that whenever Henry VIII visited Hever to court Anne, they passed love notes to each other, leaving the letters in the animal's mouth for the other to find."

"How very romantic."

"Romantic until he had her head chopped off."

True. Poor Anne, to find herself one moment in such favor of the king that the whole country had to reform, then a few years later with a sword over her head. All her love wasted on a man as changeable as the weather. Too bad she didn't see before she married him the kind of man he was to become. Then again, perhaps she didn't have a choice. Or maybe the promise of queen was too much even for Anne to resist.

Charlotte ran her hands over the stone statue. Cold and rough, just like the old king. "How did it end up here?"

Mr. Morland fingered one of the lion's large teeth. "Hever Castle is only a few miles from here. When Henry divorced his fourth wife, Anne of Cleves, he gave her the castle to live in. Apparently she didn't like this reminder of Henry's early devotion to the other Anne, so the piece was removed and ended up here."

Charlotte circled the statue, coming to a stop and staring right into its face. To think that the queen of England might have looked into this lion's face too all those years ago.

"They say," Mr. Morland continued, "that the ghost of Anne Boleyn still haunts the lion. If a woman writes her troubles, her matters of the heart, in a note and tucks it into the statue's mouth, the queen will take pity on her."

Charlotte stepped back. “A ghost? What does she do?”

Mr. Morland laughed and shrugged his shoulders. “I don’t know. ’Tis only a story.”

Charlotte had always been taught that Anne Boleyn was a good queen. Beautiful and clever. “She would want the lady to be happy, I think. She would help her as best she could.”

“I’m sure you are right.”

Darkness was descending quickly now, and Charlotte could no longer make out all of Mr. Morland’s features. He was watching her though, studying her. She folded his handkerchief and handed it back.

He reached out to take it, holding the cloth and her hand for a moment. “Keep it.” He let go, leaving Charlotte’s hand cold where his warmth had just been. She shivered.

“You are cold, and I must get home. It’ll be fully dark soon.” He parted the hanging branches of the willow trees and let her through.

They walked in silence back toward the house. About halfway along, Mr. Morland pointed down a narrow walkway that led off through a grove of young elms. “Just down there is Willow Grange, where I live with my sister, Jane.”

Charlotte could see nothing of the Grange in the dusk, but she nodded. He’d been gone a full week bringing her here from Hull. He must be more than ready to part ways.

“You go on home, sir. I can find my own way to the house.” A ridiculous thing to say since it was looming over her as she spoke.

He smiled at her. “What kind of man would leave a lady alone outside in the dark?”

“Well, I’m not really a lady, now, am I?” She knew full well the humble circumstances of her birth. All the money in the world couldn’t change that.

“Of course you are. As was your mother.”

Charlotte could scarce picture her mother living here—God rest her soul. Running about as a child. Playing with her brother in the very same willow tree she’d just been in with Mr. Morland. Eating at the giant table with china and silver. Her mother must have loved her father fiercely to leave it all behind for the little townhouse in Hull. A different kind of love than Anne and Henry VIII had. Anne gained a kingdom and a crown. Charlotte’s mother gave up everything. In the end, though, what did it signify? Both women ended up dead. And both may very likely have survived had they chosen another path.

A few paces away, a white marbled rock gleamed in the rising moonlight. The perfect size. She picked it up and tossed it a few times, catching it in her hands, getting a feel for its weight.

"Starting a new collection?" Mr. Morland asked.

"Collection?"

He nodded. "I saw your stash of rocks. You didn't bring them, so I assume now you are starting over."

She tossed it to him. He caught it and turned it over in his hand.

"That wasn't a collection," she said. "They were for protection." When he gave her a puzzled look, she went on. "You know how it is. People are not always kind. 'Specially children. More than a few times we found ourselves surrounded by little devils calling Susie names and trying to hit her with stones. In Hull, when we went out, I always carried one with me in case I needed to fend them off."

Maybe she shouldn't have told him that. Mr. Morland didn't need to know all the darkest corners about her and Susie's life before. But it was him standing there with his face all furrowed that was like cold water to a scalding burn.

After her father left, she'd had no one at all to turn to. She'd done her best though, and sometimes that had meant stones.

"I'm sorry for that. I don't . . . rightly know what to say." He handed her back the white stone. "You're a remarkable survivor, Miss Darby."

Perhaps he didn't want to hear about the ugly side of life before she'd come to Willowkeep. He knew all about managing a house and servants and lands and tenants, but he had no idea what it was like for common folk just struggling to get by.

"It weren't all bad, sir." She tossed the rock in her hand. "I've got a sharp aim." Charlotte turned and looked round. "There, see that beech tree?"

He squinted into the darkness. "Yes," he said, though he sounded rather dubious.

"Watch." Charlotte launched the stone with a grunt. It sailed through the air and hit dead center with a thunk. She turned to him, tugging her stays back into place. "What do you think of that, Mr. Steward?"

He let out a guffaw. "It's too dark to see. You could have hit any tree."

"I hit it. I never miss. I'll prove it." She lifted her skirts and placed her foot carefully into the flower bed.

"Wait." Mr. Morland's hand kept her from taking another step. "I believe you. You needn't trudge through the brambles to prove it."

She wouldn't have him always questioning her about this. She had one accomplishment, and this was it. "Sure as sure, that rock is at the base of the beech tree. I won't have you thinking I'm a complete pudding head."

"I would never think that." He chuckled. "However, if proof is needed, then please allow me."

He tromped off into the undergrowth. About twenty paces in, he reached the tree. It was darker underneath, where the twilight couldn't reach, and Charlotte could barely make him out as he bent over.

He held up a white-colored stone. "I found it. A very accurate throw indeed."

"See. I do have some skills."

"I should never have doubted." He stepped out of the flower garden and brushed himself off. "Here is your weapon."

She took the stone from him.

Mr. Morland cleared his throat and stepped away. "I should head back. Jane will be wondering. But, well, if you ever need anything, anything at all, you know where to find me."

"Yes." She curtseyed.

He answered with a quick bow and set off through the trees.

She watched him till he disappeared round the bend.

Henry stopped as soon as he was out of Miss Darby's sight. What the deuce was he thinking taking her to the willow grove alone at night? Then she'd looked up at him with her sorrowful blue eyes.

And she his employer! The last thing the poor girl needed was a scandal. With the steward nonetheless. If even the tiniest whisper of a rumor began to spread, it would only mean trouble. It wouldn't be fair to Miss Darby. Regardless of her previous circumstances, she was the rightful heir. With the stroke of his pen, Mr. Kelton had elevated her far above Henry's reach.

His reach. He mustn't think about her in that way at all. She was mistress of the manor. Perhaps a friend but nothing more—and heavens, how she needed a friend.

He took a deep breath, filling his lungs with the cool night air. Better. He had enough to worry about without getting carried away in such thoughts. Why couldn't she have been the homely spinster everyone had expected? Instead she was the most—

No. Not down that road again.

He burst into a sprint and covered the remaining distance to his house as fast as he could. The release of energy cleared his mind, and by the time he wedged the front door open, he was completely himself again.

Not a single candle was lit. The only hint of light was a faint glow from the kitchen.

"Jane?" he called.

A retching sound was his only answer. He followed it into the kitchen. A small fire glimmered from the cooking hearth. Jane leaned over a wooden bucket, her face the color of boiled egg whites.

He hurried over. "Not again."

"Don't eat the stew," she whimpered, then slapped a hand over her mouth. She removed her hand long enough to say, "I've been bent over this bucket almost since you left."

He should have come home sooner instead of wandering the grounds with Miss Darby.

"I'm sorry I wasn't here." Henry handed her a cloth to wipe her face. "Come. Let's get you to bed." He helped her to her feet and practically carried her up the narrow stairs to the loft—the only room on the upper level besides some storage areas in the garret.

Henry unfastened the hooks on the back of her dress, and through the gap of muslin, he loosened the laces of her stays. This was not the first time Jane had brought the family to their knees with her cooking.

With a rustle of fabric, her dress fell to the floor, followed by the shuffling of bedsheets. Henry picked up her discarded clothing and flung it over a chair. Jane burrowed into the covers. One of these days, he would have enough money to afford some help for her. But first he had to get his father out of prison.

"Do you need anything else?" He brushed the hair from her face.

Jane pointed at the chamber pot.

Henry used his foot to scoot the stoneware pot over to the edge of her bed. She shivered, and he put another blanket on her, even though she'd likely be sweating the next moment. He knew from experience how it was when the cooking went bad.

"I'll be downstairs."

Jane gave him a weak nod, her cheeks already burning from heat. Nothing for it. She'd have to wait it out, like always. He'd narrowly escaped the same fate.

Henry descended the wooden steps to his room. His own bed. After a week of dirty, noisy inns, he would sleep well tonight. Hopefully Miss Darby would too. She was the one who had to acclimate to new surroundings now. She and her sister.

With his neckcloth carefully hung over the top of his screen and his clothes stowed in the wardrobe, Henry climbed into bed. Clean sheets that smelled like summer wind. He'd had enough of bed linens that stank of the stable yard where they'd been dried. *Thank you, Jane.* She took good care of him.

A pounding on the front door roused him. He opened his eyes, straining to hear. Silence. Then the pounding again.

Henry climbed out of bed and pulled his breeches on. Someone on the staff must be in need of something. He made his way to the door, rubbing the fog from his eyes. He pulled the door open with a vigorous tug. "Miss Darby?"

CHAPTER SEVEN

Charlotte stood on Mr. Morland's front step and wrapped her dressing robe tighter across her chest. Mr. Morland wore his white shirt loose over a pair of breeches. His eyes gave her a quick look over, pausing on her hair. She'd done nothing to smooth it down before running out. It must be churned into a thistle top by now.

"I'm so sorry to trouble you, but it's Susie."

Mr. Morland invited her in. "What about Susie?"

"She won't stop crying, sir. I can't calm her down, and I thought, seeing as how you made her so happy before, on the journey, maybe you could come up to the house and . . . see if you can make her well."

"Is she ill?" he asked.

"I don't know, sir. But I can't do nothing to quiet her. And Mrs. Tafford's threatening to send for the doctor if she won't calm down, and that'd be worse than anything." Susie hadn't been this upset in a long time. All Charlotte's regular tricks weren't helping. "Please, will you come?"

Mr. Morland reached behind him and lifted his coat off the rack. "Of course." He tugged on a worn pair of boots, then headed off toward the house, going so fast Charlotte nearly had to run to keep up with him. "Are you sure she doesn't need a doctor?"

Charlotte stumbled. "No! No doctors."

She'd already had to pry her sister out of the arms of more than one physician who thought the best place for the child was in the asylum. The last thing she needed was another spiry-faced man telling her that children like this run in the family. That she'd best take care or her own babies would turn out like Susie. Or like her brothers—God rest their souls.

Mr. Morland slowed his pace long enough to glance back at her.

Charlotte stumbled again. The ground was uneven, and the night so dark.

Mr. Morland put his arm out, and she took it. He slowed his pace. "Apologies. I forget that you're new here. I can walk this path with my eyes closed, so often I've made the trip."

"'Tis hard to see. I fell down on my way here. Skinned my knee." Charlotte started to pull up her robe and nightdress to see the damage.

Mr. Morland looked away. "No need to show me. I'll take your word for it."

Of course. Everything was so proper here. She kept forgetting that Mr. Morland was a gentleman. Up north, there wasn't always time for properness. If you got hurt on the docks, you got help from whoever was closest without worrying so much about this and that and all the finery.

She took his arm again and let him lead her the rest of the way. He opened the back door for her—the one by his office—then she followed him through the corridors and up the grand staircase. Susie's cries reached them as they turned down the nursery hall.

Mrs. Tafford had the child pinned to the bed. Susie was thrashing about, her head flailing and her feet kicking up a storm. Mrs. Tafford huffed and puffed, and a sheen of sweat covered her brow.

"Mr. Morland, thank goodness!" Mrs. Tafford shouted over Susie's screams. "I think she must be possessed of the devil."

"She's had fits like this before," Charlotte said, rushing over to her sister. "Quite regular, in fact. But I've always been able to calm her down. This time she won't have anything to do with me." She shooed Mrs. Tafford away, doing her best to keep Susie from hurting herself with all her flailing. "Come now, Susie. I brought Mr. Morland to see you. Remember the powpy man?"

Poor Susie's face burned red as a garden beet. Her eyes and nose streamed. Charlotte took a handkerchief from her sleeve and wiped Susie's face. It only made her wailing grow. "See, sir. There's nothing I can do."

Mr. Morland looked a bit disconcerted. Perhaps he didn't want to be bothered with a fitful child. But he'd been so good with Susie before, she thought he genuinely cared about her. Maybe she was wrong.

Mr. Morland nodded. In two strides, he reached the bed. He nudged Charlotte out of the way and sat on the edge. He made no attempt to hold Susie down. Instead, he lifted her into his arms and started pacing about the room.

"There now, Susie." He took her out into the nursery, patting her back and walking about. "That's enough of that. You're going to make yourself sick if you don't calm down."

The girl's screams continued, and she flung herself backward. Mr. Morland caught her and pulled her close. He took her to the window. Charlotte followed them, trying to hear what he was telling her.

"If you get sick, you'll miss out on my big surprise."

Susie stopped flailing. Her cries turned into shuddering sobs as she tried to get herself under control. Gaw. Charlotte had tried the exact same thing, but Susie hadn't listened to her.

And here came Mr. Morland, making it look easy as tea after Charlotte had spent half the night trying to convince the child to calm down. Charlotte was ready to pull her hair out over the whole thing. The new house. An unfamiliar bed. What if this happened night after night? She couldn't run down to the Grange every time. Not even Mr. Morland was that obliging.

"I can't tell you my surprise until you are all done crying," he said.

Susie tried again to quit her tears, her breath coming in shuddering huffs. Charlotte moved in to wipe Susie's face again, but Mr. Morland waved her off. He waited a few minutes, standing in front of the window.

"Are you done?" he asked.

Susie nodded.

He held out his hand behind Susie's back and motioned for the handkerchief. Charlotte laid it in his hand, then stepped back.

Mr. Morland worked as though he had seven children of his own instead of being a single man. As far as Charlotte understood, it was only him and his sister. And their father. He hadn't told her much about him.

He brought the cloth to Susie's face. "I'm going to clean you up a bit, then we'll sit in the chair and talk, all right?"

Susie looked at the handkerchief, then back at Mr. Morland. She gave him a nod. He made quick work of wiping her nose and drying the tears, then held the cloth back out to Charlotte. She took it from him without a word.

Mr. Morland sat in the rocking chair with Susie on his lap. He turned her sideways and rocked gently. "Tomorrow, I want to take you down to see where the horses live. Would you like that?"

Susie nodded. Then shook her head. She pointed toward the door.

"We can't go now. Look out the window."

Her pale face turned toward the darkened glass.

"It's night. The horses are asleep. If we wake them up now, it will make them sick. Do you want the horses to be sick?"

She shook her head.

"Good. Now, if you go to sleep like a big girl and no more crying, tomorrow we can see the horses. Yes?"

She nodded and immediately nestled into his chest. All her fits must have worn her right out because in only moments, her eyes closed and her breathing deepened, though still broken by the occasional shudder.

"A few more minutes," he whispered to Charlotte. "Just to make sure."

Charlotte couldn't take her eyes of the scene. He'd worked a miracle. That child had never taken to anyone, ever, like she had Mr. Morland.

Charlotte stepped into Susie's bedroom to straighten the mess she'd made out of her bedsheets. Mrs. Tafford already had the whole room put to rights.

Charlotte dropped onto the bed. "Looks like Mr. Morland's got her settled. She's finally asleep."

Mrs. Tafford shook her head. "Isn't that something. I've known Henry his whole life, and I never knew he had such skill with children. Good as a mother goose, he is."

"He were a godsend when we come down from the north. I think I'd of lost my mind if he hadn't been there to help keep Susie entertained."

Mr. Morland carried Susie into the bedroom and laid her down. Charlotte pulled the blanket up and tucked it under the sleeping girl's chin. She looked peaceful now, the little troublemaker.

Charlotte's whole heart lay nestled between those covers.

They all three tiptoed out of Susie's room. Charlotte closed the door softly and smiled up at Mr. Morland. "How'd you do that?"

He shrugged. "I just keep falling back on the horses. She seems fascinated with them."

Mr. Morland's hair was smashed flat on one side from sleeping. His long shirt hung down, untucked. No cravat for Susie to ruin, and no shirtpin, so his neck showed all the way down to his chest.

"Susie's always struggled with any kind of change. But it weren't till Papa left that she started having hysterics like this," Charlotte explained. "I think she needs a father in her life."

Mr. Morland glanced at Mrs. Tafford.

"Both your parents are gone, as I recall," Mrs. Tafford said. "So do you mean she needs a brother-in-law?"

Laws and gardens. She never meant to imply that. 'Specially not in front of Mr. Morland. What must he think? "No. I didn't mean . . . I won't never marry. I only meant, 'twould be nice if her own father were here. That's all." Charlotte lifted a miniature portrait off the sideboard in the nursery. Her father, before he'd lost her mother. She handed it to Mr. Morland. "That's him," she said.

Mr. Morland studied it for a few moments, then passed it along to Mrs. Tafford.

"Quite the handsome fellow." Mrs. Tafford glanced from Charlotte to the miniature and back. "I see where you get your eyes. Bigger and bluer than a summer sky." She handed it back to Mr. Morland.

He examined it again, comparing her and her father.

"And here's my mother." Charlotte held out a second miniature in a matching frame. "But I s'pose you already know what she looked like."

Mr. Morland took it. "On the contrary." He studied it. "A feminine version of Walter, to be sure."

Mrs. Tafford agreed. "I haven't seen a likeness of dear Louisa in a stone's age. Look at those locks of golden hair. No wonder she captured your father's heart."

Mr. Tafford opened the door to the nursery in a long white nightshirt and nightcap, his spindly legs poking out the bottom. "I just came up to see if the missus needed anything. Shall I send for the doctor?"

"No," Mr. Morland said. "Little Susan's all quiet now and sound asleep."

Mr. Tafford nodded. He didn't leave though. He just stood by the open door, looking expectantly at his wife.

"Well, well, then," Mrs. Tafford said, handing back the miniature of Charlotte's mother. "I guess I'll be off to bed if there's nothing else you need, miss."

"Thank you, Mrs. Tafford," Charlotte said.

Mrs. Tafford gave a quick dip and left with her husband.

When the door closed, Mr. Morland held out the painting of her father. "I beg your pardon, Miss Darby. I don't mean to overstep my place, but I am curious about something. Why did you leave a letter for your father?"

She looked down at her father's portrait again. His smile could melt an ice block. "I don't know. I have this feeling. Do you ever have a feeling, Mr. Morland? A feeling that things aren't exactly right?"

"There have been times."

"After our mother died, it were too much for him. He couldn't manage the sadness anymore. He left a letter saying we'd be better off without him and that he was going off on a fishing smack for a spell. A storm come up, and they said him, the captain, and a cook boy were all lost."

"But you have doubts?"

She shrugged. "Perhaps. A few things have happened since then that give me a feeling that maybe he's still about." She didn't know what to believe. It was hard to accept that after all that had happened in her family, her father would just up and leave them. Even the strongest of ships could only take so much beating before they broke. She hadn't even told Mr. Morland about her five brother yet.

Her father had never cared about fishing before. He'd cared about the whaling in the North Sea and the shipments of goose quills from Norway. The loads of cotton and wool to be shipped out. Business was good, far as she knew. Still, he'd up and left.

"How old were you?"

Charlotte lowered her head. She didn't want to see the look in his eyes as she told him about the worst moment in her life. Well, the second worst. "Thirteen."

He was quiet for some time. Then he said, "Just you and your sister. With no income? How did you survive?"

Charlotte took one last look at her father, then placed his portrait back on the table beside her mother.

"For a while, we had money coming in from the shipping business. And some saved up. But when word come of our father's fate, Mr. Burton bought us out. He gave us a hundred pounds for my father's half of the company. A company he'd built up from nothing."

She'd already lived through it, and she thought she'd been strong. She'd had to be—for Susie. But here, in this grand house, talking to Mr. Morland, it seemed too much to bear.

For the last six years, she'd had a stack of bricks pressing heavier and heavier on her chest, until her uncle had come along and lifted them off. This new money made her life entirely different. She could finally breathe again.

Mr. Morland stood quietly in the center of the nursery, just watching her with a little wrinkle in his brow. "You are a remarkable woman," he said. "Even if you do bite your nails."

Charlotte snorted. She put her hands behind her back and looked up at him. "Sorry." Even though he wasn't wearing all his fine attire, he looked handsome as ever.

He smoothed down his coat front. "Well, I'd best let you get some sleep so you can keep up with her when she wakes." He crossed to the door and put his hand on the knob. "Tomorrow, when she's ready, bring her to my office, and I'll keep my word to take her to the stables."

Charlotte nodded. "Thank you."

Mr. Morland opened the door and disappeared into the dark hall.

Charlotte closed the door behind him and leaned her head on it.

CHAPTER EIGHT

Henry jerked on the front door to the Grange and stepped out into the morning air. Nearly two weeks had passed since Miss Darby's coming, and as promised, today Mrs. Kelton's son would arrive. Hurst Hardwick. Henry knew him well enough. He was a year younger than Henry and rather a dandy, Henry always thought. Hardwick must be eager indeed to meet the new owner of Willowkeep for him to leave London before the end of the Season.

Every time Hardwick's name was mentioned, panic sparked in Miss Darby's eyes. He couldn't quite decide if it was meeting new people that worried her or new people meeting her sister.

He'd taken little Susie down to the stables after that first night, good as his word, and spent over an hour with her there, feeding fistfuls of hay to the stock horses and oats to the brood mares. The girl couldn't get enough of the animals.

She only said one word the whole time. *Powpy.* Which Miss Darby explained was not a made-up word but actually meant *horse* in her northern vernacular.

By the end of the hour, he'd found himself calling them that too, causing Miss Darby to burst into giggles.

Every day since, he'd walked with Miss Darby and her sister across the grounds and to the stables to see the powpies. He never stayed long, needing to get back to his duties.

Henry sat at his desk now, sorting through the correspondence. It was going to take half the day to answer all of these. When Miss Darby came, he'd have to keep it short.

Thus far, she had managed to keep Susie hidden away from most of the staff. Henry thought it did more harm than good. If Miss Darby would just let her sister be seen, there'd be no need for speculation. If they saw with their own eyes her sweetness, her innocence, and her open heart, they would come to like her as much as he did.

Mrs. Tafford was fond of the child, in spite of their rough beginning that first night. Henry had every confidence the rest of the staff would follow suit. He'd hired a nursemaid for the child—Fanny Brown—and based on Mrs. Tafford's reports, the nurse had made great progress at gaining the trust of both Miss Darby and her sister.

Henry had been summoned to the big house thrice more in the dark of night to calm the child. He didn't mind, but the lack of sleep was beginning to take a toll. Today, he hoped to remedy that.

Mrs. Kelton asked about the child every day. She'd still not seen more than that first glimpse when Henry had carried her in from the carriage. And now Hardwick would be thrown into the mix.

Henry scowled. It didn't take a soothsayer to figure out why Hardwick was here. Mrs. Kelton had lost her lands and home. But they were still up for the taking to the man who could win Miss Darby's affections. Though Henry had heard Miss Darby declare on more than one occasion that she would not—*could not*—marry.

A soft knock pulled him from his work. He checked his pocket watch. Nearly noon. Only one person tapped on his door like that—Miss Darby. Which meant she was there with her sister to visit the stables again.

"Come in," he called, straightening his waistcoat and smoothing his hair. Sure enough, the door opened, and Miss Darby's perfectly blue eyes peeked through.

"I don't mean to bother you, sir." She said that every time.

"Come in, come in. It's no bother." He stood and retrieved his hat. "In any case, I'm particularly in need of a break this morning. Susie is with you, I trust?"

Miss Darby opened the door wider, and the child burst in, clamping onto Henry's leg.

"I hope this morning hasn't been difficult for you." Miss Darby looked around Henry's office, clearly uncertain what in this room of luxury could possibly be difficult.

"Not at all," he said.

"Powpy," Susie said, still clinging to his leg.

He took the child's hand, and Miss Darby followed them out the door. When they stepped into the warmth of the sun, Henry hitched little Susie up into his arms. "I have a different surprise for you today."

Her little lip jutted out and quivered. A look he was all too familiar with. "This is a better surprise than a powpy."

The child looked at him with a penetrating stare. Whatever was wrong with her brain, she had an uncanny ability to gauge the earnestness of other people. Especially him.

"I assure you, it is a good surprise. Yes?" he said.

At last a smile smoothed the child's mouth, and she nodded.

"Good." He set her on the ground, and instead of heading toward the stables, Henry took them off down the path toward the Grange.

"Where are we going?" Miss Darby asked.

Henry winked at her. "It's a surprise."

She laughed, and her blue eyes lit up. Sometimes Miss Darby seemed as much like a child as her sister. Then there were moments when her past weighed down and her eyes darkened beyond her years.

"Henry!" a voice called. Jane.

Henry wrested his gaze from Miss Darby and looked up at his sister walking toward them. In less than an instant, Miss Darby had Susie up in her arms and shielded from the stranger.

Jane stopped in the middle of the gravel walk and waited for them. A basket hung on her arm. Henry stifled a groan. She'd brought him lunch.

"Miss Darby," Henry said when they caught up. "May I introduce you to my sister, Jane. Jane, Miss Charlotte Darby and her sister, Susan."

Henry had to tug a bit to get Miss Darby to release the child, but at last she let Henry take her. With her hands now free, Miss Darby curtseyed low as though she were meeting the princess herself.

She would never get used to her new status as mistress and one of the wealthiest women in Kent, let alone all of England. The Keltons had always moved in the upper circles of society, and should she wish, she could present herself at court. In fact, it would be expected. Henry could scarcely imagine Miss Darby having even the smallest inclination to go to court.

"So nice to finally meet you," Jane said. "Henry talks about you all the time." She turned to the child in Henry's arms. "Hello, little Susie."

Jane fished through her basket and pulled out an almond biscuit. "May I?" she asked Miss Darby.

Miss Darby nodded, though she still looked ready to grab her sister and make a run for it should the encounter with Jane prove disastrous.

Jane slid the basket up to her elbow, freeing both her hands. "Susie. I've got a sweet here for you. Would you like a biscuit?"

The girl leaned toward Jane, reaching out her hand. Jane gave her the treat.

"There now. I know how to make friends." Jane smiled at Susie and was rewarded with a very crumbly grin and a set of merry blue eyes. "Oh, you're a beauty. No wonder you've taken the heart of my brother."

"Jane." Need she be so free with her tongue in front of his employer? Of course Jane meant only little Susie, but Henry couldn't help a quick glance at Miss Darby.

Jane laughed. "I was bringing you lunch. Where are you—Oh, yes. I know exactly where you're going." She turned and fell in step as Henry set them walking again. Jane paced herself to walk alongside Miss Darby, leaving Henry behind, holding little Susie's hand.

Miss Darby's hair strayed from her bonnet, creating wispy strands that floated on the air and tickled the curve of her neck. She hadn't tied her bonnet ribbons, and they fell down her back, swaying as she walked. Mrs. Tafford had sent for the dressmaker the morning after Miss Darby's arrival. Miss Darby now wore a soft muslin dress, and the thin fabric did much more for her figure than the stiff cotton she'd been wearing before.

"Don't you think, Mr. Morland?" Miss Darby spun around as she asked the question.

Henry's eyes went quickly to her face. "I beg your pardon. Do I think about what?"

Jane grinned. "Come, we don't need his opinion. He's not half as important as he thinks he is." She looped her arm through Miss Darby's.

Henry looked down at Susie. The young girl smiled up at him.

In a few minutes, they came to Willow Grange. Henry took them around the side of the house to a small byre, then knelt down in front of Susie. "You wait here with your sister and Jane. I'll be right back."

He took one step before Miss Darby caught his arm and said quietly, "You know she don't always take well to new things. You sure you know what you're doing?"

"I'm sure. She will like this."

Miss Darby nodded, and Henry ducked into the old stone shed. He came out a moment later holding his surprise secreted under his coat. He knelt again in front of Susie. "Ready?"

The girl's eyes danced.

Henry pulled back the folds of his coat to reveal a black-and-white spaniel pup. If possible, the child's eyes grew even bigger. "He's for you."

Susie stared at it with a huge smile.

"Oh, Mr. Morland. He's beautiful!" Miss Darby was on her knees in an instant, running her hands through the animal's soft fur. "Look at him, Susie."

"You can pet him just like you do the powpies." Henry lifted Susie's hand and put it on the pup's neck.

A moment later, Susie had both hands and her face buried in the spaniel's coat. The puppy lost all restraint, licking her face while his tail thumped wildly into Henry's chest. Henry set the pup down and stood. Freed from Henry's arms, the dog bounded in circles around Susie, stopping every few seconds for more licking and tail wagging.

Henry turned to Miss Darby. "He's from a tenant's litter. I thought maybe a companion might help her sleep at night." It might help all of them sleep at night, and possibly Miss Darby could move out of the nursery. She'd been sleeping in the nursemaid's quarters all this time, leaving Fanny to sleep up in the servants' hall.

"You are so kind to us, Mr. Morland." Miss Darby didn't look at Henry; her eyes followed Susie as she tried to keep up with her bounding puppy.

"William!" Henry called to a golden-haired lad who'd been hovering in the door of the byre.

Will walked over, taking off his cap as he bowed to Miss Darby and Jane.

"Miss Darby, this is William Stayner." The boy bowed again. "Will is the son of George Stayner—your stable master."

Miss Darby gave Will a curtsey, making the boy grin. Henry really needed to have a good long lesson with her about social standings. But not till after he had a good long talk with her about chewing her nails—again. She had her finger in her mouth, gnawing away at it as she always did when she had to meet new people.

"I've asked Will to help with the pup. He'll need a good bit of training, and Will's pleased to do that for you."

"Yes, miss," Will said.

Miss Darby didn't seem exactly pleased. "Thank you, Will," she said. "Uh, Mr. Morland. Could I speak to you a moment?"

"Of course." Henry stepped aside with Miss Darby.

"What about Susie?" she asked, her eyes darting back and forth between her sister and Will.

"What about her?"

"He might, you know . . . What if he don't like her because she's . . . ill-thriven?"

Naturally that was what worried her. "You must have a very low opinion of me to think I wouldn't choose with great care the person to work with your sister's pup."

Her eyes widened. "No, sir. I don't. I mean I do. I do have a good opinion of you. The best, sir."

"Then trust me," he said. "This will be good." Henry had full confidence in his plan to provide Susie with both a pet and a friend. Moreover, he believed this would benefit Miss Darby as much as it would her sister.

Will was a good lad. He would be kind to the child despite her difficulties. Then Miss Darby would see that not everyone was as uncharitable to a simple child as she feared.

"Yes, sir," she said.

And he wished she wouldn't call him sir. He was no gentleman. But that was another lesson for another day.

"Well, then," Henry said. "I'd best be getting back to work." He took his leave and turned toward the big house.

"Henry," his sister called out. "Don't forget your lunch."

Blast. She'd noticed. He took the basket from Jane, lifting the cloth to survey the contents. Bread and cheese. Cold ham. And a few almond biscuits. Seemed safe enough. He pecked his sister on the cheek. "Thanks."

"Mr. Morland." Miss Darby tried to wedge some stray locks of hair into her bonnet. "I hoped you might be able to join us for dinner tonight. You and your sister."

He should have seen that coming. With Hardwick scheduled to appear, Miss Darby wanted a second again. He sometimes wondered if that was all he was to her, the buttress to lend support when the weight of her new life was too much.

She was kind to include Jane, though Mrs. Kelton wouldn't be happy about it. She didn't believe in sharing her table with the peasants. She tolerated Henry because he was the steward and, therefore, not quite servant, though most certainly not a peer. Jane had nothing in the way of connections. All she had was a pretty face. One Mrs. Kelton preferred not be present when her son was around.

Jane's eyes lit up, so of course Henry would accept. "We'd be honored. Thank you, Miss Darby."

Miss Darby's whole countenance relaxed. The poor girl. Even after a fortnight, she was as much a fish out of water as ever.

A blur of black-and-white fur bounded past, followed by the laughing child trying to keep up despite her uneven gait. "Powpy," she called, and the dog raced back, lavishing her with kisses until they both tumbled to the ground. She grabbed the pup by the neck, pulling him closer until they lay on the grass in a tangled heap.

Henry glanced up in time to see that look again in Miss Darby's enormous blue eyes: love, pure and complete, as she watched her sister play with the dog.

Henry tucked Jane's arm into his, and they set off for the big house at exactly seven fifteen to ensure they would arrive promptly at half seven for the evening meal. He hadn't seen any carriage arrive, so either Hardwick was late, or he'd come on horseback.

Jane seemed especially animated to be out for dinner. Her dress was a soft creamy white, with flowers stitched in a rich purple, and all of it edged in a purple trim. It brought out her brown eyes and hair, lovely in the low evening light.

Old Tafford announced them as they entered the drawing room. Henry took it as a good sign that they hadn't been accosted by Miss Darby in the hallway. She sat in the drawing room reading a book, alone.

"Oh, good. You're here." Miss Darby stood and made a curtsey to them.

Jane let out a little snort, and Henry nudged her with his elbow.

"Miss Darby." Henry gave her quick nod.

"Jane, you look beautiful," Miss Darby said.

Miss Darby also looked lovely, though her gown of pale peach did nothing to complement her complexion. She had looked perfectly splendid this afternoon in her blue muslin.

The door to the drawing room opened, and Mrs. Kelton entered, her nose once again so high Henry looked away lest he catch a glimpse of her brains—what little of them existed. The effect on Miss Darby was immediate. Her eyes dimmed, her shoulders drooped, and the flush that had given life to her face fled.

"Oh, I see we're to dine with the servants again." Mrs. Kelton sniffed as she took her usual seat in the stiff-backed chair. "My son will be down shortly. He's just arrived and changing out of his traveling clothes. The roads were quite dusty, I'm afraid."

"I'm sorry to hear that," Henry said. Not so much because he cared but because the silence that had fallen at Mrs. Kelton's entrance had become uncomfortable. If only Hardwick's horse had thrown a shoe. Or broken a leg.

Miss Darby went back to her book. Jane walked over to the window. Mrs. Kelton spent a good ten minutes adjusting the screen to shield her face from the fire. That the fire existed at all was a sure sign of Miss Darby's desire to please her aunt. Miss Darby hated the heat of a fire on these warm summer nights.

Old Tafford opened the door once again. "Mr. Hurst Hardwick."

CHAPTER NINE

Charlotte clapped her book closed.

Mr. Hardwick was the finest-looking man she'd ever seen. He wore silk breeches that perfectly matched the flowers on his silk vest, and the cut of his coat showed off his broad shoulders. And his hair? How had he gotten it to go all up and forward like something from a sculpture?

No wonder Aunt Nora was so proud of her son.

Her aunt rose to her feet. "Hurst, this is the new mistress of Willowkeep, Miss Charlotte Darby."

Charlotte scrambled to her feet and gave him a deep curtsey. "Pleased to meet you, sir." She stopped herself just as her fingernail was headed to her mouth. Mr. Morland wouldn't want her chewing her nails in front of Mr. Hardwick. She glanced over at Mr. Morland, but he seemed to be more interested in checking his pocket watch than in Mr. Hardwick.

Mr. Hardwick took Charlotte's hand and kissed the back of it. "Cousin Charlotte. The pleasure is mine." He stared at her a moment, then released her hand and went over to Mr. Morland. "Still here, I see."

Mr. Morland nodded. "Naturally. Our family has long been a part of Willowkeep. I see no reason to change that. It's important to keep a place like this in the family, don't you think?"

Mr. Hardwick's eyes flashed. "Indeed." He turned away and seemed to notice Mr. Morland's sister for the first time. "Miss Morland." He strode over to the window and took her hand, kissing it just like he'd done to Charlotte. "I didn't expect to see you here."

Miss Morland pulled her hand from his grasp. "This is my home, Mr. Hardwick. Where else would I be?" She turned away and crossed the room to stand by her brother.

Charlotte looked at Mr. Morland, then over to Mr. Hardwick, then back at Mr. Morland. Mr. Morland finally took his eyes off Mr. Hardwick and smiled at her. The door opened, and Mr. Tafford announced dinner.

Now what? Charlotte was the mistress of the house but unmarried. She'd fall under Mrs. Kelton, wouldn't she? Then Mr. Hardwick would have to take his mother in, and she'd so hoped he might take her in to dinner. Either way, Miss Morland would be left alone. She should have invited another gentleman, but she didn't know any.

She wouldn't leave Miss Morland alone for anything. Not on her first day dining with them. Mr. Hardwick took two steps in her direction, but before he reached her, Charlotte held out a hand to Miss Morland. "Come. You and I shall go in together."

Aunt Nora's fan fluttered round her face. "Well . . . I never."

Mr. Hardwick steadied his mother and patted her on the back. She laid one hand on his arm, and the other she pressed over her heart as though it might pop right out. He led her out of the drawing room.

Charlotte turned to Mr. Morland. She'd done it again. She always did the wrong thing and this time in front of Mr. Hardwick. How long until she got the knack of this society business?

Mr. Morland had a smile big as ever.

"I'm sorry, Mr. Morland. I'm trying. Really, I am."

"Miss Darby. You really are anomalous. You did well." He waited for her and Miss Morland to pass, then followed them across the hall to the dining room.

Throughout the meal, Mr. Hardwick told them stories of this and that and so-and-so and who was out riding with whom in the park and this ball and that ball and the concert at the Hall. Mr. Hardwick must have been the center of society in London. But he'd left early, he said, because he couldn't wait to meet her.

"Will you go back?" Charlotte asked. Now that Mr. Hardwick had gotten his look at her and her ill-mannered ways, perhaps he might turn round and ride back to London this very night.

Mr. Hardwick smiled and took a sip of wine. "No. I don't think I will. The Season is nearly over, and there are some lovely sights here in Kent as well." He dabbed at his mouth with his napkin.

Miss Morland coughed and reached for her water. She drained her whole cup.

Mr. Morland motioned for the footman to refill her glass. "Nice to see you're finally interested in this place, Hardwick. You haven't been around much these last years."

"I've been busy. Business keeps me away."

"And what business would that be?" Mr. Morland asked, sawing through a cut of poultry.

Miss Morland jabbed her elbow into her brother's side.

Aunt Nora cleared her throat. "The quarter day is fast approaching, Mr. Morland. I do hope all our tenants will be ready with their rents."

"You mean Miss Darby's tenants," Mr. Morland said, stabbing a forkful of roasted woodcock.

Charlotte hadn't eaten a bite for going on ten minutes as she watched them all. Now all eyes were on her. Her tenants. She didn't know a single one of them. Perhaps she should have been out meeting them or something. Though, wouldn't Mr. Morland have told her so?

Mrs. Kelton stood. "I'm afraid I can't eat another bite. I shall retire to the drawing room." She left with a swish of black silk.

Mr. Hardwick glared at Mr. Morland. "Well done, Morland. Now you've upset Mother."

"I beg your pardon," Mr. Morland said, though he didn't look sorry at all. "In any case, rents were paid on Lady Day, not Midsummer. Have been since the beginning of time."

Miss Morland put her napkin over her mouth.

"Pray, Miss Morland," Mr. Hardwick said. "What is so funny?"

She glanced at Charlotte, then over to Mr. Hardwick. "I can't think of a time when your mother was *not* upset."

Charlotte gasped. How did Miss Morland dare be so bold to him?

Mr. Hardwick's eyes narrowed at Miss Morland, then a smile cracked through. "Touché, Miss Morland." He scraped his chair back. "I'll go see to her. If you will excuse me, Charlotte."

Charlotte nodded at him. Then as soon as the door closed behind him, she leaned forward. "I don't understand anything about what just happened."

"Neither do I," Mr. Morland said.

"Oh, Henry. Stop teasing her."

If Charlotte hadn't come down from Hull as heiress, Mr. Hardwick would stand in line to inherit. Or so she thought. It made sense that if the estate had gone to Aunt Nora, it would be hers to pass on to whoever she wanted, including her only son.

"Should we go after them?" Charlotte asked. Perhaps it was her duty to smooth things over.

"No need. I see the dessert is here, and I, for one, am very fond of spotted dick." He leaned to the side while a footman placed a wedge of the steamed pudding in front of him. Mr. Morland spooned treacle sauce over the top. "I'm sure Mrs. Kelton will still be duly offended by the time we finish this." He winked at Charlotte.

Charlotte laughed. She didn't mean to. She'd been trying to be better, to avoid the disapproving looks of her aunt. But the pudding did smell like a dream. "And now we can eat in peace." She slapped a hand over her mouth. "I shouldn't have said that. It's just that my aunt makes me so uneasy."

"And Mr. Hardwick?" Miss Morland asked. "Does he also make you uneasy?"

He was very fine. Finer even than Mr. Morland. Mr. Morland never made her uneasy. Mr. Hardwick, however . . . "Perhaps a bit. He is such an elegant gentleman and so very high above me. Who was his father?"

"Marshall Hardwick," Mr. Morland said. "The third son, I believe, of the Hardwicks of Devonshire. Not nearly as wealthy as Mr. Kelton's lot, mind. Marshall Hardwick went into the church and had the living on his father's estate. After his death, his wife, Mrs. Nora Hardwick, married Walter Kelton and became our own dearest Mrs. Kelton."

"How old was he when he came here?" Charlotte asked.

"Eighteen," Miss Morland said. "Right after his mother and Mr. Kelton were married."

Both her aunt and Mr. Hardwick had lost their home to Charlotte. "I've taken what is rightfully his. He must hate me."

"Miss Darby," Mr. Morland said. "I think you'll find that is the precise reason he will *not* hate you."

"Hush, Henry." Miss Morland dug her spoon through her pudding, picking out the currants. Mr. Morland held out his plate, and she scooted the berries onto it. He ladled on more treacle sauce until the dried fruits floated in currant soup.

"Mr. Hardwick may seem a bit gruff," she said, "but he has always been a perfect gentleman to me."

"Has he?" Mr. Morland gave his sister a glare, which she returned without flinching.

Mr. Morland tossed his napkin on the table and stood. "Miss Darby, I feel I should go and make my apologies to Mrs. Kelton. Excuse me." Mr. Morland left without another word.

Charlotte stared down at her pudding. Only she and Miss Morland were left at the table. If she didn't feel like the odd sheep out before, she certainly did now. Something had gotten Mr. Morland's feathers up. And

Miss Morland's. And, well . . . It seemed all of them were angry about something.

She pushed her food round on her plate. She daren't speak to Miss Morland for fear of driving her from the table as well. But when Miss Morland laid her spoon down and let out a sigh, Charlotte couldn't help but ask, "Have I done wrong, Miss Morland? I didn't mean to make your brother angry with me."

Miss Morland looked up with her brown eyes. "He's not angry. Leastways not with you." She pushed her plate away and set down her napkin. "And, please, call me Jane. I cannot bide Miss Morland and all its formality. Not with friends."

Friends. That sounded lovely. Charlotte took a bite of her pudding.

The door to the dining room opened, and Mr. Morland leaned his head in. "Did Hardwick come back?"

Charlotte shook her head, her mouth too full to speak.

"No, we haven't seen him," Jane said.

Mr. Morland stepped into the room. "Miss Darby, where is your sister?"

Charlotte gulped her food down. "Upstairs, in the nursery with Fanny." She stood quickly from the table. "You don't think . . . ?"

"I do," Mr. Morland was already turning to leave.

"I'll go sit with Mrs. Kelton," Jane said. "You go."

"Thank you." Charlotte ran to catch up with him.

"He wasn't with his mother. He never made it that far. But Mrs. Kelton let slip that when he arrived, he was asking about Susan and her condition."

Mr. Hardwick had no business in the nursery—if that was where he'd gone. What could he possibly want? Would he try to ship her off? What if he upset her? Was that a scream?

She hefted her skirts and took the stairs two at a time. Mr. Morland's footsteps followed close on her heels.

Another cry carried down the corridor. Charlotte glanced back at Mr. Morland as she ran down the hallway. He gave her a reassuring nod.

Charlotte threw open the nursery door and nearly collided with Fanny.

"Sorry, miss." Fanny curtseyed. "I was just coming to find you."

Mr. Hardwick stood in the center of the room as though lost. Susie had scooted into the corner of the window seat with her arms and legs flying. Even the dog seemed frightened of her.

Charlotte ran to her sister, giving Mr. Hardwick her darkest scowl as she passed. Lucky for Mr. Hardwick, she didn't have a stone with her.

Susie kicked and scrambled to get away, all the while screaming. Charlotte couldn't get close enough to calm her down.

Mr. Morland shouldered his way in front of her. Susie's foot landed him in the gut, but he grabbed her legs anyway and held them down. He turned her face with his other hand so her eyes were only on him. He smiled at her, winking like he always did. "Hush, now, Susie. You're scaring Puppy."

That was the name Susie had given the dog. Charlotte had tried to talk her into other names in hopes of getting her to say another word, but all Susie would say was Puppy. Or maybe it was powpy. They sounded the same out of her mouth.

"See?" Mr. Morland let go of Susie's legs and pointed to the spaniel cowering under the rocking chair. "He's scared."

Susie's cries died out, and she reached for Mr. Morland. He lifted her into his arms.

"What are you doing in here?" Charlotte asked Mr. Hardwick.

He shrugged. "I came to see for myself what you've been hiding."

Mr. Morland shifted Susie to his other arm. "Have a care what you say, Hardwick."

Mr. Hardwick let out a derisive laugh. "Or what? You'll throw me out? You are nothing but a hired hand, Morland. It's time you remembered that."

Susie's head was buried in Mr. Morland's cravat again. She ruined more of his neckcloths . . . but he never complained. In fact, had he not been holding her sister, Charlotte got the feeling he might've thrown a fist at Mr. Hardwick.

She half hoped he would. That man had no right to invade the nursery and frighten Susie half to death. Charlotte stepped forward. "You are a guest in my house." She pointed a finger at him. "And you have no excuse for what you have done. Leave the nursery at once."

Mr. Hardwick's face flushed. He bowed formally to Charlotte. "Miss Darby." And then he left.

Mr. Hardwick must loathe her now more than ever. Charlotte's shoulders slumped. She'd just stood up to a real gentleman, one so many times above her. But she'd had to. For her sister's sake. To keep her little family together. For that, she'd do anything.

She turned to find Mr. Morland staring at her like he'd never seen her before in his life. No doubt she'd disappointed him too. She was sick to the gills of people looking at her like she was the lunatic. They didn't know coals from cowls what it was like for Susie and her.

Charlotte waved the nursemaid away. "You can go now, Fanny. I'll stay with her until she's asleep." Charlotte waited until the door closed, then turned to Mr. Morland. "I'm not hiding her." He'd better not be thinking she was ashamed of her own sister.

He nodded. "I know."

"I'm just trying to protect her from the likes of Mr. Hardwick."

"I know."

Susie reached for her puppy, and Mr. Morland set her down. She and the dog ended up on the floor in a tangle of pied fur and brown hair.

"You need not justify yourself to me," he said. "I understand your reasons, whether I agree with them or not."

How could he say such a thing? She had to protect her sister. It was her duty. Her life.

"You don't know what's happened to us. You haven't seen the things people do to a lunatic child. You weren't there, were you, when our mother went into the river? Or when my brothers died. Or when father left us. You can't understand what it's like to have your whole family gone."

CHAPTER TEN

Miss Darby's eyes were wild again, feral like the cats that hunted in the stables. She couldn't abide anything against her sister.

"Miss Darby." Henry used the same voice he used for Susie. In some ways, they weren't so different. "You are right. I don't know anything about your life before you came here. I wish you would tell me about it."

She turned away.

There was more to her story, but anytime he came close to it, she held her tongue. Her past haunted her. Henry's only consolation was that at least here, at Willowkeep, her future was secure.

Soft snores came from under the rocking chair. Susie and the pup both slept, the dog's tail wagging as he dreamed.

"Shall I move her to her bed?" Henry asked.

Charlotte shook her head. "I'll do it. I don't mean to keep you here. Please give my excuse to Jane."

He bowed to her and left the nursery.

Henry made his way back down the stairs. There was no point in remaining at the big house. He had no desire to spend an evening with Hardwick, and undoubtedly Mrs. Kelton had no desire to spend an evening with him.

He opened the door to the drawing room. Jane's head spun around, her cheeks even more flushed than Miss Darby's had been. Hardwick stood near her at the window, his face a mask of foppish grins. That man needed to be dragged down a few rungs. Lucky, then, that with Miss Darby's arrival as the new owner, he had already descended several.

"Jane, Miss Darby is needed in the nursery and won't be coming back down. Are you ready to leave?"

Jane turned to Hardwick and gave him a stiff curtsey. "Good-bye, Mr. Hardwick."

He returned her bow with one of his own. “It was a pleasure to see you again, Miss Morland.”

She hooked her arm through Henry’s, and they headed back to the Grange.

“What was that about?” Henry asked.

“What?”

He hadn’t missed the glances between Hardwick and his sister this evening. Nor was this the first time he’d caught them glancing. Before Hardwick left for Cambridge, he and Jane had spent more time together than Henry appreciated. Or Mrs. Kelton.

Unfortunately for Jane, Miss Darby was right—she *had* taken from Hardwick his entire fortune. If Hardwick intended to maintain any semblance of his life in the Ton, he must marry for money. And Jane had none. Not to mention she suffered the same fate as Henry—a status far below that of the gentry folk.

“I don’t want to see you get hurt,” Henry said.

“Let me assure you, I am in no danger whatsoever in that regard.” She released Henry’s arm and hurried home ahead of him.

Henry closed his ledger with a thud. According to the Bible, he should be free from the sins of his father. If only that could be true. He was paying dearly for them. And Jane too.

The ledger contained a tally of his father’s debts. The list included a few local public houses, along with a gaming den all the way up in London. The Black Fox. This was the bill that would cost him everything. The total owed equaled nearly ten times Henry’s yearly income.

How was he supposed to provide any kind of life for Jane if all his money went to settle debts? Jane was old enough to marry, but her dowry—such as it was—had been squandered by their father. Add to that the fees to keep his father fed and clothed in the Marshalsea. If he died in prison, all his debts would be cleared. Lud. What kind of son was he to even think such things? He rubbed a hand across his face. A desperate son, that was what.

River Head Mill needed someone to work their accounts now that Timothy Rowbottom had left for the Americas. Henry could apply there to bring in extra income. When would he have time, though; that was the real question. Perhaps he could work nights—at least until the harvest.

Work at the mill would do nothing to elevate his status among the people of Kippingham, nor up at the big house. But he had little choice left if he hoped to pay off the debts. He walked a thin line as steward. Not a servant. Not a gentleman. Just a man of business caught in the middle.

He checked his watch. Time to head up and attend the accounts of Willowkeep. They were much easier to reconcile than his own.

Jane helped him into his coat, then handed him a basket. "Don't forget your lunch."

Henry slowly lifted the cover. "What is it?"

"Meat and potato pie. Your favorite."

Why did she think everything was his favorite? "Thanks." He leaned in and kissed her cheek.

"Is it so very bad?" Jane asked.

"Is what so bad?" Henry set his beaver on his brow, as any gentleman would, even though the walk to the big house would take only a few minutes.

"I saw you poring over your ledgers. I know you too well, Henry Morland." She tied a bonnet under her chin. "Father's debts."

He smiled at her. "It's fine. You don't need to worry about it."

"Henry. How can you say that?" She held out her hands, red and calloused from cooking and cleaning and washing. At her feet rested the bundle of laundry and mending she'd taken on to bring in extra money.

She was right, of course. They both carried the burden of their father's mistakes.

Jane straightened his cravat. "Why don't you ask Miss Darby for an advance. I'm sure she wouldn't mind."

Henry shook his head. "No. Absolutely not. What kind of steward can't reconcile the funds of his own household?" He would never risk the opinion of Miss Darby nor his position at Willowkeep. If she learned he couldn't manage his own affairs, her confidence in him as a steward would crumble. He'd lose his job, and his humiliation would be complete.

"I can do more than washing and sewing," Jane said. "I'm sure Mrs. Puddleworth would take me on to help at her boarding school. She's always complaining about her back."

"Certainly not. I will not have my sister hired out like a common laborer." He'd take on the mill job before he'd let Jane lower herself any further in society. His position at Willowkeep payed well. Two hundred pounds was no small wage for a working man. It was an honorable occupation to be the steward of one of the county's finest seats.

If only his father hadn't . . . No point in going there again. All the anger in the world wouldn't change his circumstances. "Don't worry. I'll find a way. Even if I have to steal it." He winked at her.

She shook her head as she lifted her basket of sewing and started down the lane toward Kippingham.

CHAPTER ELEVEN

By coming down early, Charlotte had hoped to avoid Mr. Hardwick. Alas. He jumped to his feet as she entered the breakfast room. Aunt Nora rose gracefully beside him.

"My dear niece, how lovely you look this morning." She gave Charlotte's arm a squeeze.

Dinner last night hadn't gone so well. Charlotte's efforts at making friends with her aunt must have taken a blow. Yet here she was, complimenting her. A compliment more than likely hollow, but still. If her aunt didn't completely snub her, that was something to build on.

"Thank you, Aunt. You are also looking very well." Charlotte was going to win her over no matter how many layers of polish she had to apply.

Aunt Nora smiled, then with a heavy nod to her son, she left the room.

"Good morning, Charlotte." Mr. Hardwick pulled a chair from the table and motioned for her to sit. "Allow me to make a plate for you."

Mr. Hardwick, on the other hand, deserved none of her generosity. Not after last night.

Charlotte picked up a blue willow dish from the sideboard. "I'm perfectly able to fix my own breakfast."

Mr. Hardwick took the plate from her. "Please. You must allow me to begin my groveling for last night's faux pas. I forgot myself. I've made you angry, and I am wholeheartedly sorry for it."

He wore another fine silk waistcoat, with matching trousers and coat. He smiled down at her, his eyes soft and gray like the morning fog over the river Humber. He must be used to having the run of the house—just him and his mother and Walter for so long. But that didn't mean he was free to invade the nursery and gawp at her sister like she was a sideshow curiosity. Even Aunt Nora hadn't been so bold.

Charlotte sat in the chair he'd offered her. It wasn't as though she'd been the picture of mannerly last night either. She'd taken the loss of his income and thrown it back in his face. Perhaps they both needed a second chance.

Above all, Susie must be safe. "And you'll not give my sister a fright ever again?"

"You have my word."

"And you'll stay away from the nursery?"

"I shall not even enter the east wing."

"Very well, then." She'd let him have another try. For the sake of family.

He browsed the sideboard, putting together a selection of foods for her. "Now let me think. I see you as a toasted-muffin, honey-and-jam sort of girl. Perhaps some cold ham?" He forked a few slices onto her plate. "Hm. No kippers—you've had enough of those growing up in a fishing port. But most definitely some strawberries and cream."

Mr. Hardwick placed the plate down in front of her. He'd made decent work of guessing her tastes—save one thing.

"Not bad," she said. "But I don't care a cow's lick for strawberries."

"My apologies. I shall take note for the future."

The future? How many times did Mr. Hardwick think he'd be filling her breakfast plate? She'd have to delay her morning meal if that was the case. Or eat with Susie up in their rooms.

Mr. Hardwick poured himself a cup of tea and sat at the table beside her. It appeared he was planning on watching her eat. Charlotte glanced at the clock on the mantel. Too early still for Mr. Morland to be here, else she might have taken her plate in to eat with him.

"So." Mr. Hardwick sipped his drink. "What are your plans for this glorious day?"

Her plans weren't none of his business. Not that she had grand ones. Same thing she did every day.

"I thought I might give you a tour of the grounds. There are some remarkable prospects."

Charlotte spread the black-currant preserves across her muffin. "Mr. Morland has already given me a tour of the grounds."

"Has he now?" Mr. Hardwick drained his cup and pushed it away. "He doesn't know all the places I know."

She highly doubted Mr. Hardwick knew the grounds better than Mr. Morland.

"Cousin Charlotte." Mr. Hardwick scooted his chair closer. "We got off on the wrong foot. The fault of which I bear entirely. I would be ever so grateful if you'd give me a chance to make amends. Such as I can."

He sounded earnest and genuinely sorrowful—though she wasn't entirely sure whether his regret was for his violation of her privacy or because he'd been caught.

He smelled like the sandalwood her father used to wear. His hair was up again in the perfect coif he'd worn yesterday. His Hessians sparkled like they'd been polished with diamond dust. Perhaps a short walk with Mr. Hardwick would be penance enough for the way she'd yelled at him last night. Especially if it would keep him away from Susie.

"Very well." She put her napkin on the table. "I accept."

"Excellent." Mr. Hardwick pushed his chair back and rose.

"I'll fetch my bonnet and be right back." Better to get out and back before the heat of the day. It was excessively hot here in Kent.

Several minutes later, Mr. Hardwick escorted Charlotte out the front door. He offered her his arm. She ignored it. They strolled round the side of the house until they ended up on the path that led to Mr. Morland's home. Just as Mr. Hardwick motioned to turn off the path, Mr. Morland rounded the bend. On his way to work, she supposed.

His step caught for just a moment. He gave Charlotte a quick bow. "Miss Darby. Hardwick."

"Just taking Miss Darby out to see some of the grounds," Mr. Hardwick said.

Mr. Morland looked at her, and she shrugged. Wasn't her idea to go walking, but she couldn't rightly say that in front of Mr. Hardwick. So she just gave Mr. Morland a curtsey.

"Good day, Morland." Mr. Hardwick seemed in a hurry to move on. Mr. Morland was still staring at them as they rounded the corner out of sight.

"I have the most lovely place to show you. I'm sure you'll love it," Mr. Hardwick said. "But I'm going to save it for last. First I want to show you the trout stream. It has the best fishing for miles around."

Fishing? Had Mr. Hardwick forgotten already what he so cleverly figured out at breakfast? She'd had her fill and more of fishing.

They walked for some time before they came to the stream. Mr. Hardwick took her to a place where the water slowed and widened, with a pocket of weeds bordering the bank. "This is the best place to catch fish."

Mr. Morland had already brought her here. But he hadn't talked about fishing. He'd been too busy skipping rocks into the river. Susie laughed and laughed, then she'd handed him more stones. Susie hadn't any idea of the proper shape of a skipping rock, but Mr. Morland threw them anyway. Just the plunk and splash had been enough to delight.

Mr. Hardwick spread out his hands more than a shoulder's width apart. "I once reeled in a pike at least this big."

Charlotte looked down at the stream. Seemed like a good-size fish, considering the smallness of the water. "In the Humber, the lads pull in cod at least twice that size nearly every day during their season. Some near as tall as a man. And loads of fish come in from the silver pits of the North Sea."

Mr. Hardwick laughed. "I should have known better than to tell fishing stories to you. I'm sure you can out-tell us all."

Gaw. He had no idea the things she'd seen. "Two years ago Old Man Crompton netted a cod, and when he gutted it open he found a gold ring. True gold. He took that ring and marched right up to the door of Widow Spainhower's house and asked her to marry him."

"Is that so?" Mr. Hardwick said.

She nodded. "Only Widow Spainhower refused. Said anything plucked from the guts of a fish were bad luck. Old Man Crompton died the next day. Keeled over dead right in the street."

Mr. Hardwick seemed taken aback. "That is quite a story."

It was more than just a story. "'Tis true. Weren't no one willing to touch that ring after Old Man Crompton dropped dead. They buried him with it still stuck on his little finger. I saw it with my own eyes."

He turned his gaze back to the murky water of the West Kipping. "You must have seen many things living so close to the port."

Charlotte used to kneel on her bed and gaze out the window at the scene down in the harbor. "I sometimes watched from my bedroom. The sun coming up, its rays bouncing off the red sails of the fishing smacks, making them look like little balls of fire just floating in the water. 'Tain't nothing like it."

He scooped a handful of pebbles from the path and tossed them one by one into the stream. "Do you miss it? Kingston upon Hull?"

Like every place, it had its goods and bads. "I don't miss the stink of rendering whale blubber, nor the piles of fish guts. Nor the mess the gulls make as they swarm for the castoffs. Gaw, the droppings I've had to scrape off. And I don't miss the sailors and their shifty eyes."

She did miss the weather. Sweat trickled down her back, and more than anything, she wanted to swish her skirt to cool her legs. Mr. Hardwick stood in the sun as though it was the pleasantest spot on Earth.

She untied her bonnet and took it off, using the stiff, straw brim to fan her brow. If it was this hot in the morning, perhaps she and Susie would have to skip their walk this afternoon.

"Shall we find some shade?" Mr. Hardwick asked. "I have another place I want to show you."

He led her off to the south and then turned onto the path toward the willows. Mr. Morland had already brought her here too.

Her steps slowed as they approached the first tree, its branches stroking the water. He parted the curtain of tumbling limbs.

She peered into the coolness. And beyond that was Henry's Lion. Mr. Hardwick might want to take her there as well. She could almost hear the lion snarling at Mr. Hardwick, warning him to keep away. Or maybe it was just the wind.

This wasn't a place she cared to share with Mr. Hardwick.

The willow arbor was Mr. Morland's. And the beech tree, where he'd waded through the shrubs to find the stone she'd thrown. And the patch of lawn by the river where he'd brought Susie and Puppy to play. None of those belonged to Mr. Hardwick.

"I've lost track of the time." Charlotte turned toward the house. "I best get back to my sister. Thank you for the tour." Then off she ran. As she fled, she thought she heard a woman's voice calling to her.

A voice of strength but also sorrow.

The voice of Anne Boleyn.

"Could I interest you in a game of backgammon this evening?" Mr. Hardwick said as they finished another meal.

Mr. Hardwick had been at Willowkeep nigh on a fortnight. He'd sat with them in the Kelton box at church. He'd walked with her often in the mornings and dined with them in the evenings. True to his word, he'd kept himself far away from her sister. After his first blunder, Mr. Hardwick had turned out to be quite agreeable.

Susie was already asleep, as she was every evening by the time dinner was served. Backgammon seemed as good a way as any to pass the evening.

"That would be lovely. Will you join us, Aunt?"

Aunt Nora rose from the table. "Not tonight. I'm tired. I'll leave you two alone." She smiled at them as she left the room.

"Shall we?" Mr. Hardwick said, pulling back Charlotte's chair. "I've had it set up for us in the library."

Charlotte followed him up the stairs.

A fire burned and flickered in the hearth. Why they insisted on a fire in the dead of summer was beyond reason. Charlotte chose the seat most distant from its heat. A tray on a small side table carried tea, fruits, cheese, and cakes. As if Charlotte could eat another bite. Mr. Hardwick had gone to some lengths to make the library welcoming.

Charlotte had only come in this room once since she'd been at Willowkeep—and that had only been on the quick tour Mr. Morland had given her. She closed her eyes and breathed deeply, smelling the wax on the wooden floor, burning coals from the fire, lavender and rose from the vases of flowers, and all with a musty mingling of books.

According to Mr. Hardwick, the Parliament sitting was over and the Season in London with it. All the folks from the city would be pouring out to the country for summer and sport. "You'll be able to meet the neighbors now. Spend some time in real society," he said as if she'd been missing a vital organ her whole life and *real society* was the only place to acquire it.

Mr. Hardwick laid out the markers on the backgammon board. "Ladies first."

She hadn't played since her father had left. They used to have a lovely set in African rosewood, with ivory inlay. One of the benefits of having a shipping merchant for a father. But backgammon with Susie didn't work so well. That set was one of the first things to go when the funds had gone tight.

The game passed quickly. Charlotte won, mostly because Mr. Hardwick had foul luck with the dice.

"Two out of three?" he asked.

Charlotte nodded. "Why not."

She got first roll again and started off with double fives.

"Thunder and turf," he exclaimed. "You must be the luckiest woman alive. Perhaps I should take you with me to the races."

Charlotte laughed. "I don't know a thing about horses. I'm sure I would do you no good."

He smiled at her, his face breaking into a handsome grin that must be the talk of London. "I'm sure you would."

Never in her life would she have used the word *lucky* on herself. But it did seem that with the passing of Uncle Walter—God rest his soul—her situation had improved.

"It would be something to see though, wouldn't it?" Charlotte said. "I can't imagine what it's like, watching the horses run at top speed. Those poor riders must be scared to death."

"Ha," Mr. Hardwick said. "On the contrary, I believe it's what keeps them alive. Either that or the money waiting for them at the end. One needs a little excitement now and then, don't you think, to really feel alive?"

"I s'pose a little hubbleshoo now and then mightn't be a bad thing." She scooped the dice into her box and rattled them before casting them onto the game board. She landed where one of Mr. Hardwick's pieces already sat. She apologized as she removed yet another of his markers from the board.

"You're whipping me soundly." He laughed a merry laugh, and Charlotte couldn't help laughing too. "I'm now perfectly convinced that a day in Newmarket is in order."

"I'm sure a day in Newmarket would be entirely inappropriate," came a voice from the door. Mr. Morland stood there, a troubled look on his face.

"Morland, you're here late," Mr. Hardwick said.

"Some of us have to work for our money. Oh, but I see you are working." Mr. Morland nodded to Charlotte. "Miss Darby, sorry to interrupt. I just need to retrieve a map from the case here." Mr. Morland crossed the room and pulled open a long, narrow drawer.

"It's no interruption," Charlotte said. "I'm just beating the breeches off of Mr. Hardwick at backgammon."

Mr. Morland riffled through the papers and pulled out a large sheet. From where she sat, Charlotte couldn't tell what kind of map it was. Mr. Morland rolled it up, nodded again, and vanished.

"Now there's a fellow who needs a little hubbleshoo in his life," Mr. Hardwick said. "Stiff as a punting pole."

She'd never thought of Mr. Morland as stiff. He worked hard, for certain. He was reliable. Always there if Charlotte needed anything. He did seem tired when he'd come in just now. Likely what he needed was the opposite of a hubbleshoo. Some quiet time and a rest.

Taking Susie down to see him so often couldn't be helping. It was not as though everything stopped for him to spend time with her and her sister. It must put him behind in his work more and more each day. She ought to put an end to their frequent visits.

"Charlotte?"

She looked up at Mr. Hardwick.

"You've been shaking your dice long enough for me to make it to London and back. Is something amiss?"

She smiled at him. "No. Just lost in my thoughts, I s'pose." She set the dice box down. "You know this library well, do you not, Mr. Hardwick?"

He nodded, seeming a bit surprised at the turn in conversation.

Charlotte stood and examined the spines of the books on the nearest shelf. "Can you point me in the direction of the history books? Henry VIII, to be specific."

Charlotte did not go out for a walk with Mr. Hardwick after breakfast the following morning. She spent her time in the parlor with her nose buried in the history books.

Three years and thirty-seven days. It was all Anne Boleyn had got as queen before they executed her on the Tower Green. After seven years of courting her, divorcing his first wife, and reforming the country for her, King Henry cast her off like spoiled herring. After he accused Anne of adultery, witchcraft, and all kinds of slander, he turned his eyes to Jane Seymour. And Anne lost her head.

When the clock chimed eleven, Charlotte closed the book with a puff of dust.

She did not go to the nursery. She went straight to her room. After Mr. Morland gave Susie the puppy, she had slept peacefully every night. Charlotte had left the nursery bedroom to Fanny and moved into this room just down the hall. The bed was big enough for three.

Charlotte sat at the writing desk. On a clean piece of paper, she scored straight, even lines. This was a letter to a queen. It had to be just so.

Her Majesty Queen Anne Boleyn
The Tower of London or The Lion at Willowkeep, Kent

She wasn't rightly sure if she should address it to the resting place of her body or where her spirit seemed to haunt.

June 1810
Dear Anne,
I hope you don't mind me calling you Anne, but if we'd have lived in

the same time, I like to think we could be friends. That is, if you weren't the queen and me a common girl.

First, I want to tell you that I don't believe any of the lies about you. I always considered you quite mannerly. Better than our own Caroline, to be sure. But I shan't say more on that. 'Tis not to the point.

I've been told that if I write you a letter regarding certain difficulties, you might be willing to lend a hand. I'm in a predicament.

There is a man, see, who's got his hook nipped into the corner of my heart. I'm trying to swim away, but he keeps reeling me in, slow and steady like some sort of flounder he's scooped out of the sea.

This cannot be.

Putting aside that he's a gentleman high above me and I'm a lowly merchant's daughter, I cannot let myself become attached to anyone. It is impossible. Especially not H. (I shall call him H.) It would end in disaster. I know this for certain.

Here is the rub: the more I push him away, the harder he pulls on his rod. I fear the hook will tear my heart and I shall bleed out.

I don't know what you can do, but I beg your help.

Yours in affection,
~C

(I'm very sorry about your head.)

Charlotte folded the letter, careful to tuck all the sides in so no one could read it. She sealed it. Not with the big fancy *W* of Willowkeep but with the small and simple *D&B* that used to be her father's shipping company.

She would be late for luncheon with Susie, but this letter had to be delivered immediately. She slipped out the back door and hurried to the willows.

CHAPTER TWELVE

Henry checked his watch. If Miss Darby was planning on a trip down to the stables with Susie today, she should have been here by now. Since Hardwick's arrival, she'd been coming less and less.

Stupid man. How could he even consider taking her to Newmarket—a full day's travel, not to mention the motley assortment of ne'er-do-wells that frequented racing events. Perhaps he'd accompanied her out walking again. Miss Darby would be roasting in this heat. Little Susie must be beside herself this long while without her sister. Had he no consideration for the child?

Henry smoothed out a piece of paper. In any case, he had letters to write. Might as well begin with the solicitor in London. He dipped his goose quill into the ink.

Mr. Bellwether Sutton
Londo—

Blast this pen. He chipped away at the quill with his penknife until it was completely unusable.

Henry pushed his chair back and strode to the window. Perhaps he should go look for her. Or at the very least check on Susie. He'd always been welcomed in the nursery, but after Hardwick's blunder, better to tread carefully.

A flash of pale blue muslin fluttered between the boxwoods. Miss Darby? Was she going out without him? Or just now coming back from her morning walk with Hardwick? It was the wrong direction for a return trip, so perhaps she'd decided to take Susie out without him. Yet he'd seen no sign of the child or her bounding dog.

He sat in his chair and leaned over the books. Miss Darby's comings and goings were none of his business. He had letters to write. Holdings to inspect. Tenants to visit. Accounts to settle. Not to mention finding a maid to replace Hannah Barwell. The girl had married a sheep farmer and gone off to live in the Dales.

He reached for his hat. Odd for Miss Darby to be out on the grounds alone this time of day. She was always with her sister. It wouldn't hurt to check on her, make sure all was well.

He slipped outside and hurried through the hedges. It didn't take long for him to spot her. She was on the path toward the willows, glancing side to side as if she didn't want to be seen. She turned to look behind, and Henry ducked behind a hedge.

Why the deuce was she stalking through the grounds so secretly? When he peered through the branches, she was gone. He followed along, always keeping just out of sight until Miss Darby parted the limbs and disappeared into the willow bower.

Perhaps she just needed a moment alone after spending the whole of the morning with Hardwick. Surely she would tire quickly around such a popinjay.

He waited less than a minute before she reappeared. Her feet barely made a sound as she passed through the branches and hurried back toward the big house. She'd walked all the way out only to turn immediately and head back.

He pulled back the curtains of green. Nothing out of the ordinary in the first arbor. He went to the second. The lion statue stood there growling at him as usual. And in his mouth a paper. Henry grinned. That was why she'd come.

He pried it out from behind the stone teeth. A lump of red sealing wax held it closed with the letters *D&B* pressed into it. Darby and Burton. Her father's old shipping business, now owned solely by Burton. The seedy man.

Henry flipped it over. It was addressed to *Her Majesty*.

Miss Darby had written a letter to Anne Boleyn.

He nearly laughed out loud. He wedged it back into the lion's mouth, then paused. What if someone else found it and read it? Certainly he and Miss Darby were not the only people who ever came here.

Matters of the heart, he'd explained to her. What matters of the heart grieved her so much that she needed to write to the beheaded queen? Had she left a beau back in Hull after all? She'd denied having one, but that didn't mean it wasn't so. Or maybe she'd met someone new. Like that rake, Hardwick.

He dropped the letter into his pocket. Best it not fall into the wrong hands.

Henry ducked out of the willows and made his way back to the house, keeping to the paths least visible from the upper windows of the nursery. He rubbed his hand over his pocket, listening to the paper crinkle. This was a private letter between Miss Darby and Anne Boleyn. Private and none of his concern. He wouldn't read it, of course. Just keep it safely away from prying eyes.

Unless Miss Darby was truly in distress.

She had mentioned quite adamantly that she could never marry. Why though? Was it possible that Susie was actually her . . . ? No. Certainly not. She would have been far too young.

But what, then?

The contents of the letter were not his business. Whatever the matter, Miss Darby would manage it. If she wanted his help, she would come to him. She always had before.

Back to work. He crumpled the blotched letter to Mr. Sutton and tossed it into the wastebin. Penknife in hand, he snatched a new quill from the drawer and went at it, stripping all but the topmost feathers.

If Miss Darby was in serious trouble, she would tell him, wouldn't she?

Henry pulled her note from his pocket and lay it on his desk. With a little help from his penknife, he carefully pried off the wax seal. He would be sacked for this if she ever found out. Or perhaps beheaded—the punishment fitting for traitors. But, by heaven, he had to know.

Henry smoothed it out, turning his back to the door, and read.

Lud. It was as he'd feared. Worse.

It wasn't hard to figure out who she meant. *H* for Hardwick. He could think of no other person she'd met with an H name who was a gentleman. A gentleman high above her. Her exact words to describe Hardwick that first evening she'd met him.

He'd always known Hardwick would be after Willowkeep and her money. He was a dandy, all right. How could Miss Darby resist? If he'd done anything untoward, Henry would see him hanged.

He read the letter again. *I cannot let myself become attached to anyone*, she wrote. Again this declaration that baffled Henry.

The door flew open, and Miss Darby burst in. She slammed it closed and leaned against it, her chest heaving and eyes wild.

Henry leapt from his chair, clutching the letter behind him as he backed into the cabinet. She'd found him out already. She must have seen him from the window despite his efforts to keep hidden.

"Miss Darby." He might as well send for the gallows right now. "I was just—"

"I've been invited to a ball." She had one hand pressed against her chest and in the other a wrinkled paper.

"What?"

"Mrs. Westwood has invited me to a ball." She thrust the paper at him. "A ball. How am I s'posed to manage that? I'll have to say no, of course. No matter how much it gets her bristles up. All those people gawking. Most of them probably wanting nothing more than news of poor Susie. They don't care two straws about me, just want the gossip about her. How's your sister? I hear she's daft. I hear she don't do more than drool. I hear she's got the devil in her. Well, she don't have the devil in her, and she never did. You know it, and I know it. They can't have her. I shan't go, I tell you. I—"

"Miss Darby." Henry secreted the queen's letter into his pocket, though he probably could have waved it in front of her face and she wouldn't have noticed it. He'd never seen her this fired up. The blue of her eyes churned and tumbled like the gathering clouds of a terrific storm. "Let me see."

Henry read the invitation while Miss Darby paced to and fro in the small quarters. Sure enough, she had been cordially invited to the summer ball at the Westwood's. The invitation was gracious and direct. The Westwoods were a long-standing and respectable family. Given half a chance, Miss Darby would likely have a splendid time.

Henry seriously doubted they cared at all about little Susan, though certainly the whole neighborhood was dying of curiosity about Miss Darby.

She flung herself into a chair, hanging her head.

"Come, come, now." If only he could calm her with horses and pups as he so easily did Susie. "All will be well. You need not attend if you truly desire not to. I can write an excuse."

Her head came up. "Would you?"

"Of course." He sat behind his desk. "Especially if you do not wish to dance to lively music. The Westwoods bring in musicians from London."

She frowned.

"Or sample the exquisite food from the Westwood's kitchens. Their cook comes all the way from France. Jacques Lévêque. He makes the most delectable *gâteau de mille-feuilles*—the cake of a thousand layers."

Her frown deepened.

"And then there's the hassle of a new gown. Only the best would do. Silk from the orient. Egyptian muslin. Blue, I think. That is your color. Lace. Ribbons. Not to mention new dancing slippers."

She looked down at her halfboots.

Henry lifted the lid of his inkwell. "It would be best to send your regrets immediately. Mrs. Westwood will be obliged to tell all the young men waiting to stand up with you the bad news. I happen to know that Mr. Westwood's nephew is coming from Addington Place. Regis Farnham. He is cleric to the Archbishop of Canterbury himself."

Miss Darby's jaw fell open.

Hopefully Henry had not presumed too much. He had no guarantee Mr. Farnham would be there. Farnham had attended every year for the past five years—ever since the Archbishop had taken his seat—so it seemed safe to assume.

Henry set a paper on his desk. "Poor Mrs. Westwood. To forgo the honor of being first to entertain you in her home. This will pain her." He hovered the quill he'd recently been hacking at over the paper.

"Wait," she said. "Let me think."

Henry dropped the goose feather into the ink pot. It was unusable anyway.

Miss Darby chewed on her nail. "What do you advise?"

"I advise you to attend." He was a fool. A fool and a half. One word from him would keep her safely at home. Away from the throng of young gentlemen who would be groveling for her favor. "It will be lovely and grand."

"Are you coming? It would be so much easier if I didn't have to go alone."

"You forget. Stewards are not invited to balls." Though what he wouldn't give to take a turn with her on the dance floor. But that was not what sent his boat careening. He still had to deliver the worst news of all. "You won't be going alone. I do not doubt for a moment that Mr. Hardwick has also received an invitation, along with his mother."

Her face lit up, stilling at last the storm in her eyes. The sudden calm did nothing to prevent his capsizing.

"Perhaps I should attend after all."

"I think that is a wise idea. Shall I send your acceptance?"

She nodded. "Yes. I s'pose so. Thank you, Mr. Morland." She turned and left.

Henry slumped into his chair and laid his forehead on his desk. No need for Miss Darby to hang him. He'd hanged himself.

A quarter hour later he opened his door and shouted for Mrs. Tafford.

She tottered down the hall. "Good heavens, what happened here?"

His desk and wastebin were strewn with the remnants of goose feathers. "This batch of quills is useless. All of them too hard. Send someone to the stationer for new ones immediately."

Mrs. Tafford stared at him. "Yes, sir." She retreated down the hall.

Henry slammed the door, then jerked it open. "And make sure they're decent this time."

CHAPTER THIRTEEN

"MR. HARDWICK?" CHARLOTTE WHISPERED INTO the library, where the footman had told her he'd last been seen.

Some papers rustled, and his head popped out from the depths of a leather chair. She was truly knobbed to be coming to him for assurances about the ball. Mr. Morland had made it sound like a fairyland of delights. But that didn't mean she was ready to be jaunting about the county.

Mr. Hardwick jumped to his feet. "Charlotte. What a pleasant surprise."

"Oh, Mr. Hardwick, I'm glad I've found you. I've something to tell you."

He folded and unfolded a piece of newsprint in his hands. "Uh, yes." He motioned behind her. "You've already met Miss Morland."

Charlotte spun round. Jane stood by a bookcase, holding a small stack of books in her hands.

"Jane. I'm so pleased you're here." She tugged on Jane's arm, pulling her closer to Mr. Hardwick.

"I came up to the house for some books," Jane said. "Mr. Hardwick lets me borrow a few books now and then. From the library. To read."

"That is very kind of him." Charlotte smoothed the crumpled invitation against her chest.

"Naturally it is your library now," Mr. Hardwick said. "So it is your permission Miss Morland will need." He slapped his folded paper against his leg a few times, then tossed it onto the leather chair.

"Oh, yes, of course. Anytime, Jane." Charlotte waved her letter in front of her. "Look what's arrived in the post today."

Mr. Hardwick took it from her. He gave it one glance and said, "Yes, indeed. Mrs. Westwood's summer ball. It is always the event of the season in these parts. Or should I say the event of the post-Season." He smiled broadly, but Charlotte didn't see what was so funny. "I received one too, for myself and Mother."

"And have you thought of whether or not you shall attend?"

"I never miss it."

Though Mr. Hardwick and his mother weren't necessarily her first pick, she needed a chaperone. As her aunt, the lot would fall on Nora. It would be infinitely better if Mr. Hardwick were also with them. "I thought, perhaps, to save the horses . . . or the drivers . . . if it's no inconvenience, we could perhaps share a carriage. It makes sense, does it not? Not to take out two?"

He looked at Jane for a moment, then back at her. "It makes perfect sense. It would be my greatest pleasure to accompany you to the ball." He lifted her hand and kissed the back of it.

Jane set her pile of books down with a thud. "I believe I'm not as inclined to read as I thought. Thank you, Miss Darby. Good day, Mr. Hardwick." Then Jane and her green-sprigged dress were gone.

Miss Darby stared after her. "Well, that were sudden."

Mr. Hardwick led her to a chair that was the twin of the one he'd been reading in. "Perhaps she didn't want to intrude on our privacy. Won't you sit for a while?"

She sat.

"Are you looking forward to an evening at the Westwood's?"

"I do feel better knowing you'll be there. Mr. Morland says they have the best musicians. He said they come from London. Mr. Morland also said the food would be heaven itself. And he said lots of important people attend, including the nephew of the Archbishop of Canterbury."

"Morland said all that, did he?"

Charlotte nodded.

"I believe he meant the nephew of Mrs. Westwood, who works with the Archbishop."

She thought for a moment. "Oh, yes. That's what he said. Mr. Morland said Mrs. Westwood will be pleased I'm coming to her house first of the neighborhood. But I don't know why that matters."

Mr. Hardwick gestured at the ancient library. "This is an old and illustrious estate. Everyone wants to meet the new owner of Willowkeep. You are now an influential part of the county. I fear I shall have competition. I hope I'm not too forward in asking you to reserve the first two dances for me?"

"No, not at all. 'Twould be a relief." Things were looking better and better.

A few dances with Mr. Hardwick, some of those French cake things, and a quick introduction to the famous nephew were all she'd need to call the entire evening a success.

Mr. Hardwick leaned close. "I had hoped that dancing with me would go a little beyond *a relief*."

The smell of sandalwood washed over her. She knew that scent anywhere—so often her father had worn it. Mr. Hardwick's mouth hitched up on one side in a roguish grin.

"I'm sure I didn't mean to say that it were only a relief. I just meant that you and I, being almost family, 'tis a comfort for me to have a cousin who can escort me."

The sun poured in through the window, bouncing off his snow-white cravat. A small fire burned in the fireplace, even though it was months past Lady Day. The whole room was like an oven. She'd have to speak to Mrs. Tafford about that. Coal was not free.

She stood. "It's hotter than— Too hot for me. Thank you." She didn't know what more to say. Before she could take a single step, he had her hand again, bending over it like she was the queen.

"Charlotte. I'll see you at dinner."

She curtseyed. "Yes, sir."

CHAPTER FOURTEEN

Henry shoved on the front door to the Grange. He'd asked the groundskeeper three times to fix it, but still it stuck. This would cost the man his job. At last Henry pushed it open, slamming it behind him.

The front room was empty. The kitchen empty as well, but a pot simmered over the fire. Henry fell onto the bench and laid his head on the table. What a day.

The kitchen door opened, and Jane stomped in. "You're late. Supper's been ready over an hour." She tied her apron on, pulling the strings so hard one tore off.

"Well, someone's got to earn the money. I can't be here at your whim simply because supper is ready. I've got work to do."

She swung the lever to pull the pot away from the fire. "Just what do you think I do all day? Sit on the sofa, sipping tea from China? Do you see me getting fat from idleness? Where do you think your clean clothes come from? And your starched neckcloths? And your supper? Not to mention the laundry and mending I do for the neighbors."

She turned and waved a copper ladle in his face. "Who do you think picks up after you around this place? Eh? It's not the fairy folk, I can tell you that. I'd like to see you get even half the work done in a day I do."

She was being absurd.

Jane ladled soup into a bowl and clunked it on the table in front of him. "Thought maybe you'd been invited to dine at the house."

"No, Jane. I was not. Those days are over." He tore a handful of bread from the loaf.

"Why? What happened?"

Henry dipped his bread into the broth. "I'm the steward, that's what happened."

"Did you hear the Westwoods are having their annual summer ball?" Jane asked.

"I heard."

"The invitations are already out. I saw Charlotte's."

"Yes." Henry sat in silence, sopping up soup with his bread. Without his father's debts weighing them down, he might have helped Jane into good society—and himself. He could have bought some land. Then who would be escorting Miss Darby to the ball?

Jane slapped a mug of ale in front of him, sloshing the amber liquid in the process.

He glanced up at her. "What's vexing you?"

She shrugged. "I'm fine."

She didn't look fine. She looked ready to set the table on fire with nothing more than the glance of her eyes.

"What is it?"

"I said I'm fine."

"Jane—"

The scowl she gave him stopped him short. Whatever was bothering her, she didn't want to talk about it. What a pair they were, wandering their own dark paths. First Miss Darby's letter to Anne, then the odious ball. Perhaps he was not the only one feeling the sting of watching from just out of reach.

He slurped the last of his soup and pushed away from the table. "I have an errand."

"Where are you going?"

He shoved his hat on. "I'm going to River Head to take work at the mill."

"Henry."

"I'll be late. Don't wait up." He closed the door behind him and strode down the lane toward Kippingham.

The village was quiet this evening. It always was near the end of the quarter. People were running low on money, and what they had left was due the draper or the grocer or the Crown or whomever they had debts with.

He went into the Grayling Arms. He had a handful of coins to pay off what his father owed there. It was a start.

Ebenezer Goddard hailed him from behind the counter. "Henry Morland. Didn't expect to see you tonight."

Henry walked over. "Small crowd, I see."

Goddard grinned. "A pox on all men's wives for keeping them home and their money safe."

Henry secretly blessed the wives. Perhaps if his mother still lived, his father wouldn't have gotten them into this predicament. He put his coins on the counter. "This should pay up in full."

Goddard counted them, then made a mark in his book. "All settled. How is your father?"

"Well enough."

"Glad to hear it." Goddard scuttled the coins away into a tin box.

Henry tipped his hat and left. He walked down the high street and out the other end of town. Only another three miles to go to reach the mill. He pulled his watch from his pocket to check the time. Something fluttered to the ground.

Miss Darby's letter.

He opened it, even though it was too dark to read. He couldn't figure out Miss Darby's great reason for denying herself thoughts of matrimony. Her sister, more than likely. She would do anything to keep Susie safe, including denying herself any chance of attachment.

But marrying a man didn't mean she'd have to leave Susie—so long as she married the right man. Even Hardwick, for all his senselessness, would not force her to send her sister away.

Charlotte would not see it that way though. Her eyes were blind to all but the threat.

She had enough money to have her pick of any man in the country. Even Prinny himself would have her simply to settle his debts—if he weren't already wedded.

What a farce that was. Prince George had piled up more debts than anyone. Hundreds of thousands of pounds. He didn't get sent to prison. No indeed. Instead, parliament granted him additional funds—tens of thousands per annum.

A footstep scraped the dirt behind him. Before Henry could turn, a strong arm closed around his neck and a filthy hand pressed over his mouth. Henry threw his elbow. It sank into the man's body. The man grunted, sending a wave of fetid breath past Henry's face.

"Like father, like son," a gruff voice said. Not the man holding him. "Ain't that right, mate?"

Henry tugged again, but the man's grip only tightened.

"Oh, that's right," a second, higher pitched voice agreed.

The man holding him slowly lifted his hand off Henry's mouth.

Henry jerked his shoulder. "Release me!"

"We will," the gruff man said. "Soon as we teach you a lesson someone shoulda taught yer old gaffer."

A fist came out of nowhere and landed right in Henry's ribs. He doubled over, gasping for air.

"Fox says a man's got ta pay wot he owes. Or else he pays."

Fox. From The Black Fox gaming den in London, no doubt.

Henry rammed his head back. The man stumbled, and Henry tore himself free. He spun around to find three men facing him. The largest had blood gushing from his nose.

"Now you really gots ta pay," the man with the raspy voice said. He was a good foot shorter than Henry but broader than an ox.

Henry stepped back. Three against one wasn't exactly the best odds. "I'll get your money. I give you my word. I just need a few more days."

He didn't mention that even a thousand more days would not be enough to pay the amount his father owed.

The man with the bloodied nose gave a nod. The third rogue took one long, lanky step forward and landed a fist right on Henry's ribs.

Then all three were on him. Henry managed to dodge the worst of it. He even got in a few good blows of his own. A satisfying crunch vibrated up his arm as he broke the ox's nose. One of them spat out a tooth before withdrawing from the brawl, leaving the finishing to his comrades.

Henry retreated until his back was against the hedgerow. They wouldn't kill him, else their money would be lost forever. But he doubted very much he'd be recognizable by the end.

His foot hit something. A stick. A stout one by the feel of it. He fell to the ground, grabbing the piece of wood. With a grunt, he rolled to his feet and came up swinging.

The men backed off. Their eyes locked on Henry's new weapon—a branch as solid as a cricket bat.

"Stay back," Henry said, panting. Blood leaked into his mouth. He spat it out.

Hoofbeats thundered on the road behind him. The rogues looked up over Henry's shoulder.

The broken-nosed man sneered. "We'll be back if'n ya don't pay up."

Then they were gone. Dissolved into the darkness of the night.

Henry collapsed onto the roadside just as the rider reined his horse into a skidding stop. A man jumped off, but Henry couldn't make out who it was with the blood clouding his eyes.

"Morland?"

Lud. Hurst Hardwick. Of all the people who could have appeared, it had to be Hardwick.

"Thunder and turf, man. What have they done to you?" Hardwick stretched out a hand and pulled Henry to his feet. He handed over a handkerchief, and Henry wiped his eyes.

"They taught me a lesson," Henry said, flinging his bat into the hawthorns. No sense pretending with Hardwick. He knew Henry's circumstances as well as anyone.

"Climb onto my horse, and let's get you home." Hardwick pulled his animal closer.

"I'm all right." Henry took a step and stumbled, his hand going to his ribs. He took a deep breath. Bruised but not broken. He'd be well enough. Eventually.

"Don't be ridiculous."

"I just need to catch my breath." Henry straightened with a grimace.

"Look at yourself. You can barely walk." Hardwick reached out to Henry. "I insist."

Henry's stomach churned. A wave of sweat washed over his face. Deuces. Not now. This was not a good night to contend with Jane's cooking.

Henry stuck his foot into the stirrup and pulled. Hardwick gave his rump a push, and Henry swung into the saddle. Hardwick kept the reins and led the horse at a quick walk through the fields, taking the faster way home.

Henry kept the handkerchief pressed against his forehead, where most of the blood seemed to be coming from. He was moments from being sick when they finally reached the Grange. He floundered to dismount while Hardwick pounded on the front door.

The door shook and rattled until Jane wedged it open. "Mr. Hardwick?"

"There's been some trouble," Hardwick said.

"Henry!" Jane ran out, lifting the hem of her apron to wipe his face. "What has happened?"

Henry waved Jane away and ducked his head into the ferns.

"I believe he had a run-in with some men on the road," Hardwick explained. "Debt collectors, so it seems."

"Thank you for bringing him home, Mr. Hardwick," Jane said. She put her arm around Henry, and he leaned heavily on her as she helped him toward the door.

"Do you need any more assistance?"

Goodness no. The last thing he needed was Hardwick in his house. He opened his mouth to say so but had to race to the ferns again. By the time he turned back, Hardwick was mounted up and riding away.

Jane watched him, even after his figure had been swallowed by the night.

Henry left her on the front stoop and headed straight to the kitchen to clean himself up. He lifted the water bucket off the peg by the kitchen door. Jane came in just as he was headed to the pump.

"I'll get that. You sit."

Henry handed her the bucket, then tugged his neckcloth loose and wriggled out of his coat. He groaned as his ribs protested the movement. Then again as his stomach revolted. At last he managed to strip to his waist but found it impossible to reach his boots.

Jane made several trips, dumping the water into the copper tub, then warming it with what she had boiling on the fire. She pulled off his boots and stockings.

"Look at your face. Look at your ribs. Who on earth did this to you?"

"Debt collectors, as Hardwick said." Henry loosened the ties of his breeches. "They said I had to pay."

Jane unfolded the screen and positioned it to give him some privacy. "I'd like to show them how to pay."

All she'd need do is give them a bowl of her stew and she would have her revenge.

Henry lowered himself into the water. Not nearly warm as he'd have liked.

"I think your breeches are ruined," Jane called. "And your cravat."

A disorganized patter of red welts mottled his front and sides. He would be solid black and blue by morning. He hadn't looked in a mirror yet to assess his face, but one eye was already swelling shut. He touched his nose. At least that wasn't broken.

"Your boots are badly scuffed, but I think I can polish them out." The irons of the fireplace clanged. "I'm coming in with more hot water."

Henry leaned forward as Jane rounded the privacy screen. She poured the pot of steaming water into the tub. The warmth relieved some of the tightness in his aching muscles.

"That's all I've got, but I can put more on the fire."

"This will do, thank you." He'd be done by the time it heated up.

"Goodness, Henry. You're a sight." She stood there staring at his back. "Let me rub some liniment on that to heal it faster." She went back into the main part of the kitchen.

Henry could have sunk into the tub and fallen asleep, but another wave of stomach cramps seized him. He dipped a towel into the water and soaped it up.

The water dripped red from his face and hands. It couldn't all be his blood. He must have done more damage than he'd thought. His fingers tangled in the dried filth of his hair. How was this not suffering the sins of his father? He was doing his best to meet the demands of the debtors. But they weren't his debts. Still, they expected him to pay—if not with money, then with flesh.

He'd lose the mill job for certain. To Miles Standish, who lived but half a mile from the mill and had his cap set at the miller's daughter. Perhaps they'd be lenient under the circumstances and still give Henry consideration. Though it might be several days before he'd be well enough to walk to River Head.

"Ready for the rinse?" Jane called.

"Yes." Henry leaned forward again.

With a pewter pitcher, Jane scooped up water from the tub and poured it over his head. Thrice she did this until the water ran clear.

Henry climbed out. Jane had left him a towel and clean clothes draped over the screen. She was too good to him. He dried off, then slipped into a clean nightshirt, all the while his stomach objecting violently.

After another moment of retching into the chamber pot, Henry said, "How is it that you are not ill?"

"I wasn't hungry." She pulled the bench away from the table. "Now sit and let me treat these wounds."

She lifted his tunic and rubbed a salve on Henry's cuts and bruises. "The butcher told me it was a fine pork joint when I bought it last week. I wanted to make your favorite."

"Ouch." Even Jane's gentle touch sent shooting pains across his chest. A clap of thunder rattled the windows. He'd made it home just in time.

"We owe Mr. Hardwick greatly for his service tonight," Jane said.

"Yes. Much as I hate to admit it, his coming at that moment saved me from far worse."

"I don't know why you're so opposed to him, Henry." She turned him and started on his face. The balm soothed and cooled as she dabbed it around his swollen eye.

"He is not an altogether unreasonable man. I know you are fond of him. But, Jane." She would only get hurt if she set her sights on Hurst Hardwick. He'd seen the way she looked at him. The heart did not always lead down the path one should follow, as Henry well knew.

"I know," Jane said. "Please. Let us not speak of it."

Sweat broke out on Henry's brow. He lunged for the pot, but his stomach was already empty. He'd never eat pork again.

He needed his bed. He turned to find Jane with a handkerchief pressed to her face.

"Are you crying?"

"No." Then a sob broke through. "Oh, Henry. You are right. This is all my fault. You deserve better than me. It's my fault father is in prison. I should have done more to keep him home. Then you wouldn't be broken. And sick. I can't even make dinner without bringing the house to its knees. I can't do anything right."

Henry got to his feet, steadying himself on the wooden table's edge. He had indeed used her ill. His life would be nothing but miserable without her.

He took her into his arms. "My dear Jane. No one is better for me than you. I should never have said such things. I was angry at myself, and I let it fall on you."

She sniffed, burying her head in his shoulder.

"We would all be lost without you. You are an angel and the brightest part of my life. All of this is my fault. What kind of man can't take care of his own family?"

Another peal of thunder shook the house, and rain splashed on the tile roof.

"Off to bed," Jane said. "That's an order."

Henry woke to a gentle knocking on the front door. His head throbbed, his body ached, and his eyelids weighed more than a full measure of barley.

Jane's footsteps creaked the floorboards from the kitchen to the front hall, then the telltale scraping as she pried that abominable door open. Tomorrow he would fix it himself. And take the money he would have paid the groundskeeper to do it. He could earn double the wages if he did both his job and everyone else's.

Jane tiptoed into his room. "Oh. You're awake." She smiled. "You have a visitor."

In the next moment, Miss Darby strolled in with a basket hanging on her arm.

CHAPTER FIFTEEN

"Gaw! You look awful."

"Miss Darby." Henry tried to sit up, but the blows to his ribs were taking their toll. He propped himself up on one elbow. "Thank you. You, on the other hand, look very well."

Color flushed to her cheeks, only improving her appearance. "Oh, no. I didn't mean that your looks aren't pleasing. Just that you look so much worse than I expected."

Jane stifled a laugh.

"Mr. Hardwick said you'd run into some trouble. But look at you."

Henry did. He glanced down and, at the same moment, had the vague recollection he'd thrown off his shirt sometime in the middle of the night because it was irritating his wounds. He pulled the blanket up.

"Miss Darby," Jane said. "Let's you and I go make some breakfast. Henry can meet us in the kitchen when he's ready."

Miss Darby nodded and followed Jane out of his room.

Henry laid his head back on his pillow. Ouch. His body hurt. And he was famished.

Hardwick had obviously informed Miss Darby of his skirmish last night. He prayed the man hadn't mentioned the reason behind the beating. Miss Darby knew nothing of his father's situation, and he dearly wanted to keep it that way.

He washed his face and combed his hair, doing his best to avoid the mirror. After donning only stockings and a tunic, he abandoned the effort altogether. Already he'd kept Miss Darby waiting near half an hour.

The smell of toasted bread and bacon lured him from his room. He put on his dressing robe and shuffled to the kitchen.

Jane was fast asleep on the soft chair in the corner, curled up like a baby. The table was laid with a breakfast unlike any he'd seen since his mother died. Nothing smelled burnt. Nothing seemed of questionable origin. He looked at Miss Darby.

"She was exhausted. I made her sit, and she fell asleep right away." Miss Darby poured Henry a cup of steaming tea. "I could see right off that her pan was smoking. She were burning the eggs. That's when I sent her away. Also, you'd best take care. I think there's a ham in the pantry what's gone off."

He did not doubt it. Henry loaded his plate with eggs, toast, bramble preserves, bacon, and some kind of dark treacle cake that smelled of ginger. "I can't believe I slept so late."

"I'm glad you did." Miss Darby spoke quietly. "Gives me a chance to make amends for all your kindness to me and Susie. Besides, Mr. Hardwick says a late breakfast is all the crack in London."

"Well, I suppose it's all right, then." Henry tucked into his plate of food. "This cake is delicious."

"Thank you." Miss Darby grinned. "It's parkin. A specialty from the north. I made it myself."

"I didn't know you were a cook."

"I don't have many talents, but I do know my way round a kitchen." She put another piece of parkin on Henry's plate. "Sometimes Cook lets me use her kitchen. She don't like it much though. Says it's no place for a lady."

Cook was right. But Miss Darby had yet to consider herself a lady. She'd been raised a shipping merchant's daughter, and in her mind, it seemed that was what she would always be. Thus far, her new circumstances hadn't changed her—at least not the heart of her. Henry hoped they never would.

"Cooking and stone throwing. You are very accomplished indeed." If the Ton didn't appreciate Miss Darby's particular set of aptitudes, he certainly did.

Dark wisps of hair strayed from her topknot, falling across her forehead and down her neck. She never could keep them in place. Her eyes gleamed like the Aegean sea. Not that he'd ever been there, but Walter Kelton had. He never stopped talking about the color of the water. Henry imagined it the exact shade of Charlotte's eyes. Er, Miss Darby's.

"More tea?" she asked.

Henry nodded.

She tipped the teapot and filled his cup, then poured in a speck of cream. She held it out to him. He reached for it, his hand brushing along her fingers. Already they were softer than that first day back in Hull.

She quickly pulled her hand away.

He'd done it again. Would he never learn? She was his employer. Superior to him in both station and situation. Not to mention Hardwick's hold on her.

"Thank you," he said.

Another knock on the front door echoed down the hallway. Jane stirred but fell back asleep. Henry got to his feet. His body moved a little better now that it had loosened up. He jerked open the door and then groaned.

"Morland," Hardwick said in his buckskin breeches and perfectly cut coat. "I'm surprised to see you up and about."

Henry swung the door wider. "May as well come in."

Hardwick stepped across the threshold.

"Allow me to thank you properly for your aid last night." Henry shook his hand. "I mean that most sincerely. I don't know what I would have done if you hadn't happened along. I'm indebted to you, sir."

Hardwick nodded. "Think nothing of it."

"You find us a bit behind schedule this morning." Henry tightened the ropes of his dressing robe. "We're just finishing breakfast in the kitchen."

Normally Henry would never receive callers in the back of the house. Today, he didn't care.

Miss Darby had the table cleared of all but the tea and parkin. A task no proper lady would ever consider. "Mr. Hardwick." She tried again to tuck her hair back where it belonged.

Jane woke with a start. She leapt to her feet and looked from Hardwick to Miss Darby, then back to Hardwick. "I'll fetch the water," she said and disappeared outside, the bucket still on its hook by the door.

"I don't mean to intrude, Morland," Hardwick said. "I just came by to see how you were getting on." He shuffled his gloves from hand to hand.

"I am well on my way to recovery."

Hardwick turned to Miss Darby. "I'm off to walk the grove. If you are finished here, your company would be most welcome."

"Oh. Well." Miss Darby glanced around the kitchen, her eyes seeming to cover everything except Henry. "I . . . That's very kind." She tucked her basket in the crook of her elbow. With a quick bow to Henry, she stepped to Hardwick's side.

"Let me know if you need anything, Morland," Hardwick said. "We'll see ourselves out."

Through the kitchen window, the figures of Hardwick and Miss Darby vanished behind the tall elms. Jane was nowhere to be seen. Henry took the plate of parkin and went back to his bed.

CHAPTER SIXTEEN

IT HAD BEEN SEVERAL DAYS since Charlotte's letter to Anne. In that time, Mr. Morland had nearly been beaten to death by highwaymen, and Mr. Hardwick had kissed her hand as he'd agreed to accompany her to the ball. She didn't mean to press Queen Anne, but neither of those was exactly what she'd had in mind when she'd asked for help.

Charlotte prepared another paper. With a fresh goose quill—Mr. Morland had ordered a new batch for the whole house—she set pen to paper.

Her Majesty Queen Anne Boleyn
The Lion at Willowkeep, Kent
July 1810

Dear Anne,

I hope all is well for you, wherever you are. I pray that king of yours is no longer pestering you. I wish you could tell me, did you ever really love him? I've been reading the histories, but they are so full of facts and so lacking in feelings.

I fear all is not well for me. I thought I had my heart shored up. Alas, I am mistaken. I feel H constantly pulling on it. Sometimes my heart near bursts when he looks at me or if our hands touch. I've never known such a kind and caring gentleman.

I'm at a loss to know what to do. Sometimes I think I should return to Hull, but I daren't, lest my heart rip open. And Susie loves it here so. She has a puppy that licks her face, a nursemaid who gives her anything she wants, and a place to run and play where other children don't cast stones.

I've made a mull of things. I knew my situation before I came. But he hooked me before I had a chance to get the walls up.

Do help quickly.

Yours in dire circumstances,
~C

After a careful sanding and blotting, Charlotte sealed the letter with her own family seal.

She headed toward the back door but stopped and peeked into Mr. Morland's office. Empty and dark. Still home convalescing. She entered his room. A few neat stacks of paper covered his desk. She ran her fingers along the feathery tip of his quill. The room still smelled of him. Of ink and leather and parchment and lavender. Mrs. Tafford always kept a bouquet of something in his office. *To soften it,* she said. According to Mrs. Tafford, Mr. Morland needed a woman's touch. Charlotte closed her eyes and breathed it in.

Enough of this. She had a letter to deliver.

She stepped outside through the back door and came face-to-face with Aunt Nora.

"Good morning, Aunt." Charlotte hid the letter behind her back.

"You are out early," her aunt said.

"I prefer the morning; it's cooler." She offered her aunt a smile but got nothing in return. "I hope you are well."

Other than dinner and occasionally an hour or two in the drawing room, Charlotte rarely saw her aunt. She spent most of her time with her sister, either in the nursery or outside. Lately she spent most of her evenings in the company of Mr. Hardwick. Aunt Nora had rooms in the west end of Willowkeep. Charlotte's quarters were in the east. With such a large house, their paths didn't often cross.

"I am very well, I thank you," Aunt Nora said. "I was just going to take a turn around the garden. Perhaps you'd like to join me?"

Her aunt had never offered to walk with her before. Charlotte had an errand at the willows, but a circle or two round the garden couldn't hurt. "That's very kind."

Charlotte bent over, pretending to fix her lace but quietly tucking the letter into her stays. She fell in step beside her aunt, and they headed toward the fountain.

"How are you finding Willowkeep now that you've had a chance to settle in?" Aunt Nora asked.

She'd been here over a month. She had a routine that seemed to work for everyone. Susie loved the nursery and Fanny. The endless grounds provided all kinds of privacy. And, of course, there was Mr. Morland. He'd made her feel welcome from the start.

"I s'pose it is starting to feel a bit like home." In many ways even better. "It is nice to have security, I think, after living on a sinking ship for so long."

Her aunt gave her a nod.

They rounded the fountain as it splashed and gurgled. In the center stood a statue of three maids, each pouring water from a Grecian urn and wearing naught but a bed linen draped round their bodies. They must have had warning about the weather.

Charlotte always thought the maids looked sad. Like they were disappointed with life, even though they lived in such a beautiful place. If they'd spent some time in Hull, perhaps they'd appreciate what they'd got.

"My son is looking forward to the Westwood's ball," Aunt Nora said, drawing her shawl more tightly across her shoulders. "He is a very accomplished dancer and is particularly anticipating his sets with you."

The ball flickered on her horizon as a beacon of anticipation. "Mr. Hardwick says you're also coming."

"That is true. I have never missed it these many years."

"We shall go together, then, like a proper family," Charlotte said, savoring the words. A family at last.

Her aunt gave her what seemed a rather reluctant smile. She was not so desperate as Charlotte for family—especially not the kind Charlotte had brought. Always between them hung the estate—the estate her aunt had been forced to hand over to Charlotte.

"I should inform you," her aunt said, looking off into the landscape, "that I have a man looking for a house in London for me. I believe my son and I can be quite content in town year-round."

Always about the money. Why couldn't they understand it wasn't her fault? She had no desire to displace anyone. Charlotte stopped and took her aunt's hands. She tried to pull them away, but Charlotte held tight. "Aunt. Please do not say such things. I did not come into Kent to drive you away. You are all the family I've got. This house is big enough for all of us." Charlotte glanced over at its towering walls. "Laws and gardens, it's big enough for ten of all of us."

Aunt Nora pulled harder, tearing her hands away.

"Willowkeep has saved us. Me and Susie. But I beg you, do not think you are not welcome to live here in your own home."

Her aunt turned aside. "I'm tired this morning. I'm going in now." She took a few steps, then said quietly over her shoulder, "It will not be your home once you marry." Then her black shawl swished, and she walked away.

"I shan't never marry," Charlotte whispered to the retreating figure. Her aunt needn't worry that another man would come along and make her leave.

The price for wealth was heavy. Charlotte wanted nothing more than to share this big house with Aunt Nora and Mr. Hardwick for as long as they desired. Forever, even.

When her aunt disappeared into the house, Charlotte pulled out the letter to Queen Anne and hurried to the willows. She was behind schedule. Susie would forgive her—'specially since she understood naught about time. But Fanny would be wondering.

The sun was high, with no clouds to block it. She'd never survive this heat, not with the rest of July and August still ahead of her. The coolness of the willow trees welcomed her.

With one last look round to make sure she was alone, Charlotte parted the curtain of long narrow leaves and entered the lion's bower.

Henry's lion, Mr. Morland had called it. Charlotte preferred to call it Anne's. She circled round the weathered beast, coming to stare at him right in the eye. His mouth curved in a snarl, or so she'd thought at first. Today as she studied him, it looked almost like a smile. A welcoming grin.

Her first letter was gone. She bent to tuck the new one back behind his teeth, but there was something already there. A flower.

Charlotte pulled it out and gently unfolded the petals. A rose. A soft, velvety rose. And as the petals fell open, she saw it clearly. A Tudor rose. Red round the outside with a layer of white petals in the center. From the house of Henry Tudor. Anne's Henry.

She'd been here.

Queen Anne Boleyn had left this sign for Charlotte.

Anne must have truly loved Henry. Why wouldn't she? He was a king. Anne fell in love with him before he'd turned old and fat and cross. Charlotte had seen pictures of him in those history books. He looked as handsome as anyone. He'd been so romantic courting Anne with notes and flowers and such. He must have broken her heart into a million pieces when he turned against her.

Charlotte stuffed her letter into the lion's mouth, then set off for the house, cradling the rose in her hand. She'd been almost everywhere on these grounds, either with Mr. Morland or Mr. Hardwick. She'd never seen roses like this anywhere. Plain yellow, yes. And some pink ones in the hedges. But not this two-colored white and red. Where else could it have come from if not from Anne?

In her room, Charlotte opened the history book and pressed the flower between the pages of Anne Boleyn and Jane Seymour—the woman who died giving birth to Henry's sole male heir. Charlotte tried not to think on her, as it was likely her fault Henry's eyes strayed. It was Anne, after all, who'd given birth to Elizabeth, the greatest queen they'd ever had.

She closed the book and hurried off to the nursery. Susie squealed when she entered.

"Sorry I'm late, Fanny."

"No trouble, miss." Fanny curtseyed, showing her gap-tooth grin. "She's had her tea. She wouldn't wait. And now she's begging for powpies."

Powpies and puppy were the only words Susie said beyond the occasional "Parr," which was her name for Charlotte. In Susie's world, everything started with a *P*.

"Thanks, Fanny. You can go now."

Fanny gave a quick bob and left.

Susie tugged on Charlotte's hand. "Powpy," she said.

"Not today, my dear." Charlotte knelt at her sister's level. "Mr. Morland is hurt, and he can't take us to the ponies." He hadn't been up to work in two days.

Susie tugged harder, nearly pulling Charlotte over.

"When did you get so big and strong? Come." Charlotte whistled for Puppy, who was napping on the window seat. The dog's head perked up, his long ears flopping forward. "Let's go out for a walk. We can play with Puppy down on the lawn."

When they walked along the back hallway past Mr. Morland's workroom, Susie halted in front of his door. She was so used to this routine. They never went to the stables without Mr. Morland.

"Not today." Charlotte opened Mr. Morland's door and showed Susie the empty room. "Come along."

The girl backed out of the office with a frown. She'd been doing so well these last few weeks. But anytime the routine changed, it was three steps back. Still, Susie didn't cry, so that was a right piece of luck.

Charlotte found a stick and tossed it for Puppy. He bounded after it and brought it straight back to Susie. They played tug-o-war, a game that always ended in Susie being dragged across the lawn laughing. Then Puppy let go, and Susie threw the stick, and it started all over again.

Mr. Morland had been touched by an angel when he'd given that dog to her sister. The furry black-and-white body slept every night in Susie's bed. There hadn't been any more nighttime fits, and that alone was worth the price of the Crown Jewels.

Susie gave the stick another throw. She launched it up into the air, and it splashed down into the river. Puppy stood on the bank, wagging his tail, then leapt into the water.

Henry had had enough of sitting around. Two days was far too long to be idle. It wasn't as though he was ill, just a bit roughed up. He still had half the day left. He could finish his accounts and perhaps even ride over to see how the new oast house was coming.

He dressed in soft cotton breeches and one of his older, looser-fitting coats. He found Jane in the kitchen preparing the afternoon tea.

"Where are you going dressed like a farmer on Sunday?"

"Up to the house. I'll go mad if I sit here doing nothing the rest of the day. Mrs. Tafford will be needing money for the grocer. The Ledfords say their roof leaks. And Smithson is worried about the hops in the south field." Truth be told, a glimpse of Miss Darby wouldn't be wholly unwelcome either.

"But look at you."

The bruises on his face had faded to a nice deep golden brown. Those on his body were still a vibrant purple. Admittedly, he did walk with a stiff gait. And he wasn't entirely without light-headedness. "I'm fine. I'm sore from sitting." He fit his hat gingerly over his aching head. "The walk alone will do me good."

He reached for the doorknob and yanked. "Ow." That did nothing for his injured ribs. The blasted thing was getting worse by the day.

"Henry?"

"I'm fine."

He took it slowly at first, bent like an old man. After a while, the movement loosened his muscles and he could walk upright, mostly. Henry kept to the shaded side of the path, out of the sun. Miss Darby would likely be indoors on such a warm day.

He stopped for a moment at the crossroads. He hadn't checked the lion for several days. It was possible Miss Darby had written another letter. What if someone else found it? In the wrong hands, it would be devastating.

He turned down toward the willows. Sure enough, wedged into the lion's mouth was a paper sealed with the same *D&B* wax stamp as before. He pried it out, careful not to tear it.

It might be best if he waited until he reached his office to read it. He only made it to the cover of the other willow tree before sitting down on the wicker bench and tearing off the seal. He tried to be as careful as possible, but without his pen knife, he could not disguise that it had been broken.

Again it was to Anne Boleyn. Apparently she'd been reading up on her.

There was more about that clod, Mr. H.

Sometimes my heart bursts when he looks at me.

Henry folded the letter. He shouldn't be reading this. He didn't want to read it. He didn't want to know her feelings for Hardwick had grown so strong. Time to give up his charade and put this note back where he found it. As Miss Darby rose to take her place in society, he would only sink further and further out of her reach. *Step away, Henry. Step away.*

He unfolded it and read on.

She was contemplating returning to Hull. How could she even consider it? Her mention of the Hull children casting stones only confirmed the insanity of such a notion.

And then more about her *situation*. Though the letter did not say so specifically, Henry knew what she meant. Her vow to never marry.

What could possibly make her feel so unworthy to attach herself to Hurst Hardwick? Surely by now she must understand her place in the highest society. It must be Susie holding her back. Perhaps he should speak with her about this. Her efforts at protecting her sister need not preclude marriage should she truly find someone she loved.

A cry rolled across the grounds, its whisper filtering through the thicket of branches. Henry tucked the letter away and rushed out. He couldn't tell where it had come from, so muffled it was inside the bower.

There it came again. A girl in distress—or so it sounded. He crossed the stone bridge and ran as fast as his injuries would allow along the edge of the water. It seemed to have come from across the lawn. The lawn where Charlotte and Susie often played this time of day.

"Susie!" came a chilling scream.

That was definitely Charlotte's voice. He bolted off, pressing a hand over his ribs. Branches snapped off as he cut through the trimmed boxwoods.

Charlotte was kneeling at the water's edge, reaching and reaching while the pup barked and barked beside her. A small mound of dark hair bobbed as it drifted downstream.

In spite of his injuries, Henry crossed the lawn at top speed, stripping off his coat and waistcoat as he ran.

CHAPTER SEVENTEEN

A streak of white shirt and dark-green breeches flew past Charlotte. Mr. Morland dove into the water and came up right next to Susie. He grabbed her round the middle and hauled her to the shore.

Charlotte reached for the child and dragged her onto the bank. Mr. Morland crawled up behind her.

"She's not breathing," Charlotte cried. Mr. Morland leaned over the girl.

The pale cheeks. Blue lips. Hollow eyes. Not again. Not Susie. Charlotte couldn't live through this again. She rolled Susie onto her side, pounding on her back. Susie lay limp and unmoving.

"Nothing," Mr. Morland said.

Charlotte pounded again, harder this time. "Come on, Susie. You cannot leave me here."

Susie's whole body shuddered. She coughed and gagged. Charlotte tipped her farther onto her side so her face pressed into the grass.

Water spilled out of her mouth and nose, followed by a fit of choking. Susie took three gasping breaths, then burst into tears.

Charlotte scooped her into her arms. "You're safe now, Susie. You're safe. It's over. You're safe." Charlotte rubbed her sister's back, holding her tightly against her chest. She'd never let go again.

Mr. Morland rolled onto his back, breathing heavily and gripping his side. Puppy came up, spreading his kisses all over Susie's face. Susie clutched the dog, burying her face in his fur, still frantically gulping for air. All her panicking only made her breathing that much harder. Charlotte had to get her calmed down.

"Susie, look. Mr. Morland is here."

Mr. Morland rolled onto his knees. "Hello, little Susie. Did we go for a swim?"

Susie looked up at him.

"You got me all wet." Mr. Morland wrung his limp neckcloth, creating a tiny waterfall.

Susie's gasping slowed.

Mr. Morland shook his head, and drops of water sprayed in all directions, landing on Charlotte and Susie.

Susie took a shuddering breath, then the tiniest smile touched her face. Mr. Morland showered them again.

He rubbed his hand across his forehead and grimaced. "I can't do that again." He pointed at Susie. "You try. Shake your water all over your sister."

Susie looked at Charlotte.

"Oh, no you don't," Charlotte said.

Susie shook her head from side to side. She couldn't do it nearly fast enough to make a spray like Mr. Morland had done, but her long locks swished back and forth, getting Charlotte plenty wet on their own.

"You got me," Charlotte said.

Susie tried again to shake her head, but she couldn't do any more damage to Charlotte. Her sister had already got her dress soaked through.

Mr. Morland clutched his side. One eye was ringed in brownish yellow, and though he smiled at Susie, his smile carried an edge of pain.

Near drowning seemed to fleece Susie's spirits. She tucked herself deep into Charlotte's lap and settled there.

"Are you all right, Miss Darby?" Mr. Morland asked.

"Yes," Charlotte said, though her heart still galloped in her chest. She'd never been so scared. Leastways not since her mother. "I almost lost my sister."

Mr. Morland nodded. "But you didn't, so thanks be to God for that."

"You were right, Mr. Morland. You are never late. If you hadn't come along just then, I daren't think about it." She kissed the top of her sister's head. "I can never thank you enough."

"I'm very glad I decided to come up to the house today, or I never would have heard."

Mr. Morland looked at the river, then back at Charlotte. "Why didn't you go in after her?"

"I can't swim," she said.

"How is it that you've lived your life surrounded by water but don't know how to swim?"

'Twas a reasonable question, but the answer would only bring more questions, each leading closer and closer to what she didn't want him to know.

"What is it?" he asked.

"I hate the water. I won't never go in."

His wet hair sent droplets snaking down his face. "What happened? I know something . . ." He looked away, across the river. When he looked back, his eyes were autumn velvet. With a voice like goose down, he said, "I know something has happened to you. Perhaps it is not my place to ask, but I can't help wishing . . . Can you not tell me?"

Susie reached a hand up and touched Charlotte's cheek. Charlotte pulled her close, brushing her sister's damp hair away from her face. So small and fragile yet infinitely precious. Life should not be so frail. Something so vital, so necessary, should not be so easily snuffed out.

"My mother drowned in the river Hull."

Mr. Morland's eyes were on her, listening as though this were the most important thing in the world to him. "How did she drown?"

"After my youngest brother died, she couldn't take no more." Charlotte spoke slowly and carefully. She wouldn't tell him all, but she'd give him a taste. "Edmund were the last of the five children we lost. He lived a few weeks, and Mother got her hopes up. But he didn't make it either."

"She must have been beside herself with grief." He waited as if he already knew there was more she had to tell. He always knew.

"Next day, she took herself off to the docks, her dead baby in her arms, and jumped in. She didn't know I'd followed her." Charlotte glanced down at Susie, whose breathing was still harsh and raspy. "They dragged her out and tried to save her, but it were too late." Charlotte could see it, plain as if it was yesterday. "I watched them. I watched them pound on her back. Weren't no use. She didn't want to come back."

Mr. Morland seemed to be puzzling things out. Her mother's suicide. Her father's leaving. After a minute, he asked, "And your brothers?"

Aye. Her brothers. What should she tell about them?

It wasn't so much the death of her mother that marked her for a spinster's life. It was the death of her brothers. All of her brothers. Words about Susie and her brothers were dangerous ground.

"They died as infants."

Mr. Morland looked down at Susie. "That must have been very hard on your family."

"Father weren't the same after mother drowned herself. A few weeks after her death, he left us."

"Out on the boat." Mr. Morland reached for his coat. He wrapped it around Susie. Her little body shook with cold.

Charlotte tucked his coat over Susie's shoulders. "You live in Hull your whole life and you see a lot of men go out and never come back. Ships go down all the time." She needn't repeat that whole story.

"That does not make the loss of your father less painful."

"No. No, it don't."

Susie had fallen asleep. An angel's face with her eyes closed and the blue of her veins softening her lids. Her cheeks flushed from the cold water, life flowing back into them. Her dark hair glimmered like raven wings.

"I am very sorry," Mr. Morland said. "I wish . . . I don't have the words to tell you how sorry I am for your suffering." He looked up, right into her eyes. "You are the strongest woman I know."

She had laid her troubles at his feet. He'd lifted them and carried them away, even if only for the moment. She wished she could make this moment last forever. Forgetting all the past and no worries for the future.

The river rippled and churned as it rounded the bend. The water that had pulled Susie under was long gone. Replaced by new water that knew nothing of all that had happened.

Larks called from the trees across the way. Puppy ran through the grass, digging up sticks and worms. Everything moved on. Time couldn't stop and wait for her. Nor could it be forgotten.

"Susie's cold. I best get her into dry clothes and warmed up."

Mr. Morland stood and then lifted Susie out of her arms. Charlotte got to her feet and brushed off her dress. It was wet through and utterly wrinkled. She reached for Susie.

"No, no. I've got her." Mr. Morland started off toward the house. It must have pained him some, though, with his bruises and such from the highwaymen.

Charlotte picked up Mr. Morland's waistcoat, and they walked in silence back along the gravel pathway toward the house. Susie's sleep became fitful, shivering even under Mr. Morland's fine coat.

As the path joined with the main walkway leading through the formal gardens, Mr. Hardwick found them.

"Ah, Miss Darby, I was just coming to look for you." He glanced over at Mr. Morland carrying Susie, all of them wet to the bone. Though Mr. Morland's hair had dried and stuck out in all directions. And he was wearing naught but breeches and shirtsleeves.

"Have you been swimming?" Mr. Hardwick asked.

"No," Charlotte said. She wouldn't be found swimming, even if it was the second flood.

"Susie fell in the river." Mr. Morland tried to step round Mr. Hardwick. He must be aching from head to toe by now.

"Please allow me." And without another word, Mr. Hardwick lifted Susie straight out of Mr. Morland's hands. "I'll take her inside and see her to the nursery. Morland, you go home and get out of your wet clothes. You look terrible."

Mr. Morland shook his head. "I don't think she will be pleased if she wakes up and finds you—"

"Nonsense. The child and I get along fine." He tossed Morland his coat. "I insist. Don't you agree, Miss Darby? He'll catch his death in his weakened state."

Mr. Morland did look pale. And they were nearly back to the house. "I s'pose."

"There. It's settled." Mr. Hardwick turned and started off.

Charlotte handed Mr. Morland his waistcoat. "Thank you again for saving her. I will be forever in your debt."

She gave him a deep curtsey, then trotted off after Susie.

Henry wanted to pull back and land Hardwick a facer. But what would that prove? Only that Henry had let him get to him.

Hardwick wasn't all bad. Look how he'd helped him after the debt collectors' attack. But Henry would give his left arm to have that man back in London.

As Henry rounded the corner, he heard the wailing screams of little Susie. She'd woken up and seen who carried her. Henry grinned as he hobbled home.

He turned the knob on the front door and pushed. It didn't budge. He put his shoulder into it and leaned just as the window opened and Jane called out. "Henry, no. Don't use the front—"

Too late. He'd already shoved it open.

Jane ran out from the kitchen. "Look what you've done."

The door bore an imprint of Henry's shoulder, and his sleeve was covered with a smear of fresh paint.

"Mr. Peters was here," Jane said. "He painted the door."

"Why the deuce would he do that? It didn't need painting. It needs refitting."

Jane threw up her arms. "Well, now it needs both."

"Will this come out?" His linen shirt now had a mark on it the color of an evergreen woodland. If he wore a coat, it might not show. In fact, he had a frock coat that might match perfectly.

"I'll do what I can. Give it to me." Jane held her hand out. "You're back early. And rather underdressed."

Henry laid aside his coat and waistcoat, then pulled his damp tunic over his shoulders. "I didn't make it to the house."

He related how he'd heard Miss Darby's scream and raced to pull Susie from the river. How Miss Darby had revived her when she wasn't breathing.

"Poor Charlotte," Jane said. "And poor little Susie. That was a close call."

"Yes." It had been very close.

"My brother, the hero. And now that you've saved her sister, she will love you even more." Jane grinned.

Henry wadded up his tunic and threw it at her. Jane caught it and ran off into the kitchen.

CHAPTER EIGHTEEN

Henry rode into the stables the following afternoon. He'd been down to see the new oast house and had checked on the drainage problem in the west field. He'd also met with the ironmonger regarding the new traces and plow head.

He'd spent most of his ride turning over Charlotte's confession about her mother's death. What a nightmare she'd been through. Her story answered many of his questions and reinforced what he'd suspected. No wonder Charlotte was so desperate to keep her only remaining sibling safe—even if it meant not marrying. Certainly she'd been dealt a heavy hand and suffered great loss. She deserved a future with some happiness.

He handed the horse over to Stayner. "I'll need her saddled and ready to go first thing in the morning."

The stablehand nodded at him. "Yes, sir."

Henry stepped through the stable door to find Miss Darby beside the paddock, pacing back and forth, gnawing at her fingernail. "Miss Darby?"

She spun around. "Thank heaven, you're back." Her eyes had gone wild.

"What's wrong?"

"It's Susie." She hurried over to him. "She's ill. I think she took a chill when she fell into the stream. She's coughing and fevered and struggling to breathe." She wrung her hands as she spoke, her eyes like glass dams holding back a river.

"Mrs. Tafford says she needs the doctor. But I can't have the doctor looking at her. Think of what he'll do to her." She'd been in wild states before but nothing like this.

If the child was sick, there wasn't much Henry could do. But if it would ease her worry, he would take a look. "Come, let me see her."

"Oh, thank you, sir."

She hadn't called him that in a long time.

"Mrs. Tafford says if we don't call the doctor, she might die." Her hair sprayed out in all directions, and he doubted she'd done a thing with it since she'd woken up—if she'd even slept at all. "But I can't."

"Let's just see how she's faring." If little Susan was very ill, they shouldn't have waited for him to summon the physician. "I'll talk to Mrs. Tafford. We don't have to decide anything this very moment."

"No. 'Course not. Let's check on her first."

They made their way through the maze of rooms and up to the nursery. Mrs. Tafford and Fanny were busy tending to the child.

"Mr. Morland, thank goodness," Mrs. Tafford said. "This child needs a doctor immediately." She took a rag from an aromatic basin of water, wrung it out, and laid it on Susie's chest. "Thyme and barberry, to clear her lungs."

"No doctors," Miss Darby said.

Mrs. Tafford handed a kettle to Fanny. "Could you fetch some more tea, please."

Fanny nodded and left the room.

"Look at her, sir," Mrs. Tafford said. "She can scarce draw breath."

The child's skin was pale as the sheets, her eyes dark and sunken. They stared at nothing, with a sheen like wet glazing. Her chest rose and fell slowly, painfully, by the way her rib cage showed with each breath.

He laid his hand on her cheek, then her forehead. Far too hot. In her troubled haze, Susie reached out and grabbed his cravat. The knot came loose, and Henry had to pry the cloth out of her hands. He glanced at Mrs. Tafford, and she gave a small nod.

Henry stood. "I'm afraid I must agree with Mrs. Tafford."

Miss Darby shook her head, feral and fierce. "No. No doctors."

She was as set against them as she was against marriage. He couldn't allow her fears to put the child in danger. "I believe we must."

"They won't come," she said. "It don't matter because they won't come. They don't care about weeans like this, children who aren't right in the head. They won't treat them; they'll just watch them die or, worse, send them off to the asylum, where they die anyway. I've seen it already. I don't need more." Her voice trailed off to a whisper.

Perhaps that had been her experience in Hull, but things were different here.

"The doctor will come when he is summoned by the mistress of Willowkeep," Henry said. "He will come, and he will do his best to help her because his reputation hangs on the word of Willowkeep."

He took her silence as a small step forward. Regardless of whether she consented or not, Henry was sending for the physician. "I don't think she will survive the night without one."

She slapped a hand over her mouth, choking back a sob.

He looked at Mrs. Tafford and mouthed the words, "Send for the doctor."

Mrs. Tafford nodded and left. She would send a runner to Dr. Leigh down in Kippingham. He'd be here within the hour.

The child rattled with a fit of coughing.

Miss Darby was at Susie's side in an instant, sitting her up and rubbing her back with the herb-infused water. After several minutes, the coughing ceased and she laid her back down, rinsing the cloth in the basin.

Henry did his best to retie his cravat.

"I wonder how many of your neckcloths my sister has ruined."

"My neckcloths?"

"I was just remembering how, on the way here from Hull, Susie kept falling asleep on you. Every day your cravat ended up soiled and crushed."

Yes. That last day on the coach he'd had to tie a rather creative knot to keep a stain hidden.

"And she ruined another one just now."

He laughed. "Jane may not take the prize as best in the parish for her cooking, but she is quite accomplished in the husbandry of neckcloths."

Miss Darby wrung out the towel and reapplied it to Susie's chest. The child shuddered, and Miss Darby smoothed her forehead, running her hand gently along Susie's brow. She sang to her sister in a soft, silken voice. Henry walked around to the other side of the bed and sat across from her.

"Hush my joy, lie still and sleep. It grieves me sore to hear thee weep. If thou be silent I'll be glad. Thy moaning makes my heart full sad."

If Susie did not overcome this illness, Miss Darby would never recover. He suddenly saw very clearly how, in a moment of overwhelming grief, her mother had made such an error in judgment. If anything did happen to Susie, he'd keep Miss Darby under watch every moment.

After some time, Susie sank into a deeper sleep, her breathing still coming at great effort. Miss Darby looked up at him. "I'm frightened."

"I know. Dr. Leigh is a competent man. I'm sure he will be a great help to her."

The main door to the nursery opened, and Mrs. Tafford entered. "Dr. Leigh is here; he's just giving Fanny some instructions and will be in directly."

Miss Darby went whiter than chalk.

A moment later, Dr. Leigh entered the room. Miss Darby gripped the back of the chair, leaning heavily on it.

"Dr. Leigh." Mr. Morland stepped forward and shook the doctor's hand. "Thank you for coming. May I introduce Miss Charlotte Darby, the new mistress of Willowkeep."

The doctor bowed respectfully to her. He had long graying hair he kept tied back with a black ribbon to match his black suit and a long black waistcoat.

"And her sister, Susan." Henry motioned toward the sleeping child. "Your patient."

"I see." Leigh set a worn leather case on the edge of the bed. "Tell me about her symptoms."

All eyes turned on Miss Darby. She looked at the doctor, opened her mouth, then retreated a few steps.

"Uh," Henry said. "Yesterday Susan took a bad chill when she fell into the West Kipping. We got her out, but not until after she came very near to drowning. Miss Darby skillfully revived the girl, but she's not been well since." He turned to Mrs. Tafford.

"She has fits of coughing that shake her whole body," Mrs. Tafford explained. "Her skin's as hot as the evening coals. And look at her eyes, empty as a poor man's coffer."

The doctor lifted the herbal cloth and watched as her ribs fought for breath. He touched her brow and pulled up on her eyelids, looking closely into her eyes. "How old is she?"

"Eight," Miss Darby said, at last moving closer.

This seemed to surprise Leigh. He studied the child's face. "She's a lunatic. Does she speak?"

Miss Darby slammed her mouth shut, ready for battle.

"She's very bright," Henry said, waving at Miss Darby to stand down. "She doesn't say much, but she understands quite well."

Dr. Leigh nodded. "Is she often ill?"

Henry turned toward Miss Darby. Only she could answer that.

"No. She's rarely ill," she snapped.

Leigh didn't seem to notice her acerbity. Or he chose to ignore it. In his profession, he must meet more than his fair share of bitterness. He opened his bag and took out a jar of medicine. After pouring a small dose into a glass, he lifted the child's head and tried to pour the liquid down her throat.

Susie gasped and choked, spewing the liquid all over Leigh's face. She took one look at the strange man and burst into tears, shrieking and thrashing about the bed. The doctor removed a handkerchief and wiped the medicine off his face.

He moved his doctor's bag to the dresser and poured another drachm. "Please calm your sister," he said to Miss Darby, who was already doing her best to stop the crying. The child's feet kicked off the covers.

Henry thought it a good sign that Susie could muster so much energy, but at this rate, she'd expend herself and have nothing left to fight her illness.

"We'll have to restrain her," Leigh said. "She must drink this."

"No," Miss Darby said. "No. I'm not going to hold her down to be clubbed like a fish pulled in from the ocean."

For heaven's sake. How quickly she jumped beyond any point of reason when it came to Susie.

Leigh narrowed his eyes at Miss Darby. "No one will be doing any clubbing. Goodness, woman."

His words seemed to bring some sense to Miss Darby. She sat on the edge of the bed. "Susie. Do you want Puppy?"

Then, quickly as it had started, it ended. Little Susie went still. She stared out through her fevered eyes, her chest heaving. She was more ill than Henry thought for her to let a stranger so near.

Susie drank her medicine in a stupor. The doctor gave her a thorough examination, then went to work treating her. A small nick to the inside of her elbow to let some blood—Miss Darby biting her nails to the bone the entire time. A few drops of a blackish concoction into the water basin. He told Miss Darby to use this to soak her chest.

Henry stood ready to catch Miss Darby should she faint. Or to stop her should she be the one inclined to do the clubbing—on Dr. Leigh.

After a half an hour, Susie's fever slowly faded and she breathed easier. When she fell back into a deep sleep, Dr. Leigh said there wasn't much more to do and they must wait.

"We've got some supper ready for you," Mrs. Tafford told the doctor. "I'll show you the way."

With an admonition to call him if Susie worsened in any way, he followed Mrs. Tafford out the door.

Miss Darby sank onto the edge of Susie's bed. "He's not the friendliest fellow, is he?"

Henry grinned. "No. But he's competent. And despite his gruff manners, he's a very careful and attentive physician. Your sister is in good hands."

She changed the cloth on Susie's chest. "She seems to be resting better."

"She does."

Miss Darby stroked the child's hair away from her face. Her hands lingered on Susie's cheek, smiling at her with more love than Henry knew existed. She bent down and kissed Susie's brow, her lips red against the child's pallid skin.

He should go. He was no longer needed. He was an intruder in this room. The bond between these two sisters did not include him.

But when Miss Darby looked up, he found he could not leave. He was staring at her. She must think him an idiot. Still, he could not look away.

She put the tip of her finger in her mouth, her eyes fast on his. Did she not know she was killing him?

He reached up and pulled her hand away. "Do not fret," he whispered, keeping hold of her hand.

"Do you think she will live?" Miss Darby whispered.

"I feel certain of it."

"Mr. Morland." She leaned closer, her cheeks flushed from worry, her hair wild from struggling with her sister. She was the most beautiful woman he'd ever seen.

Their breath met in the small space that separated them. His fingers thrummed to caress the softness of her cheek. If he just—

The door to the nursery opened.

Henry jumped to his feet, and Miss Darby nearly fell forward onto Susie. Half a moment later, Mrs. Tafford rounded the corner into Susie's room. Henry leaned against the wall while Miss Darby's face burned redder than beetroot.

"The doctor is eating, and cook is sending up a small repast." Mrs. Tafford looked down at Susie. "Doesn't she just look peaceful as a babe."

He pushed off the wall. "Well, seems all is in hand. Thank you, Mrs. Tafford. I've got a few things to finish before heading back to the Grange."

He left the nursery and went straight outside through the back door. He needed cool air. A moment to clear his head. He'd nearly put Miss Darby in an extremely compromised situation. If Mrs. Tafford had come in even a few seconds later . . . Well, he would have had to tender his resignation. Or Miss Darby might have sacked him. She still could.

He deserved nothing less.

CHAPTER NINETEEN

"Could you sit with her a bit?" Charlotte asked Mrs. Tafford moments after Mr. Morland had made his hasty departure.

"Of course, dear." Mrs. Tafford sat herself down in the rocking chair and took up some mending.

Charlotte hurried down the hall to her room, shutting the door and locking it. After all her careful planning to avoid an attachment, she'd practically thrown herself at him. She might as well go set up camp with the convenients.

How could she ever look him in the eye again? She'd really made a mull of it this time. Mr. Morland's friendship was the only thing keeping her sane in this new country of hers. He must think her a complete and utter cod's head.

At first, Willowkeep had been the end of all her troubles. Now she was here with money and more to spare, food on the table—and a whole new set of problems. Susie was safe though. That was most important.

She splashed some water onto her face, gazing out the window in the dimness of the evening light. Someone was in the garden. Mr. Morland.

She jumped behind the curtain so as not to be seen. She'd not lit a candle, and with her room dark, he likely couldn't see her anyway. She peered round the edge of the window covering.

Mr. Morland was alone, pacing the paths of the gardens. He picked up a stick and gave the boxwood hedge a good whack, spewing tiny leaves into the air. He hurled his stick over the wall of green, then turned and kicked a statue of a dancing satyr.

He yelped and grabbed his toe, hopping in little circles.

Charlotte laughed. Mr. Morland turned and looked up at her window. She ducked out of sight, pressing her hand over her heart. Had he seen her watching him? Maybe he'd sensed her. He always seemed to know exactly when she needed him.

She couldn't need him anymore. It had to end. The afternoon visits with Susie to his office. Her constant questions about every little thing. She had the whole household at her command. If she needed something, a footman or Mrs. Tafford should suffice. Or even Aunt Nora and Mr. Hardwick. Surely between them all she could survive without needing Mr. Morland.

No more.

Charlotte woke up tired and cramped on Susie's bed, Susie's head resting on her arm. The child had woken a few times during the night with fits of coughing. Each time Dr. Leigh had come in and had her drink more medicine.

This morning her cheeks had a touch of pink. Charlotte felt her sister's brow. Warm and alive—and no fever.

Dr. Leigh knocked on Susie's open door. "I believe she is out of danger."

Charlotte untangled herself from Susie and stood. "Thank you, sir."

"It will still be some time, perhaps weeks, until she is fully recovered."

"Yes, sir."

He took a few steps into the little room. "She will need rest."

Charlotte nodded.

"And plenty of tisane. I've told Mrs. Tafford how to prepare it."

She nodded again. "Yes, sir."

He stood there for a few moments. "Are you sure that keeping the child here is the best situation? There is a new asylum in London. It is the very best of modern care for patients such as her."

Charlotte knew too well the kind of care Susie would receive in an asylum. "I would die first."

She had a whole mouthful more of what she wanted to tell Dr. Leigh, but she swallowed it down. Mr. Morland would be proud. Except that after last night, he'd never be proud of her again.

For the first time, Dr. Leigh smiled. "I suspected as much. You are a remarkable woman, Miss Darby. Please keep me informed of her progress or if she worsens."

He turned without another word. Charlotte curtseyed, but he was long gone. He was nothing like the doctors of Hull. Under his rough edges, he did have a caring heart.

But who didn't have some rough edges?

Aunt Nora was covered in them like a hedgehog. Perhaps underneath lurked a caring heart as well. She loved her son and presumably her late husband—God rest his soul.

Mr. Hardwick. His edges were more difficult to see. He tried hard to hide them under his fine outer shell.

Mr. Morland. He had some rough spots as well. For all his kindness and goodness, he was stubborn and proud. Somehow, on him, they suited well.

After seeing that Susie was settled and resting under Fanny's care, Charlotte went to her own room to wash and dress.

She hadn't eaten nearly all day yesterday, and she was famished. Aunt Nora would likely be in the breakfast room at this hour, but her need for nourishment trumped her need to avoid her aunt.

Sure enough, the woman was there, sitting at the table, reading the morning's letters.

"Charlotte. How are you this morning?" She laid her letters aside.

"I'm well, thank you. And you?" Charlotte filled her plate near to overflowing.

"I'm quite well. But I'm dreadfully concerned about your dear sister. Fleurette tells me Dr. Leigh's been here all night tending to the child."

Charlotte had been very careful with Susie round Aunt Nora. Her aunt had seen her sister only a handful of times. Each time Susie had buried her head, refusing to give Aunt Nora a proper greeting. Or as near to proper as Susie ever gave.

Charlotte set her plate down. "The doctor says she is out of danger but still very ill."

"I do hope you'll permit me to visit the nursery and offer my best wishes for a quick recovery."

"Oh. Well." Aunt Nora in the nursery. Thus far that place had not been sullied by the outside world save that one time when Mr. Hardwick had given them the slip.

If her aunt insisted on seeing her, today might be just the day. Susie wasn't really awake enough to notice a strange visitor. Though the very notion of Aunt Nora bending over her sister's bed gave Charlotte the shivers, if she really wanted to be a family with her aunt, that included Susie.

"That's very kind of you, Aunt. Perhaps later today."

Aunt Nora smiled, then looked up over Charlotte's shoulder.

Mr. Tafford held out a silver salver with a letter on it. It was addressed to Charlotte from London. Mr. Tafford left the room, and Aunt Nora went back to her own letters. Charlotte turned the note over and broke the seal.

She skipped straight to the last line to see the sender. Mr. Sutton, the sheepdog solicitor who'd first told her about inheriting Willowkeep.

Dear Miss Darby,

I'm writing to inform you of a particular piece of information that may be of interest to you. When Mr. Walter Kelton amended the will granting you ownership of Willowkeep, its lands and structures, it seems he forgot about a small detail, the which neither I nor my associates had noted.

Although Willowkeep does not have an entail specifying the nature of the individual who can inherit, there is a clause which previously slipped past our notice. It is incumbent on me to inform you that this clause, set up by the elder Mr. Kelton—Alan Kelton—shall be carried on until the third generation, at which time it will be null and void but until that time continues in effect, the result of which pertains to your personal situation as an unmarried woman in ownership of the home and lands of Willowkeep, asserting that said ownership cannot be continued beyond the age of specification, in this case, the twentieth year, at which point in time the home and lands inclusive will devolve to the next in succession to inherit should they be male, or if otherwise, meet said requirement, unless the situation is rectified before the year previously mentioned.

I shall await news of any changes in your situation.

Regards,
Mr. Bellwether Sutton

Charlotte read the letter three times and still couldn't make sense of it. The word *unmarried* caused a complete loss of appetite. And *ownership* brought a lump to her throat. Whatever it meant, it couldn't be good.

"Bad news?" Aunt Nora asked.

She hardly knew. For a brief moment, she considered handing the letter over to her aunt for clarification. But no. That didn't sit right. "It's just a letter from the solicitor. I should pass it on to Mr. Morland."

Aunt Nora nodded. She kept a watch on Charlotte for a few moments before going back to her own letters.

Did she really want to show this to Mr. Morland? It talked of her married state and inheritance. After last night, what would he think?

She could show it to Mr. Hardwick. He was almost as clever as Mr. Morland. He didn't usually come for breakfast till later, after his morning ride.

"Excuse me." Charlotte pushed away from the table. "I have to go check on Susie."

Charlotte went straight to the stables.

The stable master greeted her. "Mr. Morland just left, miss. He should be back by the afternoon."

Gaw. This only confirmed that she relied far too heavily on Mr. Morland. "I'm actually looking for Mr. Hardwick."

"Gone up to London. Won't be back till tomorrow." Mr. Stayner hung some tack on the wall.

It looked like she'd have to make do with Mr. Morland. But this time, it would be done proper.

"When Mr. Morland returns, can you please tell him I need to speak with him on a matter of business?"

"Morland. Sure thing, miss."

"Thank you, sir."

He grinned at her. "George is sufficient."

Naturally. If Mr. Morland were here, he'd have told her the same thing. Another lesson on how to address the staff.

Mr. Morland, Mr. Morland, Mr. Morland. Could she think of nothing else?

At the house, she passed on the same message to Mr. Tafford. That she needed to speak with Mr. Morland when he returned. Mr. Tafford's eyebrow quirked when she said she'd meet him in the drawing room.

From now on, everything proper.

Charlotte tucked the letter into her corset, then went off to the nursery to tend to her sister.

CHAPTER TWENTY

"MISS DARBY WISHES TO SPEAK with you as soon a possible," Stayner told Henry as he led his horse away. Henry went from the stables straight to his office, assuming Miss Darby would meet him there. He'd just opened the terrier records when Tafford knocked and entered.

"Miss Darby will see you in the drawing room," Tafford said.

He looked up at the old man. "The drawing room?"

"Yes, sir."

Henry had known the butler most his life. Old Tafford did his job very well. Many times they'd shared a good laugh regarding the goings on of the Kelton family, especially since Nora Kelton had arrived. Henry had had his hands full trying to pacify the staff after some of Mrs. Kelton's odd requests.

"I'm on my way," Henry said. He wound his way through the back corridors toward the drawing room, Old Tafford following behind him.

Miss Darby was making a statement. A reminder to keep him in his place. He was staff. She the employer. He'd overstepped his bounds by about fifty miles last night. Her message was clear.

He straightened his hair and smoothed his waistcoat, then nodded at Tafford.

Tafford pushed the door open. "Mr. Morland, miss."

Miss Darby sat straight-backed with her hands folded in her lap. "Please sit down, sir."

Lud, she really was serious about keeping him in his place. It was Mrs. Kelton all over again. Henry did as he was told.

The minute he sat, Miss Darby stood and began wandering about the room, chewing on her nail. Perhaps she really was going to sack him. If he lost this position, he'd never get his father out of prison.

Henry's thoughts stalled as Miss Darby reached into her bodice and removed a letter.

"I've received word from Mr. Sutton—the man from London?"

"I know who Mr. Sutton is."

"Of course." She held out the letter but didn't actually hand it over. She seemed uncertain about whether or not he should read it. "I can't make out what he's saying, but it's given me the fidgets all day."

Finally a glimpse of the Miss Darby he knew. "Do you want me to look at it?"

"Yes." But still she did not hand it over.

He reached out and tugged it out of her grip.

Henry unfolded the correspondence and read. No wonder she didn't understand it. Mr. Sutton had gotten to the point by way of Scotland. Henry reread just to be sure he'd not been mistaken.

This news would fall hard on Miss Darby. Very hard indeed.

"Miss Darby, will you sit?" He indicated the empty space beside him on the sofa, but she chose the chair she'd been sitting in earlier. "As you suspected, it is not the best news."

"What does it mean?"

If only he were not the one to deliver this. "It appears Mr. Sutton has unearthed some information regarding the inheritance of Willowkeep and all its holdings."

She shook her head. "You sound like the sheepdog. Give it to me straight. Sir."

He'd always been forthright with her. He should be so now. "According to this letter, if you don't marry by your twentieth birthday, you will lose Willowkeep."

A thud sounded from the hall just outside the room. Old Tafford had left the door open—as was proper. Henry peered into the hallway and saw nothing. He closed the drawing room door. This would have been better handled in his office, where footmen or maids or other prying ears could not overhear.

Miss Darby had abandoned her seat and resumed stalking about the room. "Aunt Nora will turn us out on our fishtails before breakfast." She turned to Henry, then turned away. She crossed to the window, then back to Henry. Then she strode to the fireplace, then back to Henry.

"What has happened to my home in Hull?" She sat, then immediately stood. "Has it been sold? I could return there, perhaps buy it back before my birthday. Do I have enough money to buy it back? It's just Susie and me. We can manage something smaller."

"Yes, you have enough money to buy it back. But if you buy it with estate money, it would also belong to the estate." Seemed every time a ray of sun shone down, clouds moved in to block it. Just when Miss Darby thought her future was safe, this letter had come.

She sat back down beside him. "Mr. Morland. What am I to do?"

He had ideas of ways to work around this, but first he had to state the obvious—though he could already guess her answer. "You could marry."

"No. It's not possible."

"With your wealth, any man would have you. Just wait until the ball."

She shook her head. "No."

What about her beloved Mr. H? Hardwick would be giddy as a gate horse to have Miss Darby's hand—and the money that came with it.

"I felt sure there was a gentleman who had caught your eye."

She looked up at him. Her eyes spun with alarm, and her cheeks flushed. She left the sofa and moved to the window. "You don't understand. I absolutely will not marry. 'Tis not a choice; 'tis a certainty. It is out of the question and will never happen. And that's the end of it."

Perhaps her reluctance went beyond her need to protect Susie. Perhaps she had been used ill. Sailors and dockworkers were not the most honorable lot.

More than once Henry had had to put an end to gossip below stairs. Susie was eight, but she looked the size of a four-year-old. Miss Darby would have been eleven when Susie was born. Far too young.

But if the child really was only four, Miss Darby would have been fifteen. Still young but certainly not unheard of. And they looked so much alike.

"Why?" Henry asked. "Why is it so out of the question?"

She looked at him, the sadness on her face almost as bad as when Susie had nearly drowned. Blue crystals ready to shatter with only the smallest crack. Miss Darby had suffered much, but there was still more. More she wouldn't tell.

The devil take it. This line of questioning only caused her more pain.

"There is one part of this letter that has me curious," he said, unfolding it again.

She came and joined him on the sofa.

"This mention of the third generation. It is not uncommon in an entail to specify a time limit to the stipulations. Perhaps we might find that it has already lapsed and does not apply. You may be the fourth generation. It was my understanding that you are the last in the Kelton line, so I don't know who this next in succession could be."

She scooted closer and peered at the writing. "Could it be Susie?"

Henry shook his head. "No. The law would not see her fit to inherit."

She slumped back into the cushions.

"This mention of the twentieth year is odd. A person is not considered of age until twenty one. We could call that into question and, at the very least, garner more time."

That seemed to brighten her.

"There are several parts of this letter that I have questions about. I have to go up to London soon. I'll stop at Sutton's and get this figured out. In the meantime, I'd like to offer one more solution, though I think you will not at first be open to it."

"What is it?"

"You are set against marriage; this I understand, though the reason is unclear. I am suggesting you consider a marriage of convenience."

She was already shaking her head.

"Hear me out. You would not be the first woman who needed a legal marriage to keep her property. There are men out there who are still decent and respectable but who desperately need money."

Why had he started down this path? These were not things he wanted to be suggesting to Miss Darby. He took a breath and pressed on. "It would be a marriage on paper only. You need not . . . share . . . fulfill . . . all aspects of married life."

She was staring at him. He could see her mind spinning through those clear blue eyes.

He didn't wait for a response. He got to his feet. "There is much to consider. But we have time, five months before your birthday. I'm sure when I see Sutton in a few days we will find that there is a mistake. Otherwise Mr. Kelton would not have willed it to you in the first place. All will be well. I'm sure of it."

Her only response was another nod. It had been some time since she'd spoken, and Henry didn't like the look on her face.

"Miss Darby?"

She stood.

Perhaps he should apologize for last night. He'd ruined their friendship as fast as Jane's cooking ruined his appetite—leaving him just as sick too.

"Miss Darby, I beg your pardon if . . ." He found he could not say it. "I do hope you know that I am here for you in whatever capacity you need. Steward or friend."

She gave him a curtsey. "I know. Thank you, sir."

Her eyes meant it, but her *sir* at the end told him things were different—not how he wanted them but as they should be.

CHAPTER TWENTY-ONE

Charlotte went straight to her room. She tugged on the drawer of her writing desk so hard it fell open, spilling papers and quills and sealing wax all over the floor. She grabbed a single paper and left the rest.

Her Majesty Queen Anne Boleyn
The Lion at Willowkeep, Kent
July 1810

Dear Anne,

I know you didn't have an easy go of life. I'm sorry; I truly am. You were wronged by your family, your husband, and your country. But I am in dire need here.

The London men are telling me I can't stay at Willowkeep unless I marry. You and I both know that cannot be.

You had the power to turn the heart of a king and change the fate of England forever. I know you can help me.

I s'pose you can't do all the work though, so I've put my mind to what can be done, and I have two options. The first, I die, not too painfully, I hope. The second, I haven't figured out yet. I can't leave my sister alone, so that rules out the first.

It's up to you now.

Yours expectantly,
~C

She folded it tightly and sealed it. Next week was the ball. She'd been looking forward to it, especially now that she'd be going with Mr. Hardwick and her aunt. Mr. Sutton's letter killed her anticipation.

Then there was Susie. She improved slowly, and it didn't seem right to leave her while she was still recovering.

Charlotte set off for the willows, ducking into the shelter of the branches and hurrying to the lion's bower.

Another Tudor rose waited there for her. Queen Anne had been here. Hopefully Charlotte's pleadings wouldn't go unanswered for long. She gently removed the rose and put her letter in.

Aunt Nora was coming to see Susie in a few minutes. What an event that would be. Charlotte had no time to linger and enjoy the coolness of the river and the cover of the willows.

She arrived at the nursery short of breath. Her sister lay in her bed sleeping. Good. Things would go better with Aunt Nora if the child did not know she was there. Fanny sat in the rocking chair mending the girl's stockings.

"How is she?" Charlotte asked.

"She's resting. She ate well and lay with her dog until Will came to take him out."

"Thank you."

She could dismiss Fanny since she planned to stay here till dinner, but she'd rather not be alone with her aunt, just in case. If Susie woke up and found a strange face peering down at her, Charlotte would likely need Fanny's help.

Charlotte gently arranged Susie's hair on the pillow without waking her. As she was straightening the blankets, the door to the nursery opened.

Here we go.

Charlotte stepped out into the main room. Aunt Nora waited at the threshold, but she was not alone. Mr. Hardwick was there too. Charlotte smiled to see him, though perhaps the nursery wasn't the best place for him, seeing as how Susie was so frightened by him.

He came forward and took her hand. "Charlotte. I can't tell you how relieved I am that your sister is recovering so well."

"Thank you, Mr. Hardwick." She dipped her head at him. "I'm surprised to see you back so soon from London. How was your trip?"

"London?" Aunt Nora said. "I thought you said—"

"Well, yes. I did have plans to ride up to London today and arrange a fitting for the ball, but I was waylaid by other business." He shook his head sadly. "Alas, I am at the mercy of the tailors, and I must hope my vestments will accommodate me without a final fitting."

Charlotte hadn't ever seen Mr. Hardwick wear a set of clothes that didn't accommodate him perfectly. Even now, when there wasn't a soul here but their own family, he looked ready for a visit to St. James's Palace.

"Enough about clothes," Mr. Hardwick said. "How is that sister of yours doing?

"She's resting," Charlotte said.

She led them into Susie's little room. Fanny slipped out quietly, as, no doubt, she'd been trained to do. Or maybe she was just frightened of Aunt Nora.

Aunt Nora circled the bed, her eyes sharp on the sleeping child. After a long, quiet moment, she said, "She looks very well. Almost like a normal child when she's sleeping."

This was precisely why Charlotte kept her sister out of sight. "Are you saying she don't look normal when she's awake?"

Mr. Hardwick smiled at Charlotte. "What Mother means is that she looks very peaceful."

"I understand Dr. Leigh was here?" Aunt Nora said. "Was he of service?"

"Yes. He was very useful in clearing her cough." Charlotte was trying, she really was, to make peace with her aunt. But how could she when the woman was all prickles and thorns?

"I'm very glad to hear it. What did he say was wrong with her?"

"Wrong with her?" Her aunt had better not be asking what Charlotte thought she was asking.

"Yes. Her abnormity. Was he able to determine what is wrong with her?"

That was the last straw. Nora Kelton was just like everyone else. "People always think there's something wrong with her. But the way I see it, it's everyone else what needs to reconsider. She's my sister. A person. Same as you or me. And she doesn't need some tight-faced woman telling her she's not good enough or regular enough to be loved as part of the family."

Aunt Nora gasped. She whipped out her fan and waved it round her face as though she could whisk Charlotte and Susie out of her life. "Well, I never. How dare you speak to me like this in my own house."

"But it's not your house, is it? It's mine now. I stayed out of your way and let you live like always." Charlotte started a flood that could not be stopped. "Do you have any idea how pleased I was to find I still had family? I would have done anything for your kindness. But you turned your nose up at me. I didn't ask for this; your husband is the one who put me here. So why don't you go find his fancy grave and give him the view of the underside of your sniffer."

She wasn't sure, but she thought she heard Mr. Hardwick snort. Aunt Nora looked like she'd had a bucket of ice water dumped on her. Splotches of red burst out across her face.

"How dare you. You are an uneducated, uncivilized child and have no right to a place like this. And you bring your sister here, sullying these walls with—"

"Mother." Mr. Hardwick stepped between Charlotte and Aunt Nora. He turned to Charlotte. "This has been a difficult adjustment for her, coming so suddenly after the death of Walter. She needs time to come around."

"I don't need time," Aunt Nora said over Mr. Hardwick's shoulder.

He shushed her with a wave of his hand. He looked down at Susie, who was stirring with all the commotion in her room. "She does look infinitely improved. She is lucky to have such an attentive sister."

Behind him, Aunt Nora huffed. Mr. Hardwick shifted his body so Charlotte could hardly see her aunt. Which was just as well because she might have thrown her hands round her broomstick neck and strangled her.

"Puppy, come!" came a shout from outside the open nursery door. Will, bringing back the dog.

Puppy bounded into the room and leapt onto Susie's bed. Susie grabbed the dog round his neck and hugged him close. She opened her eyes and smiled at Charlotte. Then she saw Mr. Hardwick and his mother peering over his shoulder.

Susie's lower lip jutted out, and her cry rattled the room.

"Sorry, miss," Will said. "He's not too good with commands yet."

"Get your mother out of here," she said to Mr. Hardwick. She should never have let them in.

He escorted his mother out of the room but returned alone a moment later. Charlotte held Susie tight to her chest, rocking her back and forth. If Susie's health took a turn because of this, Aunt Nora would be taking tea in the hedgerow.

"Let me apologize for Mother," Mr. Hardwick said. "She can seem a little uncivil at times, but that is simply because she—"

"Mr. Hardwick. I believe my sister will calm down faster if we're alone."

He gave a quick dip of his head. "Of course."

Mr. Hardwick left, closing the nursery door behind him.

What a disaster. That woman would never set foot in this nursery again.

It was clear that her aunt hated her as much now as on the first day they'd met. Probably more. Charlotte thought she had warmed, but no. Whatever hopes Charlotte had of kinship with the people of Willowkeep shriveled up and died.

So now what? Live in the same house with a woman who despised her and her sister? Or ask Aunt Nora to leave her own home? As conceited and obstinate and beastly as Aunt Nora was, Charlotte had no right to make her go. Only a few days ago she'd promised her aunt she'd never want her to leave.

Mr. Hardwick wasn't so bad. At least he made her feel welcome. Without him in the house, it would be a very lonely place indeed. 'Course, if she didn't marry, she'd lose it all anyway, and then who'd be taking tea in the hedgerow?

It had taken almost an hour to get Susie quietened down. She'd worked herself up into a fit of coughing that had Charlotte worrying she might slip back into her fever. Finally she'd fallen asleep.

The day slipped by with administering tisanes, soaking Susie's chest, and trying to get her to eat something. Regardless of her exhaustion, Charlotte couldn't bring herself to leave the nursery. She held Susie in the rocking chair, singing the songs her mother had sung. "Over the mountains and over the waves, under the fountains and under the graves."

Charlotte had tried to do her best for Susie, but it wasn't the job of a child to raise another child—at least it shouldn't be. Part of Charlotte would never forgive her parents.

There was a soft knock at the nursery door.

Now what?

Mr. Morland wouldn't be back, of that she was quite sure. Not after last time.

Charlotte laid her sister in bed and closed Susie's bedroom door. She didn't want to take any chances of a repeat.

She pulled the nursery door open to find Mr. Hardwick standing there, still looking like a dandy in his fine evening attire. His hair was perfectly perched on top of his head. He had his hands behind his back.

"I came to check on you," he said.

"I'm fine. Just tired. It was a long night last night." And a long day.

"You don't seem quite yourself. I don't mean to press, but are you sure there's nothing I can do?"

She just wanted to be left alone. "Nothing is wrong, I assure you."

"Well, it did seem like you needed some cheering up, so I brought you this." He pulled out a plate from behind his back, covered with a napkin. He lifted the cloth to reveal a piece of brownish cake. "Parkin. Cook said it was your favorite, so I had her make you some."

"Thank you." Charlotte took the plate. He did try. She couldn't help a smile. "You are very kind."

He gave her a solemn bow. "Good night, then, Charlotte."

"Good night, Mr. Hardwick." She shut the door.

The cake was the color of burnt straw, not the dark treacle color it should be. And dry. The oats crumbled out. Cook must have baked it this very night. Parkin wasn't ready for eating till after it sat for several days getting moist and sticky.

She set it on the table for the maids to clear away in the morning.

CHAPTER TWENTY-TWO

HENRY SET OFF AT DAWN. He took the curricle and the two Cleveland bays. They'd get him to London with the smoothest gait and fastest time. He had only one day to do his best to settle—at least partially—his father's debts, talk to Mr. Sutton, and get back to Willowkeep.

He'd chosen this day on purpose—the day of the ball. Better to get away from Willowkeep and all the preparations. Miss Darby had been wavering on whether or not to attend, given her sister's condition. But Susie was doing much better now, and Miss Darby seemed excited to go.

Henry stopped first at Mr. Sutton's.

When the clerk ushered him into Sutton's office, he almost laughed out loud. The sheepdog, Miss Darby had called him. Now that Henry saw him again, he had to agree. The gray shag on his head and chin, small nose, and little black eyes set deep just beneath his bushy eyebrows.

"Mr. Morland. Please sit."

Henry took the seat across the great walnut desk from Sutton.

"I'm surprised to see you here," Sutton said.

"Are you?" The solicitor must have known his letter would raise many questions. "We received your letter about the new information regarding Miss Darby's ownership of Willowkeep."

Sutton nodded. "Yes, I'm sorry we didn't notice it sooner, but there were quite a large number of documents to sort through."

"May I see it?" Henry asked. He'd understand it better if he could read it in its original wording and not through the jumble of Sutton's translation.

"It's not here at the moment," he said, his gray beard wafting about as he spoke.

"Where is it?" It seemed to Henry that legal papers should be kept in the legal office. He knew for a fact they had a large safe in the building to keep such documents just that—safe.

"We sent it over to the bank to legalize the funds that are being transferred into the name of Miss Darby with the stipulation of the requirements being fulfilled by the date as stated in order to keep the funds, otherwise, they will need to be transferred again to the name of the next in succession who takes control of the house with all its lands and properties inclusive." He shrugged apologetically.

What was Sutton up to? Henry had worked with him for years as they'd both waded through the many legal and logistical workings of Willowkeep. He wasn't always so roundabout.

"And who is the next in succession?" It wasn't Mr. Hardwick. They'd already covered Mr. Hardwick's inheritance months ago when Kelton had passed away. He got nothing. Which explained much about his attitude toward Charlotte—Miss Darby.

"Let's see." Sutton thumbed through a stack of papers, all of them yellowed with age. Much like Sutton's teeth. "There is a young man, a Mr. George Kelton. The grandson of the elder Mr. Kelton's brother. He is not of age yet, so there will be a time of interim."

A time when Henry would be running things on his own. Or, more likely, under the jurisdiction of George Kelton's mother.

Odd that he'd never heard of this man. "Unless Miss Darby marries," Henry said. Whatever happened, he doubted he'd stay on at Willowkeep. It was his childhood home, and he loved it more than anything. But he didn't want to be there with another old harpy telling him how to do his job. And he could never stay and watch Miss Darby marry another man.

"Naturally if she marries, all is a moot point."

"How old is this Mr. George Kelton?"

"Fifteen, I believe."

"Let me see it," Henry said.

According to the paper, Walter's father, Alan Kelton, had a younger brother named Edmund—Walter's uncle. This Henry already knew. If Uncle Edmund had a son that young, he must have fathered him in his very old age. "Are you sure George is not Edmund's grandson?"

"I don't believe so. We've not yet made contact with him to work out the details."

"And it is Alan Kelton's father who set the entail on Willowkeep?"

Sutton nodded.

"I will need to see the entail document as soon as possible. The original, mind you, not a summary. And the family history with legal documentation. Especially proving George Kelton's date of birth."

Mr. Sutton jotted down Henry's list on a small piece of parchment.

"I have serious concerns about the legality of the entail," Henry said. "If, as stated in your letter, a three-generational entail was not renewed by Walter, it may have lapsed. I find it very odd that Walter would renew the entail, then turn around and will the estate to his niece."

Sutton dropped his pen into the inkwell. "I shall gather the papers you request and send them to Willowkeep."

Henry left the law offices wishing he had better news to take back to Miss Darby. He wouldn't be able to tell her anything definitive until he had the papers in his hands.

This led him to his next and most odious task of the day—his father's debts.

Henry had scraped together all he'd managed to save to pay them. It totaled barely a third of what his father owed.

He lived in Willow Grange—property of Willowkeep. He had no property of his own he could sell. No carriage. Nothing worth more than a few shillings. He'd lost the job at the mill, as he'd predicted, to Miles Standish.

The bank was unwilling to offer an extension, so Henry had to do the best he could with what he had.

He drove the curricle across the Thames to Southwark. His father hadn't the wealth nor status to be allowed into the west-end pigeon holes. No. He'd made a name for himself in the gaming dens of the tradesmen and warehouse workers.

These places were the degradation of society. They didn't care about the family at home, the mouths waiting for food. If a man had money in his pocket, they took it all. And more.

If it hadn't been daylight, Henry would never have driven the carriage into this part of town—not with its Willowkeep heraldry on the side. Too easy a target.

He stopped in front of a seedy tavern, The Black Fox. Aptly named. The street was littered with horse dung and mounds of various other refuse. The hot sun baked down on it, creating a stench that rivaled any cesspit in England.

Henry called out to a boy gazing green-eyed into the window of the baker's shop across the street. "You, lad."

The boy came closer.

Henry held out the reins. "There's tuppence for you if you keep these animals here and ready to go. I'll only be a moment."

The lad's face lit up. "Yes, sir."

Henry crossed the street, careful to miss the worst of the muck. Not all of it could be avoided.

Two men stood guard at the door. They looked familiar, like the ruffians who'd paid him a special visit on the road to River Head. They sneered, their fists clenching and unclenching as he passed by. One of them pushed off the wall and followed him inside.

The stink inside was worse than the moldering manure outside. It seemed no man who frequented this place knew the meaning of a privy. Pipe smoke and sour ale filled the air. Men stood cheering around a hazards table in the center of the room while dice clinked. Along the outskirts, they gathered at tables of faro. The fortunate ones held their cards at a jaunty angle, a grin on their lips. The not-so-lucky pulled at their hair and sweated in desperation.

It wasn't hard to find the proprietor of the dung heap—he was the only man still sober.

The ruffian from the front door spoke first. "This 'ere's Henry Morland, son of Mr. Morland Senior."

"Ah." The proprietor nodded at Henry. "Ready to try your luck at my tables? It don't always have to be like father like son, eh?"

"Hardly." Henry would rather dive headfirst into the Thames. "I'm here to settle my father's account."

The man grinned. "A good son, eh? You're late." The man eyed Henry, taking in his worn breeches. His wool waistcoat instead of silk. Granted, knowing where his errand would take him, Henry hadn't worn his best. Nonetheless, this man had a shrewd eye.

Henry handed over the handful of banknotes. "Here you are, Mr. . . . ?"

"Most here just call me Fox." He passed the bills to the brute standing beside him.

Henry felt a twinge of satisfaction at the missing tooth in the brute's mouth. The man fingered through the banknotes, then whispered something into Fox's ear.

Fox gave Henry a sardonic sneer. "Ain't near enough."

"It's at least a third," Henry said. "And it's the best I can do. If you'll give me till Michaelmas, I'll have the rest. I swear it. I just need more time to work out the funds." That plus a miracle.

"Already gave you more time, eh. I'm tryin' to run an establishment here. Can't do that if I'm givin' money away."

"It's all I've got."

"Well, then, you should'na let yer father come spendin' money he don't 'ave."

Henry stepped closer. "You shouldn't have let him play when you knew he could not pay."

Fox straightened himself up to his full height. He almost came to Henry's shoulder. "Oh, he can pay, all right. I knows who you work for down in Kent. I knows you got money; you just ain't reachin' deep enough."

Lud. Fox had let his father play into such debt because he thought Henry could pay it from Willowkeep money. Because he was the steward. Now, where would Fox get such a notion? His father always did have a loose tongue.

"I'm just a working man with a working man's wages. No more." Henry took a step back. Time for him to leave. "Could I get a note of receipt for that payment?"

The brute was pounding one fist into the other in typical brutish fashion.

"Tell ya what," Fox said. "We can make a deal. I'll give you more time if you give Rudge here something in return."

What could the brute—Rudge—possibly want from Henry?

Rudge grinned, showing the gap where his tooth had been. The tooth Henry had knocked out on the road to River Head.

Fox pointed at the gap. "An eye for an eye, jus' like the Bible says. That'll buy you three more months."

That was likely the best offer he'd get. It wouldn't be so bad. Lots of people had missing teeth. Even the first Mrs. Kelton had two false teeth donated to her by some poor soul who'd sold them for gold.

Henry nodded and set his stance, planting his feet firmly for the best balance. Under no circumstances did he want to fall backward onto that filthy floor.

Dice clanked against the hazard table. A man cursed. He must have lost.

Rudge drew back his hand, his jaw tight, and swung right at Henry's face.

Henry ducked just in time while his own fist landed squarely on Rudge's nose. The brute stumbled back, and blood gushed from each nostril.

Henry turned and ran. The gamers in the room cheered as Henry made a dash toward the door, bursting out into the street at top speed. He dug into his pocket and tossed a coin to the boy still dutifully holding the carriage.

In one leap, Henry bounded onto the curricle and whipped his horses forward.

Fox yelled at the second brute standing guard. "What're ya doin'? Go after him."

The man ran, but by then Henry had his team on the move.

"You'll pay fer that, Steward," Fox called after him.

Henry careened down the street, praying with all his might that some young mother and her children wouldn't try to cross the road in front of him. The carriage skipped and skidded over the littered cobblestones. Several blocks down, Henry reined the horses into a more manageable trot.

He had no doubt he would regret his choice. But letting Fox's cutthroat take a free swing at him didn't fall into Henry's manner of thinking.

In only a few more turns, Henry was on Borough Street. The Marshalsea prison occupied almost a full block. He couldn't leave London without stopping in to see his father.

CHAPTER TWENTY-THREE

HENRY BROUGHT HIS CARRIAGE TO a stop in front of the prison's small gatehouse, then he knocked on the door. A wooden panel slid back, and the turnkey peered through the barred opening.

"I'm here to see Mr. Henry Morland," Henry told the turnkey.

"Who's asking?" Every time he visited, the same turnkey asked him the same question. *Can't skip the formalities*, the turnkey always said.

"His son. Henry Morland. Junior."

Iron clanked on iron, and the door opened. "Hello again, Mr. Morland." He gave Henry a little bow. His body was so thin it seemed it would snap in two. Combined with the man's long thin nose and the few wisps of long hair on his head, he looked rather like a depleted mop. "Sorry about the bother, but we can't skip the formalities."

"No, of course not."

"Have a good visit, then." The turnkey hooked his key ring onto his belt. "Remember bell sounds at half four. All visitors out."

"Yes, yes. Thank you, Mr. Pebblesham." Henry gave the man a sixpence. Any donation Henry made went to keeping his father on the good side of the jailers. In a place like this, it could mean the difference between a meal or starving.

If the air in the gaming den was foul, the Marshalsea was infinitely worse. Henry crossed the courtyard, which served as a sort of purgatory, a temporary place of smells that let the individual prepare for the final perdition of stench that awaited inside the walls. He'd already learned that covering his nose did little good. It only reminded the occupants of their fall from grace.

His father sat in an upright chair in front of a barred window. A coating of filth covered the glass, and nothing but the most minimal amount of sunlight leaked through.

"Hello, Father." Henry pulled the old man's meager blanket over his shoulders. Despite the stifling heat in the cell, his father shivered.

The old man smiled up at him. "Henry. Good of you to come."

Henry didn't like the sound of his father's voice. Too weak and raspy by half.

"Here is a basket Jane sent." Henry opened the cover. "Three loaves of bread. Dates. Some fresh strawberries. A pudding. And some meat pies."

In truth, Henry had stopped at a market and purchased the meat pies in London. He didn't trust Jane's pies on his father's weak constitution.

His father took the basket. "Are the pies safe?"

"Yes, yes. They are safe."

His father laughed, but it ended in a racking cough. Finally he said, "You are very good to me."

Henry took a flask from the bottom of the basket. "And here's something to fortify you when the nights get cold."

His father immediately unstopped it and took a swallow, closing his eyes.

Henry talked about Willowkeep and its new mistress. The work on the new oast house. His father talked of the people he'd come to know in prison. Each one had a tale of their own. Mostly debtors but some traitors and criminals too.

"Twenty-four died in the prison last week, and a wagonload of men were taken away to be transported to Australia."

More than likely they were prisoners whose families could not pay the prison rent. Without rent, inmates starved or withered away from disease. Henry had already had to pay several shillings just to have his father's chains removed.

"We'll have you out of here soon," Henry assured him. Though he had grave doubts about that. Especially after his encounter with Fox. "I've already paid a large sum."

His father lowered his head into his hands. For several minutes, he said nothing. When he looked up, he had tears in his eyes. "Son. I've left you a muddle. Leave it. Don't waste another penny on it. Let it die with me, and you can at last be free."

His father had never spoken like that before. He'd never mentioned the debts he'd amassed. Not directly. He had served honorably as the steward of Willowkeep. When Henry took over, idleness had not suited him. Before Jane and Henry could fully realize what was happening, he'd ruined them all.

"Do not say such things." Henry could never leave him there to die. Though he had no assurance he could get his father out before he succumbed to illness, he would spend his last farthing trying.

"Did the physician see you?" Henry had given funds for a doctor.

"No. There is no physician."

Then Henry's money went to fatten the coffers of the prison master.

"Twenty-four died in prison last week, and a wagonload of men were hauled away for transportation," his father said. "Australia."

"Yes, so you mentioned."

The old man's mind was slipping. From age or illness, Henry couldn't tell. It made the need to free his father more urgent than ever.

The bell clanged.

"I have to go, Father. I'll come back soon." He stood and kissed him on the forehead. "That is from Jane."

His father's eyes went back to the window, staring out but seeing nothing. "You will give my love to Jane, won't you?"

"Of course."

"And to your mother."

His mother had long since passed away. "Yes, Father."

Henry pulled the blanket up over his father's shoulders again.

As awful as his father's mistakes were, Henry had spent his life looking up to him, following in his footsteps to become the next steward of Willowkeep.

This was the lot of fathers and sons. The father watched his son grow from boy into a man. But son watched his father fade from man back to boy.

Henry hurried to the gate.

"Almost locked you in," the turnkey said with a laugh, though Henry didn't think he was joking.

"Mr. Pebblesham," Henry said. "You seem like an honorable man."

The turnkey straightened, his thin body becoming more toothpick than ever. "Thank you, sir."

"I wonder if you aren't more honorable than the master."

The turnkey glanced around, then moved closer. "I'm listening."

"My father is not well. I'm willing to pay the man who brings him a doctor an extra crown."

The turnkey narrowed his eyes. "Make it two crowns and it's as good as done."

"Agreed." Henry shook his hand. Corrupt, the whole lot of them. But if it got his father help, so be it. "Good day to you, then, Mr. Pebblesham."

"Safe journey," the turnkey said.

Henry stepped through the gate, and the door locked behind him.

Henry climbed into the curricle and left Borough Street for the Kent Road. It would be late when he got home. Well past dinnertime. Jane would be up at the house now, helping Miss Darby dress for the ball.

Henry had managed to escape the day of preparations, but poor Jane. Miss Darby had begged for her help until Jane could do nothing but relent.

Miss Darby would be the talk of the ball. Her beauty. Her money. Her mysterious sister. Her money.

She'd dance every dance, of that he was sure, and with the most eligible men in the district.

Perhaps he should have let Rudge take his hit. It might have been less painful.

CHAPTER TWENTY-FOUR

Charlotte stood in front of a gilded mirror big enough to show her whole self and then some. Jane stood behind her, lacing up the back of her gown—creamy silk trimmed with a deep and brilliant blue. A new dress she'd had made just for tonight.

"Who do you think will be there?" Miss Darby asked.

Jane shook her head. "I don't know."

"But I thought they have this ball every year. I heard from your brother that the Archbishop's cleric will be there. Have you ever met him?"

"No." Jane tugged on Charlotte's corset laces.

"Have you ever been to the Westwood's? Is it grand? I hope it's not too grand, or I shall feel like a fish out of water. I wish you could come with me. As it is, I'll be arriving with Mr. Hardwick in his carriage. And Aunt Nora. But at least I shan't be entirely alone." She flapped her arms to cool off while Jane worked on fastening her gown.

Jane stepped away. "There."

"Is it done? It feels tight. Do you think it's too tight? If the food is as good as Mr. Morland says, I want space to grow."

Jane didn't answer.

"Jane? Are you all right?"

She'd been unusually quiet this evening. No wonder, though, with Charlotte carrying on about the ball and Jane not able to go. What a cod's head she was.

"I'm sorry. I'm being thoughtless." Charlotte had been in far worse circumstances than Jane only a short while ago. She hadn't meant to make Jane feel low.

Charlotte turned and grasped Jane's hands. "I have just had the most wonderful idea. We have this whole house, right?"

Jane gave a half nod.

"We must give a ball, Jane. You and I. I'll have to ask Mr. Morland's permission, of course. But I don't think he'd mind. He's always telling me to get to know the neighbors. What do you think?"

At last Jane gave her a weak smile. "Miss Darby—"

"Charlotte." Jane had lately taken to calling her *miss* again.

"You are very kind. But it wouldn't matter where the ball were held. Your society is not my society. As I'm reminded continually."

"But—"

"No," Jane said. "We need not worry about that tonight. You are ready."

Charlotte made a little twirl in front of the mirror. A few months ago, she'd never have dreamed she'd be wearing a dress fit for a queen.

Jane had put some sort of salve in Charlotte's hair that smoothed its unruly strands. It lay flat and was tucked into the blue and ivory ribbons that perfectly matched the dress.

"I don't even recognize myself."

She went to her wardrobe and opened it. Tucked into the back were her mother's jewels. The sapphire pendant and matching earrings.

"Just one last thing." She lifted the lid and showed them to Jane. "These are the only thing I have left from my life before. They belonged to my mother. I probably should have sold them long ago to feed us. But I couldn't do it."

"They're beautiful." Jane lifted the necklace and held it to the candlelight.

The gem danced like fairies in the night. "I've never worn them before. Not out in public anyway. If I would have stepped outside my door in Hull with these on, I'd have been killed faster than a goose at Christmas."

Jane draped it round Charlotte's neck, clasping it in the back. "Good that you are here, then."

"Do you think they'll be safe?" Charlotte asked. Perhaps she'd better not wear them.

"I'm sure of it. No one would dare steal them in these parts of the country."

Charlotte put the earrings on. The colors in the jewels perfectly reflected the trim of her dress and ribbons.

Mrs. Tafford came into her room and smiled grandly. "Oh, you do look lovely. Like a real lady."

Charlotte curtseyed.

"Mr. Hardwick and Mrs. Kelton are ready. They're waiting for you in the drawing room."

Charlotte picked up her reticule and headed down the stairs to meet Mr. Hardwick. On the last step, she paused. Was Mr. Morland back from London yet?

She changed directions and went to the back of the house, to his office. She knocked once, then opened the door. The room was dark and empty. Even if he was back, he wouldn't be here this late. He was likely home, waiting for Jane and his dinner.

Charlotte closed the door and made way her to the drawing room. Mr. Hardwick stood by the window, gazing out. Aunt Nora was there too, dressed in the finest black silk money could buy.

There'd been a great silence between Aunt Nora and her since the night of the nursery disaster. Tonight her aunt would be her chaperone at the ball. What a mess that would be.

"Sorry I'm late," Charlotte said.

Mr. Hardwick bowed to her. "You look enchanting." He winked.

"There's fashionably late, and then there's late. Come along." Aunt Nora gave Charlotte a quick appraisal. Her eyes lingered on the sapphire jewels before she swished from the room.

Mr. Hardwick shook his head. "Don't let her worry you. We're in plenty of time."

He wore his new suit—the one he'd ordered from London. Ebony breeches, stockings whiter than snow. A blue and silver waistcoat with silver buttons shiny as a mirror. The coat fit him perfectly, stretched tight across his broad shoulders.

He held out his arm, and she laid her hand on it.

Standing in the corner of the entrance hall, nearly hidden in shadows, lurked Jane. She must've come down to get a glimpse of them as they left.

"Jane!" Charlotte said.

Mr. Hardwick's head spun round.

Jane stared at them for a moment, then turned and disappeared down the hall.

Charlotte looked up at Mr. Hardwick as he gazed into the empty hallway.

"I have the feeling I've offended her somehow," Charlotte said.

Mr. Hardwick took Charlotte's arm and steered her toward the front door. The coach waiting for them was the same one she'd rode down from Hull in. Mr. Hardwick's legs fit in much better than poor Mr. Morland's.

Twenty minutes later, the carriage turned down a lane and came to a stop in front of a large house. She knew naught of great houses and their styles, but Willowkeep had the appearance of something from the days of old, while Ashdown Hall seemed newer built.

Lanterns lined the drive, and a row of coaches waited to dole out their passengers. So many people, and each one dressed in something finer than the next.

She wouldn't fit in with these folk even if she had a hundred years to practice. Jane's words rang in her ears. This society was not her society, no matter how many times Mr. Morland told her differently.

Mr. Hardwick handed out his mother, then Charlotte. A man in a white wig announced her and the Hardwicks as they entered.

"Miss Charlotte Darby of Willowkeep," he bellowed. Heads turned in her direction. Perhaps it was a good thing her hands were covered to her elbows in gloves—to keep her nail out of her mouth. "Mrs. Nora Kelton and Mr. Hurst Hardwick."

Entering the ballroom was like drowning in a sea of softly colored pearls and black onyx.

A stout but handsome woman pushed her way toward Charlotte. Mr. Hardwick smiled at her.

"Mrs. Westwood. How well you look." He nudged Charlotte forward. "May I introduce you to my cousin, Miss Charlotte Darby, the new owner of Willowkeep."

Mrs. Westwood took hold of both of Charlotte's hands. "Miss Darby. How good of you to come. We are so looking forward to an acquaintance with our new neighbor. How are you settling in?"

Mrs. Westwood's words were a gentle song. Not at all like the sharp voice her aunt always used. Charlotte's anxiety drifted away on them.

"Thank you for including me in the invitation." Charlotte gave her a curtsey. "We are settling in all right, I s'pose. The house is so big I sometimes get lost."

Mrs. Westwood laughed. "Come with me, child. There is someone I want you to meet." She pulled Charlotte away. "You don't mind, do you, Hardwick?"

"Not at all, madam."

Mrs. Westwood led Charlotte through the sea of women wearing every shade of white imaginable. It was slow going, as they all wanted to meet her. Charlotte dipped her head and said, "Pleased to meet you" more times than she could count. Name after name flitted into her ears but went out again just as fast. She never knew so many people lived in Kent.

They reached a young man wearing clergyman's clothes and speaking to a small group of people.

Mrs. Westwood waited a few moments, then tapped him on the arm with her closed fan. "Regis."

"Excuse me," he said as he stepped away from his friends.

"I would like to present my new neighbor I was telling you about." She tipped her head toward Charlotte. "This is Miss Charlotte Darby, lately from Kingston upon Hull but now of Willowkeep. Miss Darby, our nephew, Regis Farnham, cleric to The Most Reverend Archbishop of Canterbury."

The man bowed. He looked about Mr. Morland's age. Not as tall, of course. He had red hair and striking gray eyes.

Charlotte curtseyed deeply.

The man laughed. "Come now. My aunt makes too much of it. We all must earn a living somehow."

"Yes, but I've never met anyone so important before." Charlotte curtseyed again. "'Cept one time we met the captain of a Greenlander who come all the way from Denmark. They thought he was a spy though, so they locked him up. He only had one arm."

Mr. Farnham and Mrs. Westwood seemed to have nothing to say to this. They looked at her all puzzled-like.

"He were hanged though, in the end." She may as well finish the story.

"Miss Darby," Mr. Farnham said. "That is perhaps the single most interesting thing I've heard all evening. Coming from the north, you must have had many experiences vastly different from our ordinary days."

She hadn't ever thought about it like that before. Most likely because she wouldn't exactly call her days in Kent ordinary. But yes, they were vastly different. "I s'pose you're right."

"Come now, Miss Darby," Mrs. Westwood said. "I still need you to meet Mr. Westwood."

"It's been a pleasure to make your acquaintance," Mr. Farnham said. "Would you save me the first dance, I wonder?"

"Mr. Farnham, that is very kind," Charlotte said. "But I've already promised the first two dances to Mr. Hardwick."

Mr. Farnham's eyes roved the sea of people. "The next one, then."

"I believe I gave that one to . . ." She looked round; she couldn't remember his name.

"Mr. Smallwood, dear," Mrs. Westwood chimed in. "And then Mr. Chivery, and then Mr. Newton."

Gaw. All was happening too fast, like she was twisted up in a swing and spinning out, all the faces flashing past in a blur.

Mr. Farnham's eyebrows rose. "Is there a dance you have open that I might reserve?"

Mrs. Westwood arranged for him to dance with her before they went in to dinner, then she whisked her off again, guiding her through the crowd, stopping only to introduce her to those that deserved Mrs. Westwood's "Here's a dear friend" or "Here's a fine gentleman."

At last they found Mr. Westwood in the card room. He was kind and pleasant but quite uninterested in more than a basic introduction. Mrs. Westwood stayed with her until they found Mr. Hardwick again, surrounded by a flock of young ladies.

Mr. Hardwick broke through the barrier of silk and muslin and lace. "Miss Darby. There you are."

Mrs. Westwood kissed her cheek and hurried off. A moment later, a few strains of music announced the beginning of the first set.

"Shall we?" Mr. Hardwick said, leading her onto the floor.

They took their place, far too near the head of the line for Charlotte's taste. Of all the people at this ball, she was the most unfit to be in the lead. Her few times at the assembly rooms of Hull had not prepared her for this.

Mr. Hardwick was a lovely dancer, which more than made up for Charlotte's deficiency. With the number of couples dancing, the set took more than half an hour. She'd be here all night. Charlotte prayed that Fanny wouldn't have any trouble with Susie. She'd never been alone for bedtime before.

Charlotte danced and danced. The musicians were just as Mr. Morland had said, the finest. Their music filled the room and floated out the open door. Her partners came and went, some of them pleasant, some less so. All of them asked extensively about Willowkeep. By the time Mr. Farnham led her out, she wasn't sure she could dance anymore.

"You look tired, Miss Darby," he said. "Would you prefer to step off the dance floor for a while?"

She had no desire to offend him, but her feet ached, and the ballroom was hotter than a roasting spit. "I'm dripping like a—" Mr. Morland would not want her to say that. She smiled and clasped her hands behind her back. "If you don't mind."

"Not at all." He led her round the edge of the room and through a door into the gardens. Quite a number of people were already outside enjoying the cooler air. "I suspect I will benefit more from your conversation than your dancing. Now, tell me more about the one-armed captain."

Charlotte told him how she'd met the man, how he'd dined at their house before they'd arrested him. How he swung from the gibbet for days before the gulls chewed him down.

Mr. Farnham listened. He seemed quite fascinated by the whole account. "The things you've seen, Miss Darby. It's quite wondrous."

So she went on and told him about the great whale they had once brought in. About the smell that hovered for weeks. About the meat that tasted rich, like venison or beef, not at all like fish. About the jawbones she could walk through without bending over. He was easy to talk to and quick to laugh.

They had rounded the fountain and started their way back when Mr. Hardwick approached. "Farnham, Mrs. Westwood is looking for you. Apparently an express letter has arrived from Addington Place."

Mr. Farnham nodded. "Miss Darby, it appears my evening will be cut short. I do hope I have the pleasure of your company again soon." He bowed and kissed her hand. "Hardwick," he said with a nod, then strode off.

Mr. Hardwick extended his arm. "I've hardly seen you at all. Will you take another turn with me before we are called to dine?"

"Of course." Charlotte put her hand on his arm, and they strolled back through the hedges. They reached a stone bench set along a row of lavender and sat down.

"Are you enjoying yourself?" he asked.

"Surprisingly, yes," she said. Just as Mr. Morland predicted, it was lovely and grand. "Much more than I expected."

For all its grandness, one ball was enough. How some young ladies managed a whole Season of this was beyond her comprehension.

It was nearly midnight. She'd been gone a long time. Susie was still recovering, and if she got scared or upset, it wouldn't go well for Fanny—or Susie.

"Farnham seems taken with you."

"He's very kind." Cold from the stone seeped through her thin gown. Charlotte wanted to put her face on it to cool off.

"It's good to see you smile," Mr. Hardwick said. "I haven't seen it much these last few days."

With Susie's near drowning, then her illness, and Aunt Nora's frolic in the nursery, it hadn't been the best week. "I s'pose I have been a bit off."

He stared out into the night. Clouds had moved in, blocking the stars, but the light of the moon was still visible, an orb shining through the mist in a sea of black satin. He seemed pale in the light, and a sheen of sweat glistened on his forehead. He must be overheated too. Or unwell.

"But you do feel at home now, do you not?" he asked.

Willowkeep? Home? "It feels like . . . sanctuary. Not quite home, but at least safe for now." She had friends there. People to help. No longer just her and Susie trying to make a go of it. Fanny. Mrs. Tafford. Mr. Morland. She'd be lost without him. She didn't have anyone like that back in Hull.

Mr. Hardwick took her hand and kissed it. A long, slow kiss that brought heat to her face. "Charlotte. I have admired you from the moment I first met you."

Charlotte withdrew her hand. She wasn't such a simpleton that she couldn't see where Mr. Hardwick was going. She should have taken Jane's advice and brought a fan. This country was too cocksure hot by far.

"I'm glad we have this moment alone. It would be the greatest honor if you would consent to"—he swallowed hard—"give me your hand in—"

"No." She stood. "No. Please stop. I'm flattered, but I absolutely cannot. It is not possible. Do not ask again." One more reason she should have brought a fan: so she could slap him with it. He was ruining everything.

Mr. Hardwick looked up at her as the clouds drifted across the moon. He watched her for a while, then tipped his head back. "Oh, thank heaven for that." He let out a huge sigh. "Miss Darby, please sit down."

She did, keeping herself on the very edge of the bench. What kind of game was Mr. Hardwick playing at?

"I can't keep this up any longer. I must come clean."

"Clean about what?"

"You must know by now that my mother summoned me back to Willowkeep to pursue you."

This place wasn't so different from Hull after all. Up there she'd have been set upon for her jewels. Here, it was Willowkeep. Mr. Morland had warned her about her new income attracting desperate men. She'd sort of put it out of her mind that Mr. Hardwick could be one of them. He lived in the big house. He seemed to have everything. She'd forgot that none of it was his. "Mr. Morland might have hinted at something of that sort."

"I'm sure he did." The color returned to his face, and he seemed much better. "My dear, widowed, proud mother will kill me for this, but no matter how she tyrannizes me, I cannot go through with it. It's not fair to me and most certainly not fair to you."

"So you don't want my money?"

"No. I don't want your money." He shrugged. "That is to say, of course I want your money. Every man in the country wants your money. But not like that. My mother wants everything to be as it was before. She is afraid she will be homeless when you get around to kicking her out."

"But I would never do that." Even after the scene in the nursery, Charlotte would never do that.

"I know." He took her hand again. "You are the kindest and humblest person I know. You deserve to be happy. As much as I admire you and count you as a friend, I am not the man for you, nor you the girl for me." He let out another long rasp of air.

There was no man for her because she could not have any. "I am sorry, Mr. Hardwick. But the truth is, I shan't ever marry."

"Is that so?"

She nodded.

"Do you know how many young ladies I've heard protest the very same sentiment only to marry weeks later?"

Unlike the other young ladies, Charlotte meant it. "How many girls have you asked to marry you?"

"One. And she rejected me. Most emphatically."

"I am sorry," she said again. Though really he did seem rather pleased that she'd said no. Perhaps because his heart had already been taken. More than once she'd stumbled upon a quiet moment between Jane and him.

"At least this way I can tell my mother that I honestly tried and was rejected. She can be quite forceful, you know. I'm sorry I imposed, and I hope you can forgive me."

He had imposed, but he hadn't pressed. He seemed so relieved by her refusal that she nearly laughed. She'd lost enough family already. 'Twould be a shame if this became a wedge between them. "Are we still friends?"

"I hope that we shall always be the best of friends."

"Then I forgive you," she said. "Under one condition."

"Anything." He grinned. It had been a long time since she'd seen Mr. Hardwick so genial. Aunt Nora must have pressured him unbearably to make him desperate enough to ask to marry a girl he did not want.

"I'm dying for some of this thousand-layer cake Mr. Morland told me about. Something French, he called it. Get me a piece of that, and all is forgotten."

"*Gâteau de mille-feuilles.* Consider it done."

CHAPTER TWENTY-FIVE

THE COACH ROLLED ONTO THE Willowkeep drive in the wee hours of the morning. Even so, they'd left the ball early. Aunt Nora was tired, and Charlotte was desperate to get back to Susie.

In the front hall, Mr. Hardwick bade her good night with a wink. Aunt Nora's face was a ray of sunshine. How quickly that would fade when she discovered the truth about Mr. Hardwick's joy. Hurst. He'd made her promise to call him by his Christian name. They were cousins, after all.

Charlotte laughed out loud as she climbed the stairs. At least it was over and done and Hurst could get on with his life.

She crept on tiptoe into the nursery and then into Susie's room. Her sister wasn't in her bed. Only Puppy yipping softly in his sleep.

Charlotte looked round and nearly screamed when she saw a dark figure sitting in the rocking chair.

Mr. Morland, with Susie on his lap. Both sound asleep.

His cravat was a mess, and he'd thrown off his coat, draping it over the foot of the bed. He must be roasting there under all Susie's warmth.

She reached for his shoulder to wake him, but he looked so peaceful. All those men at the Westwood's ball in their finest silk stockings and neckcloths like snow lilies, and not a single one was as handsome as Henry Morland just now.

It wasn't hard to see what had happened here. Susie hadn't gone to bed, not without Charlotte. She'd cried and worked herself up into one of her fits, the likes of which only her or Mr. Morland could calm down. He must be exhausted. All day in London and then stuck here with a fussing child.

She swept a strand of Susie's hair from Mr. Morland's face. He took a deep breath but didn't wake. Charlotte's fingers traced the line of his jaw, rough and whiskered this late in the day. Still he did not wake. She leaned closer. The sweet tang of pipe smoke lingered on his clothes. Something he must have brought home from the city. She'd never smelled it on him before.

She brushed her lips on his forehead, barely a touch. He slept on.

Perhaps one more. She may never have this chance again. She moved to his cheek, pressing her mouth ever so softly into the hollow just above his jawline. She closed her eyes while the warmth of his skin tickled her cheek. His breathing continued, steady and deep.

She looked at his lips, parted ever so slightly.

No. What was she thinking? Too much punch at Mrs. Westwood's ball. She stepped back and grabbed a children's book from Susie's dresser, fanning it round her face.

Great conkers, she'd lost her mind.

She set the book down silently. "Mr. Morland?"

He did not stir.

Her eyes lingered on his face again.

No.

She reached instead for his shoulder. "Mr. Morland," she whispered with a gentle shake. "Mr. Morland?"

His eyes cracked open. "Charlotte?" He blinked several times. "Miss Darby."

"You're back," Henry said. Susie stirred on his lap. He patted her, and she settled back to sleep. "Let me put her down."

He stood slowly and laid Susie in her bed, careful not to jostle her too much. But after the fuss she'd made, she'd probably sleep for days. He started to pull the blankets up, but Miss Darby stopped him.

"It's too hot. Just the one." She settled it over her sister's shoulders, and Puppy scooted forward and tucked in close.

Charlotte followed Henry out of Susie's room to the main part of the nursery. "I'm sorry you had to come here after your trip to London. You must be worn to the bone."

Her gown had turned out perfectly. Just enough blue to make her eyes shine like moonlight bouncing off the water. Strands of hair wisped about her neck, softening her features. It never stayed put.

"You look beautiful," he said.

She smiled. "Thank you."

He was staring. He knew it, but he couldn't take his eyes off her. "How was the ball?" He dreaded her answer.

"Wonderful. You were right about everything." She spun in a circle, her frock billowing out to show her dancing slippers underneath. "The music. The cake. Mrs. Westwood was very kind. I met Regis Farnham, the Archbishop's cleric. I danced every dance, except when I was too tired and Mr. Farnham took me out into the garden."

What business did Regis Farnham have with Miss Darby in the garden? A man of the cloth, no less. Perhaps tomorrow he'd write a letter to the Archbishop reminding him to teach his clerics civilized manners around young women.

"Only then he had to leave, so Hurst sat with me."

Hurst? She'd never used that name before. Her entire face lifted into a grin as she recalled something that seemed to bring her great delight.

Was it possible Hardwick had made his move already? Henry couldn't imagine her saying yes, not after her many protestations to both himself and Anne Boleyn that marriage could never be. Perhaps she'd changed her mind after Sutton's letter. Perhaps Hardwick had swayed her. He was very persuasive where females were concerned.

Henry should never have asked about the ball.

"Then I worried about Susie, and Aunt Nora wore out, so we left early, and I came and found you here."

Henry was too tired for this conversation. He couldn't keep his mind clear. With wanting to floor Hardwick with a facer, forbid any form of ball in the future, and take Miss Darby in his arms and kiss her, he had to go. "I'm very glad to hear it. Good night."

"You're going?"

'Course he was going. "It's nearly two in the morning."

"Oh, yes. I forgot."

He took a step toward the door, but she slid closer, blocking him. What had gotten into her tonight?

"I . . . I s'pose I just wanted to say that I had a grand time at the ball." She fiddled with the limp ends of his cravat. Perhaps trying to fix it but only making his skin alive with her touch. "However, I would've liked it better if you'd been there too." She turned away, the back of her hand brushing his as she did.

He caught it and held it. She looked at him, straight into his eyes for one long moment. Then she vanished into Susie's room, closing the door behind her.

Henry stood there, unable to move. What the deuce did that mean? He had to go. There would be talk if any servants saw him leaving the nursery so late at night. Fanny was in her room asleep—or so he hoped. He snuck out and down the servants' stairs, then out through the back.

Something had passed between Miss Darby and Hardwick. Of that he was certain. She'd even seemed taken with Mr. Farnham, may he never show his face in Kent again.

Henry had been the halfwit who'd advised her to marry so she wouldn't lose the house. Hardwick might be desperate enough to meet her terms. By the way she went on about him in her letters to Queen Anne, she must love him.

But that look she'd just given Henry didn't seem to be about Hurst Hardwick.

He turned off the path toward home and headed to the willows. It was cool there. It reminded him of his time with Miss Darby before Hardwick had come along.

He ducked into the bower and sat on the bench. In one heartbeat, he was up again. How could he be still after that look? She'd told him frankly that she'd wished him at the ball. But, then, she'd often wanted him with her when she'd had to face the unknown. Perhaps it all meant nothing.

He went through to the second bower to check the lion's mouth.

Sure enough, a damp paper was wedged behind the teeth. He pulled it out. Another letter from Charlotte. It was too dark to read here.

His determination to distance himself from Miss Darby had crumbled. He must rebuild it. He could not afford to lose his position now. He could not allow the servants to run wild with supposition. He must be professional. He was a steward. And a good one. A man of business. And that was all.

When he reached the Grange, he went straight to his room and lit a candle. The letter was dated the day Mr. Sutton's news of the entail had arrived. Some of the ink had run with the dew, but it was still legible.

He smiled at her opening lines of sympathy. So very much Miss Darby. Always on the side of Queen Anne.

It seemed she was still committed to never marry—at least as of several days ago.

She had so much faith in this legend of Anne, believing a ghost would come and help her.

She said she'd rather die than marry. For goodness sake. She must have a very low opinion of men for death to be the better option.

He tucked the letter into his drawer with the others. Something had happened at the ball, and he needed to find out what.

CHAPTER TWENTY-SIX

HENRY WOKE LATE THE NEXT morning. He could've easily rolled over and slept longer, but regardless of how late he'd been up last night, he had to get to the house on time.

He dressed and headed into the kitchen. "I'm off, Jane. No time for breakfast." He gave his sister a peck on the cheek. She'd been in a terrible mood these last few days. He wondered if she was feeling ill, but when he'd asked, she'd nearly bitten his head off.

"But I made you a sausage roll." She glared at him.

He dared not risk another outburst of temper. "Smells delicious. I'll eat it on the way."

She wrapped it in a napkin and gave it to him.

He opened the front door with a hard jerk. The mark he'd made on the wet paint was still there, even though Peters had sworn he'd come and fixed it. Time for a new groundskeeper.

He set off for the house. The sausage roll was still warm and quite delicious. Perhaps he should tell Jane that this was his favorite.

The big house was quiet, as all three of its occupants had stayed up so late last night. He asked Old Tafford to have some tea sent to his office, then sat down to work. The morning went slowly, especially as his mind kept wandering to things other than the price of a measure of lumber and the drainage problem in the south field.

With any luck, Miss Darby and Susie would show up for a stroll. Stretching his legs was just what he needed. He'd already fallen asleep twice at his desk.

Someone knocked at his door, then entered. Miss Darby. By the wild look in her eyes, this was no social call. Had her sister taken a turn for the worse? She'd been doing so much better. Or had Hardwick broken her heart? "What is wrong?"

"Someone has taken my mother's jewels."

Henry stood up. "What?"

"My mother's jewels—the sapphire pendant and earrings—they are missing."

"But are you sure? Perhaps they are just misplaced. Or maybe your sister got hold of them."

"They were in my room on my dressing table last night when I went to bed. I set them in their box, but I was so tired I didn't put it inside my wardrobe.

They should have been safe. Nothing like this had ever happened in all Henry's years at Willowkeep. "And Susie?" he asked at great risk of being flayed alive.

"No. They were gone when I woke up. I went to the nursery, and Fanny assured me Susie'd been in there the whole time. Susie never comes to my room. She's always in the nursery or with me."

That only left the staff. "Your maid? Who came in to light your fire this morning? Did anyone bring breakfast?"

"I don't have a fire. It's too hot. And a maid did come in, but I slept late, and I didn't see who."

This did not bode well. "Miss Darby, before I go accusing the staff, I must know with absolute certainty that you did not accidentally misplace them."

She took her fingernail out of her mouth. "Mr. Morland. I own one thing of value in this life. One. And it's those jewels. I've torn my chambers apart looking for them. I know where I put them, and I know where they should be." She sat in one of Henry's chairs. "If you don't believe me, you're welcome to go to my room and conduct a search of your own."

Perhaps he should. How many times had he accused Jane of misplacing something of his only to have Jane find it in the exact place he'd left it? "Yes. Let's check one last time. Who else knows about this?"

She shook her head. "No one. I came straight to you."

He placed his hand on her shoulder. "Do not fret. I'm sure we'll find them."

"I didn't misplace them," she said. "They're gone."

"I believe you. But there can be no room for error. Once I take this to the staff, it will not sit well."

Willowkeep was filled with expensive objects. Many of them worth five times the value of her mother's jewels. Why would someone go specifically for those?

Henry stepped out of his office and summoned a footman to go find Mrs. Tafford immediately. He would not go into Miss Darby's rooms without her. Especially not after the way she'd looked at him last night.

"We've never had anything like this happen before. All our servants are carefully chosen." Henry closed his books and straightened his desk while they waited for Mrs. Tafford.

It didn't take her long to appear, huffing and out of breath.

"Mrs. Tafford. Miss Darby believes— We believe that her mother's sapphire jewels have been removed from her room without permission."

"Stolen?" Mrs. Tafford asked.

"Indeed. We need to search her chamber before we take this any further."

Mrs. Tafford understood immediately. "Of course."

They followed Miss Darby to the second floor, just down the hall from the nursery.

The moment Henry crossed the threshold, he knew the jewels were not there. Her room looked like the devil himself had been through it. Clothes strewn everywhere. Her drawers empty, their contents spilled onto the floor. Miss Darby had indeed scoured it thoroughly.

"Mrs. Tafford, let's make a quick search just to be sure."

For all her new wealth, Miss Darby truly did have very few possessions. A dozen or so dresses, underpinnings, her toilet, and that was it. A few books lay on the bedside table, all of them about the history of England and one specifically about Henry VIII.

He picked it up and looked over at Miss Darby.

She shrugged. "I found it in the library."

Henry checked under the bed and scooted the dressing table away from the wall to look behind it. Mrs. Tafford rehung her frocks and gowns, and by the time they were done, the room was set back to rights.

The jewels were not there.

"Mrs. Tafford," Henry said. "Who did Miss Darby's room this morning?"

"Rachel Cowden, sir."

Hm. Hannah Barwell's replacement. The only new girl on the staff. Even so, Henry couldn't imagine she would have the gall to lift a set of jewels right under Miss Darby's nose.

"Assemble the staff in the main hall," Henry said. "And bring Rachel to my office."

He honestly could not believe one of the workers at Willowkeep could have done such a thing. Which meant the situation might extend beyond these walls. "And send Daniels to fetch the constable."

"Yes, sir." Mrs. Tafford hustled off.

"Do we really need the constable?" Miss Darby asked.

She never took it well when strangers came to the house. "Whoever took them would be a fool to leave them here, knowing there would be a search. So unless this is someone's attempt at a joke, I fear we will need to increase the boundaries of our suspicion."

Miss Darby sank onto the bench at the foot of her bed. "I shouldn't have worn them. I should have kept them hidden."

"This is your home. You should not have to hide your belongings. You should feel safe here."

She looked so forlorn. Shadows ringed her eyes from her late night. Living at Willowkeep should have been an end to her troubles. So far, it seemed they were only getting started.

She leaned her head forward, resting it on her hands. "What if they're gone forever? Who would do such a thing?"

That was not a difficult question. "Someone who is desperate for money. Since you and the gems are not well known, they would be easy to sell."

Who did Henry know who needed funds—besides himself? Hardwick? He would have seen her wearing them last night at the ball. But if there was some kind of agreement between the two of them, he'd have no need to steal. The entire estate would go to him upon marriage.

"Miss Darby." Henry paced away, over to the window. He had to ask, but, lud, how he feared the answer. "Is there any kind of agreement between you and Mr. Hardwick?"

"Agreement?"

He kept his eyes on the landscape below. The fountain needed a cleaning. "As in marriage."

She let out a soft laugh. Henry turned to see a smile on her face. Again, that look of something new. "No."

Henry nodded. Thank heaven for that. Though now he'd have to confront Hardwick about the missing gems. Perhaps he should leave that job to the constable. The word of a gentlemen always held sway over the word of a steward. And there was still the question of little Susan. Mrs. Tafford should check the nursery, just in case.

"All right, then." There was nothing more he could do here. He should go. He crossed the room to the door. "It might be best if you wait here," Henry said.

"If you think so."

Mrs. Tafford caught up to him as he reached the stairs. The constable would be here soon as he could. He had a more pressing matter—of life and death—or so he'd said to Daniels. Henry asked her to search the nursery with Fanny's help.

"No one else is to go in there aside from you, Fanny, Miss Darby, or myself," Henry said. "If the constable wants to look in the nursery, I am to be summoned first. The last thing we need is for the child to have one of her fits."

Mrs. Tafford agreed.

Henry went to his office to interview Rachel. The girl sat with her hands clasped in her lap, looking awfully close to fainting. Her family were tenants of Willowkeep. Her father farmed a small parcel of land but was not very productive. They had nine children. Rachel was the eldest and the first to be hired out in service. Funds in their family were extremely low.

He asked her the questions. "Did you tend to Miss Darby's room this morning?"

"Yes."

"Did you put anything away?"

"Only her slippers that were near ruined from all the dancing. I put 'em in her wardrobe."

He remembered the slippers. Mrs. Tafford had commented on the state of them.

"What about the jewelry box on the dressing table. Did you touch it?"

Her hands wound in and out of her apron. "Please, sir. I took one peek. Just a peek. But it was empty. Please don't sack me. I promise I won't never touch anything never again."

She seemed in earnest. At least now he knew they'd been taken sometime between two and six in the morning.

"You're not losing your position. Go join the rest of the staff in the hall."

She bowed to him, and her feet pattered on the wooden floor as she scuttled away.

Mrs. Tafford returned and reported that a thorough search of the nursery had turned up nothing.

Deuces. It would have been much easier if Susie had snuck away with them.

Henry stood before the staff, a few steps up on the main stairs.

"As you may have heard"—the likelihood of keeping news from spreading to the help was slim, no matter how careful they'd been—"something of great value has been taken from Miss Darby's private chambers. A necklace and earrings."

A few of them nodded knowingly, though most seemed surprised.

"If any of you have information or have seen anything or anyone out of the ordinary, please come forward. Even something that seems small or unimportant can be—" His stomach twisted and groaned in a familiarly painful way. The sausage. Oh, Jane. Not now. "Useful," he finished as a sheen of sweat broke out across his brow. He shouldn't have eaten the pies.

Old Tafford appeared at his side. "The constable is here."

Henry looked to the back of the room. Mr. Poole waited with a few other men he'd brought with him.

"You finish up here," he said to Old Tafford. "Then send Poole." He closed his mouth for a moment. "I'll be in my office."

Henry took off at a run. By the time he reached his workroom, his stomach could wait no longer. He raced to the wastebin and bent over it. Everything came up.

Even if he had to take on a second job cleaning pigsties, he was hiring a cook. Jane, for all her good intentions, was going to kill him one of these days.

Perhaps today. He bent over the wastebin again.

He opened his workroom door. There was no footman to take the bin to the kitchen for cleaning; they were all assembled in the hall. He went out the back and emptied it into the daisies. He took a few breaths of fresh air, then retreated back to his office. Seating himself gently in his chair, he leaned forward and rested his face on the desk.

A quarter of an hour later, Old Tafford opened his door. "Constable Poole, sir."

Poole entered, his tall, thick frame filling the doorway. He sat across from Henry. "You don't look so good, Morland."

For a man just stepping into his fifties, Poole was very fit. His grizzled hair and imposing figure only added to his authority. He'd been the constable of the parish for as long as Henry could remember.

"I've been better." He swallowed down the urge to vomit. "My sister's cooking isn't exactly all the crack."

"That bad, eh?" Poole chuckled. "Tafford tells me there's been a theft. A sapphire necklace and matching earrings?"

Henry nodded.

"Do you know the value of said items?"

"At least four thousand pounds."

Poole's eyebrows went up.

"They are family jewels. Something from her mother and probably her mother's mother—as Louisa Kelton brought them with her from Willowkeep into Hull." Henry couldn't wait much longer. He inched closer to his wastebin.

"Right, then," Poole said. "If you don't mind, we'll conduct a search and question each member of the staff. Is there anyone else who might have done this?"

"I hate to say it, but Hardwick. Perhaps. He got nothing from his step-father."

Poole made some notes in his booklet. "I'll keep you informed should anything turn up."

Henry nodded again. He couldn't open his mouth.

Poole grinned. "In the meantime, I'll leave you alone with your bin."

He left. The moment the door closed, Henry doubled over.

CHAPTER TWENTY-SEVEN

HENRY LAY ON THE SMALL wooden bench in his office, covered with the knit blanket Mrs. Tafford had brought him. As long as he didn't move, his stomach remained settled.

Someone knocked at his door, then Old Tafford peeked in. "Mr. Poole, sir. Shall I let him in?"

Henry sat up with a groan and smoothed his hair. He moved to the seat behind his desk. "Yes." He glanced at his pocket watch. He'd been in and out for nearly three hours.

Poole entered and closed the door behind him.

"What news?" Henry asked.

"Goodness, man. You look worse than before." Poole sat across from Henry and unfolded a linen cloth revealing Miss Darby's missing jewelry. He set them on the desk.

"Quick work, Poole. Where did you find them?" He really hadn't expected them to ever be recovered. Miss Darby would be pleased. And with it all over and done so quickly, perhaps her confidence in Willowkeep would be restored.

"Well, that's just it. We found them at your place. Stuffed into the pocket of the coat you were wearing last night—confirmed by both your sister and Miss Darby."

Henry stared at the jewelry. How the devil did they get there?

"I'm going to have to take you down to the old parish hall till we get this sorted out."

Jail? They were going to put him in jail? He reached for the bin and retched, though nothing remained to come up. He wiped his mouth. "Come now. You know I didn't do this. Someone has used me."

Poole shrugged his broad shoulders. "It's the law. The stolen goods were found in your private chambers. You have motive and means."

Motive. Meaning Henry needed funds to pay off his father's debts and get him out of that wretched prison. And yes, it would have been easy for him to take them. But the very idea that he would steal from Miss Darby was absurd. Especially her mother's jewels.

"Do you really think I need money so desperately that I would walk into my employer's room and take the one thing she—" He had to stop before his stomach protested again. After the wave of nausea passed, he said, "I didn't do it."

"We'll see." Poole opened the door, and two men came in. Henry didn't know them, but one carried a set of wrist irons.

"I don't need irons." He would be ruined after this. Even if the real culprit was caught, his reputation would never survive. "At least take me out the back way."

Poole agreed. "Bring that." He motioned to Henry's bin.

They left the house through the back door, walking all the way around to the coach waiting out front. At least it wasn't the cage. With any luck, most of the staff would be down in the kitchen or working to catch up from lost time. But it only took one set of eyes for the entire household to know.

Henry climbed in quickly. Poole followed after him and knocked on the roof. The horses jerked forward. He closed his eyes and leaned against the sidewall. When he recovered from the sausage rolls, he was going to be furious about this.

"Is he all right?" the man with the jangling shackles asked.

Henry didn't open his eyes. Sweat trickled down the side of his face.

"He ate something that didn't agree," Poole said.

Henry vaguely recalled arriving at the old parish hall and being ushered into a room with barred windows. No rugs. Just a bare floor, two hard cots, and a small square table and chair. He lay there for hours, alternating between shivering with cold and dripping with sweat. There was another man in with him, but Henry didn't take the time to get to know him. All he cared about was not moving a single muscle. And the wastebin.

Sometime before dawn, it finally passed. He rolled onto his back with a groan. What a night.

"I see you decided to live," came a voice from the other cot.

Henry looked over. The man was older, maybe in his late forties. He lay on his back, staring straight up at the heavily beamed ceiling. In the dark,

Henry couldn't make out much. Dark hair, it seemed, and not dressed like a gentleman but not quite a farmer either. Since those were the only two options in this part of the country, he must not be from around here.

"Rough night?" the man asked.

"Quite." Henry stepped to the washbasin on the table and splashed cold water on his face. He poured himself a cup, rinsed his mouth, and spat. Only a thin mattress of rough straw covered the hard wooden planks of his cot, but he laid back on it anyway, as there was nowhere else to go.

This must have been quite a day in Kippingham. Two criminals at once. This jail cell could go unoccupied for most of the year. The only time they had real trouble was when the outside workers came in for harvest.

"So, then," the man said. "Who are you, and what have you done?"

Henry wasn't about to give his name to a stranger. Especially one in prison. Though now that he was on this side of the bars, it occurred to him that perhaps not everyone in prison was guilty. This stranger may also have been wrongly accused. Regardless of his guilt or lack thereof, Henry felt no need to share the particulars. "I haven't done anything," Henry said.

"That so?" He had a lilt to his speech that reminded Henry of Miss Darby, confirming his assumption that the man was not from these parts.

The sun slowly rose, filling the cell with slashes of sunlight through the iron bars. The man from the carriage appeared with two plates of food.

"Glad to see some color in your face, Morland," he said as he set the food on the table. Boiled eggs, bread, and porridge. It looked well enough, but Henry's stomach wasn't anywhere near ready for breakfast.

His cellmate sat at the table and peeled an egg. "Morland. Would that be Henry Morland from Willowkeep? Steward, if I'm not mistaken. Like father, like son."

Indeed. Only, did he mean because his father had also been the steward or because his father was also in prison? Or both? The harder Henry tried to break free from his father's shadow, the more he sank into its darkness.

He shouldn't be here. He should be out looking for the real thief. The notion that Henry would steal Miss Darby's jewels to pay his father's debts was utter nonsense. There were at least a dozen better ways he could pilfer money from Willowkeep and no one would ever know.

Henry sat up and studied the man. There was something familiar about him. "Do I know you?"

The man shook his head. "No."

"Rather impolitic, don't you think? That you should know me but I don't know you."

"I s'pose." The man swallowed a mouthful of bread. "You can call me Tom."

Well, that narrowed it down to about half the population of England—if that was even his real name. Henry crossed to the window.

The room was on the second story of the old parish hall, overlooking the West Kipping and the fields of ripening wheat and the pale tips of the hops just coming into flower. Across the river, the round cones of the oast houses rose above the growing crops. Come fall, the place would be filled with workers from London to harvest the hops and dry them in the oasts. Henry always dreaded that time of year.

Tom finished his breakfast and returned to his bed. Henry paced the perimeter of his quarters. He had to get out of this place. Miss Darby wasn't safe with a cutpurse on the loose.

He couldn't overlook the possibility that she'd likely fire him. What employer in her right mind would keep on a man accused of thieving? Maybe that was why the jewels had been stashed in his coat—to get him out of the way. Once again, Henry's mind went to Hardwick.

Keys jangled in the lock, and the door clicked open. Poole entered and closed it behind him.

Henry glanced at Tom, but the man had a blanket pulled up and his face to the wall. Asleep, so it seemed. But Henry wasn't taking anything for granted.

"You have a visitor," Poole said to Henry.

Jane. That was kind of her, but a visit was the last thing Henry needed. "Did you find the thief? Did you even look for him? This is foolishness to keep me here. You have the wrong man."

"We're looking into it. But I have to tell you, it doesn't look good."

"Poole. You know I didn't do this."

The constable kept his face as empty as Tom's breakfast plate. "Shall I show Miss Darby in?"

"Miss Darby?" She was up and out awfully early. He ran his fingers through his hair and made a weak attempt at reviving his neckcloth. He should look at least moderately presentable—though she was probably here to give him the sack.

He nodded to Poole.

Miss Darby entered. She looked like she'd been in tears half the night.

There was only one chair in the room, and Henry pulled it closer to his cot. "Will you sit?"

Charlotte sat in the wooden chair he'd offered. The room smelled heavily of unwashed men and cooked eggs.

All these months she'd considered herself and Mr. Morland on equal ground. He knew every detail about her life. Well, almost every detail. Yet he'd kept something rather large hidden from her.

"How could you?" she said.

His whole body sank, caving into itself. His proud, tall frame shrinking into the cot. "Miss Darby," he said. "I swear to you that I did not take your mother's necklace."

A rustling sound came from behind her. She turned and noticed for the first time the other figure lying across the room. His back was to them, and it sounded like he was sleeping. She scooted closer to Mr. Morland.

"I would never do such a thing." Mr. Morland leaned closer. "The thief will be caught, then you will see. It wasn't me. I give you my word as your steward"—he paused—"and your friend."

It wasn't the missing jewelry that had ripped the floor out from under her. "That's not what I mean." She shook her head. "How could you not tell me?"

"What?"

"You came to me in Hull because I was the new owner of Willowkeep. You brought me here, reminding me daily that I had all the money I could ever need and more. One of the richest ladies in the country, I believe you said."

He nodded. "It is true."

"And never once did you think you might mention your father's debts? Or that he were in prison?"

He wiped a hand across his face, his shoulders sagging. "It was not your concern."

She lowered her head, looking down at the filthy floorboards, stained with what, she didn't want to know. "I could've helped."

Mr. Morland seemed completely done in. Mrs. Tafford told her he was fully sick when they took him away. He still didn't look entirely well.

"It wasn't your concern," he said again.

She may not completely understand the duties of a steward, but it seemed that rocking a child to sleep in the middle of the night or calming the fears of a foolish young woman didn't quite fall under *his* concern. But that never stopped him. Well, she would see about that. The proud, stubborn man.

"What will happen to you?" she asked.

"Well, if they decide I am guilty, I will be hanged."

"Hanged?" She nearly fell off her chair.

"If the worth of the stolen item is over forty shillings, then, yes. That is the law." The worth of her jewels was far beyond that.

Mr. Morland spoke quietly. "Or I could plead the benefit of clergy and be transported." He held out his thumb where only a few decades earlier they would have permanently branded him. "Living the rest of my life with less reputable society in foreign climes."

"What if I tell them not to? I mean, what if I say they weren't stolen after all. Or I could say I loaned them to you."

He shrugged. "It might help. But we've already told the constable they were stolen. In any case, what matters to me is that you know I did not do this. Someone has set me up to ruin me. The only way I can have any sort of life is to find whoever did it and clear my name."

Charlotte stood. "Then that's what we must do. Willowkeep cannot survive long without its steward."

Mr. Morland shook his head. "If I am thought a thief, I will lose all respectability with the staff, with the solicitors in London, with the tenants, with everyone. It might be better for all if I resign."

"You shall do no such thing." Charlotte could not imagine Willowkeep without him. The very notion— "Great conkers." She knew exactly what had happened to that blasted necklace. She fell back into her chair with a moan. "This was not what I meant."

"Miss Darby?"

She looked up at him. "I know who took the jewels."

"You do?" He leaned forward. "Who?"

"Anne Boleyn."

Mr. Morland sank back.

"That greedy queen. I asked for her help, but this was not what I meant." She rose again. She had begged for Anne's help to keep her heart from being broken, not for him to be hanged.

"I have to go." She held out the basket hooked over her arm. "Jane sent you some food."

"No," he said. "Take the food. I don't even want to see it."

She knocked on the door, and the jailer opened it. "I'll be back tomorrow," she told Mr. Morland as she left.

Charlotte hurried out the door. She needed to speak to Mr. Tafford immediately. And she needed to have some words with that crafty queen. What was she thinking, hiding Charlotte's necklace in Mr. Morland's room? And how would she ever prove a ghost had taken it and clear Mr. Morland's name? No wonder the king had her head chopped off. She was too clever by half. What else must she have been scheming behind his big, giant back? Charlotte was ready to chop her royal head off herself.

Mr. Poole was waiting for her downstairs. "How is Morland feeling this morning? Better, I hope."

"Yes, I think so." She set the basket on the side table, then let out a light-hearted laugh. "Constable Poole. I'm such a cod's head. As I talked with Mr. Morland, I remembered that I asked him to take the jewels for safekeeping while I tried to calm my sister. She gets these fits, see, and it takes some real work to settle her down. You can ask Mrs. Tafford. Or Fanny. That's her nurse."

Mr. Poole watched her carefully as she spoke.

"As I took my sister from him, she'd fallen asleep on his lap, see, and when I'd got home from the ball he were handing her over to me. Well, I had to put the necklace somewhere, and they slipped into his coat pocket." She smiled at him. "So they weren't stolen after all."

Mr. Poole pulled out a parchment and dipped his quill. "Let me make sure I've got this correct. You gave him the jewels for safe keeping?"

"Yes."

"But he didn't know?"

She hadn't realized she were such a dolt at lying. "The child was so hysterical, weren't none of us really thinking about the necklace and earrings."

He scribbled on his paper, then looked up. "I thought the child was sleeping on Morland's lap. Which was it? Sleeping or hysterics?"

Laws and gardens, he'd never believe this. But for Mr. Morland, she carried on. "She was asleep at first, but she woke up in hysterics when we moved her."

"And Mrs. Tafford is witness to this?"

Mrs. Tafford had been in and out but not there the whole time. Would he question her? Mrs. Tafford loved Mr. Morland. It was worth the risk. "Yes. And Fanny." Gaw. Why did she include Fanny?

Mr. Poole set his writing aside. "You realize, do you not, that if this is your claim, we cannot charge anyone for the theft?"

Mr. Morland had said the only way to clear his name would be to find the real thief. But if that thief was a headless ghost, there wasn't no one to find. Better to have a mark on his name than have him hanged. Or worse, Australia.

"Yes." She gave him a nod, trying her best to copy the assured and dignified way of Lady Westwood as she'd moved about her ballroom.

"Very well. I'll look into this."

She stood. Mr. Poole came round his desk and opened the door for her. She left and headed for the carriage and coachman waiting for her. It was only after she was settled in the curricle beside coachman Jim that she remembered Jane's basket of food.

Under no circumstances was she about to go back in there and say she'd forgotten her basket. Mr. Poole could do as he liked with it.

The moment her carriage pulled up to the front doors of Willowkeep, Mr. Tafford came out and handed her down.

"Mr. Tafford," she said. "I need your help. I need to get to London."

"London, miss?" He looked up at Jim.

"Yes." She pulled Mr. Tafford aside. "I also need some ready money. Lots of money. Do you know how I might get my hands on that?"

Mr. Tafford thought for a moment. Then a light came to his eyes. He grinned. "I see." He turned to Jim. "We'll need the traveling coach ready to go as soon as possible. Up to London and back."

"What? Today?" He checked the watch dangling from his waistcoat. "It'll be dark before we get back."

"Then bring the lamps," Mr. Tafford said.

CHAPTER TWENTY-EIGHT

Henry sat on his cot, listening to Mr. Poole and his men shuffling around on the lower floor. His cellmate, Tom, had barely moved in the quarter hour since Miss Darby had left. Henry took the bread from the table and returned to his cot, watching the unmoving mound across the room from him.

Tom's blankets stirred, and he sat up. He swung his legs over the edge of the wooden platform and stared at Henry.

"Bread?" Henry offered.

Tom shook his head. "You seem to be on close terms with your employer."

The man had been eavesdropping. Henry had been right not to trust him.

"What is that to you?" Henry stared full on at Tom. He had a thick head of dark, unruly hair, and large blue eyes.

Lud. Could it be? Why else would this stranger know so much about his personal life? Why else would he care? Henry had only seen that one miniature of Miss Darby's father. Though older and graying at the temples, he looked just like the portrait. And exactly like Miss Darby.

"You're Thomas Darby."

The man's head jerked back. Clearly he'd not planned on being identified.

Everyone thought him dead. He'd abandoned his own children to suffer and starve. Charlotte had been in this very room minutes ago, and he'd lain there without saying a word. He was the lowest kind of man, and it was all Henry could do not to smash his nose. It would break Miss Darby's heart when she learned of this.

"You think me wrong not to make myself known." He'd gotten over his surprise and now spoke with the same slick smile as Fox from the gaming den in London.

"Yes, I think it wrong." Miss Darby had never recovered from his leaving. Perhaps that was the reason she refused to marry. She didn't trust a man to stay.

Henry took a bite of bread. "How did you know where she was? The letter?"

"Aye."

"How long have you been here?"

"Long enough."

"No need to ask why. As soon as she has money, the relatives show up."

"I didn't come for the money." Tom stood up, tossing his blanket onto his cot. "I know you won't believe me, but it weren't for the money."

Tom should have drowned at sea in that small fishing smack.

"I wasn't the only one who read that letter."

There had been another person who'd been interested in Miss Darby's new money. Tom's old business partner. "You mean Burton." He'd had a sick feeling about that man. They were a well-matched pair, this Darby and Burton. Both deceitful, lying swine.

"I came to warn her," Tom said.

"Well, consider your daughter warned. I'll pass it along, and you get your breeches away from here."

Tom smiled. "She looks well, doesn't she?"

Very well, but Henry would never admit that to him.

"How's the child? The little one?" Tom asked.

Did he not even know his other daughter's name? "Susan. She's well enough."

"Still alive, then. Well, that's something." He smiled sadly. "She's the only one out of six what lived. And, of course, Charlotte. All of 'em born like Susan."

Six children all born with the same problem as Susie. He understood now why Miss Darby's mother was so beside herself with grief. The poor woman.

"Midwife said it were her mother's fault. Too much imagination during her time with child ruined the growing babe. Apothecary said Louisa ought to drink pennyroyal every day so's any more babes end in misbirth."

Tom leaned his elbows on the windowsill, staring out as though he could see all the way to Hull. "Doctor said better to drown the infant like an unwanted whelp. Or give it over to the workhouse, which is the same thing only slower."

How could someone ever suggest such a thing? No wonder Miss Darby had her mind set against doctors. And everyone. Anyone.

Susie wasn't an easy girl. She required constant care. Some would consider such a child a burden to the family, a continual drain on the family's resources without ever being able to earn her keep.

Henry had never seen love like he'd seen between Miss Darby and Susie. It defined them, neither complete without the other. If the child had been left to die, the best part of Miss Darby would have died also. Or perhaps never been born.

"My poor Louisa," Tom said, still staring out the window. "She couldn't take it no more. Day before she died she told me she was a murderer by giving birth to children what couldn't live. Said I'd be better off without her. So's I could have a proper family."

So much death and sorrow must have taken quite a toll. Thomas Darby had lost more than Henry could imagine. But to abandon his own children, the only ones left living—there was no excuse for that.

Footsteps sounded in the hall. A moment later, the constable opened the door. "Morland. You're free."

It took a moment for the words to seep in.

She'd done it. That wild-eyed girl had stood up to the constable and gotten Henry out.

"Miss Darby explained the mix up." Poole gave Henry a skeptical look. She had fooled no one with her lies to free him. "Whatever her story, the point of the matter is that without anyone to press the accusation, I appear to have no crime to lay against you."

"Which is just as well," Henry said. "Since I am innocent." Henry collected his coat from the cot.

Poole opened the door wider and gestured for Henry to exit the cell. "Off you go, then."

Henry turned back and looked at Tom. "What about him?"

Poole grinned. "He'll be here a long while yet. He's in for murder."

What the deuce? Murder? He turned back. "Who did you kill? Burton?"

Miss Darby's father only shrugged. Then Henry was out the door and free. Poole locked the cell behind him.

He ran the few miles to Willowkeep, bursting through the front door. Hardwick was there, just coming down the stairs. It was still early enough in the day that he might be coming down for breakfast.

"I'm surprised to see you back so soon," Hardwick said. "Couldn't find anyone to buy the necklace?"

"Don't be a fool, Hardwick. We both know it was a setup. I'm not entirely convinced you weren't the one who took them."

"If I were to steal something to pad my pockets, there are much easier and less conspicuous objects than the jewels from around Charlotte's neck." Hardwick took the last few steps.

"Precisely. Now, where is Miss Darby? I need to speak with her immediately."

"You look awful flush, man. What is it?" Hardwick stood with his hands clasped behind his back, like all the calm in the world.

"Where is Miss Darby?" Henry repeated. Hardwick wasn't going to be any help. Henry started up the stairs to check her usual place—the nursery.

"Welcome back from jail," Hardwick called over his shoulder.

Henry hurried to the nursery, passing several servants on his way. All of them gave him a sideways glance. No matter that he was cleared and free, he'd never be the same to them after this. But until the moment Miss Darby discharged him, he'd fulfill his duty as both steward and friend.

Fanny sat in the nursery window seat, sewing. She gave Henry the same look as the rest of them. Then she smiled her gap-toothed smile. "I knew it wasn't you."

"Thank you." Though it came from Fanny Brown, nursery maid, her words were a balm to his injured soul. "Miss Darby. Is she here?"

"No, sir. She left."

Henry glanced around. "Left where?" In her last letter to the queen, she'd threatened to return to Hull to get away from Hardwick. She couldn't have packed up everything and set off so quickly. Not without saying good-bye.

Fanny shrugged. "On an errand, I think."

Henry looked around again. Something was noticeably absent. "Where's little Susie?"

"Miss Darby took her with her." She lifted the piece of lace she was mending. "Gives me a chance to catch up on some other work."

"Carry on, then." Henry left the nursery and nearly bumped into Mrs. Tafford.

"Oh, Mr. Morland. Thank heavens you're back." She threw her arms around him.

"Good to see you too, Mrs. Tafford."

"Though you do smell like a night in the nethers." She backed away.

"Fair enough." Who knew how long that mattress had been moldering there. "Do you know where Miss Darby went?"

"Up to London." She gestured in the wrong direction.

"London?" What the devil would possess her to travel to the city? Perhaps she wanted to deposit her mother's jewelry in the bank for safe keeping. They had plenty of places to lock up valuables here at the house though, so that made no sense. A new dress? But she'd never cared about London fashion before. "Why? Who else went?" He hated to think of her wandering the streets alone.

"Mr. Tafford is with her. And Coachman Jim, of course." They made their way down the hall. "She didn't say why. Just that she had something she needed to do. Left in a hurry, she did."

What a nonsensical thing for her to do. Henry would have to wait for her return. Mrs. Tafford was right; he needed to clean himself up. He went home for a bath and a change of clothes.

CHAPTER TWENTY-NINE

IT HADN'T TAKEN CHARLOTTE LONG at the bank to get some notes. They didn't even blink an eye at her when she asked for such a large sum. Mr. Tafford came in with her, and they estimated as best they could how much she would need. The bank man simply handed it over. She doubted her family had ever had so much money in their entire life.

Jim drove the carriage south again and over the London Bridge. Charlotte watched out the window the whole way. She'd never seen so many buildings. People. Everywhere she looked were more people. Costermongers pushing their carts, selling fruits, vegetables, and fish. Sheep bleating as they were led through the streets to market. Boats on the river, ferrying people across who couldn't afford to pay the tolls—or simply wanted to avoid the crowded bridge.

It was quite a sight. She'd read about the Tower of London, where Anne Boleyn had lost her head. A glimpse of its tawny stones and domed turrets appeared as they crossed the bridge. And the Church of Saint Paul. Mr. Morland had told her it was the most beautiful place he'd ever been. Perhaps she'd come back one day.

They passed a beggar on the corner. A young woman about Charlotte's own age. Only this woman wasn't right. She reminded Charlotte of Susie. Walking a bit off and ill-thriven. A handful of children trailed behind, jeering at the poor waif.

If anything happened to Charlotte, there wouldn't be nothing between Susie and a life like that. 'Cept perhaps Mr. Morland. He wouldn't let that happen.

"Here we are," Mr. Tafford said. "The Black Fox gaming den, just like the banker told us."

The neighborhood was one of the worst yet, the street littered with waste and a nasty smell to accompany it.

Charlotte took the banknotes and tucked them into her stays. Seemed the safest place. Jim opened the door and offered his hand. He had the arms of a coachman, broad and strong. Charlotte stepped down and nearly tripped on a loose cobble. She looked across the street at The Black Fox. Two hulking men stood like sentries on either side of the door.

Old Mr. Tafford had planned on coming in with her, but upon second thought, he might not be her best option.

"Jim, perhaps you would be so kind as to accompany me."

The coachman closed the carriage door. "Yes, miss."

She picked up the broken cobblestone. One never knew when there might be trouble. Always be prepared. She stuffed it into her reticule.

She left Mr. Tafford minding the horses and crossed the street with Jim close behind. She nodded at the sentries and entered.

The inside nearly made her retch. Smoke filled the room, along with the stench of defiled chamber pots and dirty, sweaty men. The only other women in the den looked like ladybirds. This place wasn't so vastly different from the docks of Hull. It seemed her time in Kent had softened her.

A gentleman neared. No, not a gentleman. He just wore fine garments and strutted about as if he were a gentleman.

"What can I do for you, milady?"

"Are you the owner of this place?" she asked.

He cocked his head. "I am. Name's Fox."

"Well, Mr. Fox—"

"No mister. Just Fox." He grinned. It had been quite some time since she'd seen such a pair of shifty eyes.

Charlotte straightened her spencer. "I'm here to pay a debt."

"Is that so? And whose debt would that be?" He looked at her overstuffed reticule. "Perhaps you'd like to try your hand at hazard. 'Tis a game that favors the ladies."

Charlotte glanced at the table in the center of the room. A circle of men surrounded it, most of them cursing even as they dug into their pockets for more.

"No, thank you." Charlotte had a keen eye for desperate men; she'd seen enough of them wandering the streets, looking for work. It wasn't any different here.

"His name is Henry Morland. Senior."

Fox's eyebrows flew up. He nodded at someone behind her. She turned to find one of the sentries from outside coming forward. When she turned back, Fox's face was too smoky by half. He was up to something.

"Mr. Morland owes quite a bit. Are you sure you can pay?"

"I believe so. How much does he owe?"

Fox reached onto the desk behind him and opened a ledger. "Twelve hundred pounds."

Charlotte turned her back and fumbled into her bodice. She spun round with a handful of bills.

Fox reached for them with a slick grin, but Charlotte pulled them away. "Oh, no. Not until I have written acknowledgment of complete release from all his debts." Mr. Tafford had been very clear on that.

Fox shuffled through his papers. He dipped a worn-out quill into the inkpot and scribbled something. After waving it in the air to dry, he held it up for Charlotte to see.

Near as she could tell, it seemed in order. It even had the seal of The Black Fox on it. She handed over the money and reached for the release.

Fox twisted it out of reach. He folded the money and receipt and tucked them into his waistcoat pocket. There was a grunt from behind her. The large sentry had grabbed Jim, pinning his arms behind his back.

"Problem is, milady, his son owes more than just money."

CHAPTER THIRTY

Henry leaned back into the bathwater. He'd filled it slowly this time, using plenty of hot water from the fire. He closed his eyes, savoring the sweet scent of the bar soap Mrs. Tafford always nipped for him from the stash up at Willowkeep.

Thanks to Miss Darby, his reputation might survive the quick taint from prison. She'd gotten him out very fast. He'd have given anything to see her standing up to Mr. Poole.

Odd, though, that she'd gone up to London so suddenly. He would have expected her to talk to him about the trip. She always came to him first with such things.

If Coachman Jim kept her to the west end, she'd avoid the worst of the city's grime. But why Mr. Tafford? If she was visiting the mantua maker or the milliner, Mrs. Tafford—or even Jane—would have been the logical choice. Perhaps she'd gone up to be fitted for a wedding gown. That would explain why the trip all the way to London. But not the suddenness. She had claimed there was no agreement between herself and Hardwick.

He couldn't keep from turning back to that night after the ball, as he was leaving the nursery. The look in her eyes in that one fleeting moment—as though she was hungry for something she could not have. There was nothing of Hardwick in that look.

Most puzzling of all was why on earth she would take her sister with her. Susie was a nightmare in the coach. It would be a miserable trip, trying to keep her tame for the three-hour ride to the city. Not to mention Miss Darby would rather lose her teeth than take the child out in public.

London was nothing if not public. His last trip had nearly ended in disaster. Even if he did manage to pay his father's debt, Fox would never let him off without extorting some form of revenge.

Oh no.

Henry sat up, sloshing water over the kitchen floor.

"You're cleaning that up," Jane called from the other side of the screen.

"I have to get dressed." He flung on a robe and, dripping wet, made a run for his bedchamber, his feet slipping and sliding on Jane's nicely waxed floors.

Jane followed after him. "What? What is the matter?"

"I cannot say exactly. Something is not right."

"What?"

"She would never take her sister to London." Not unless something dreadful had happened. He closed the door to his room.

"Who? Miss Darby?" Jane called through the door.

He knew where Miss Darby had gone. Or at least he suspected. What a blockhead he was for not putting the pieces together sooner. She'd just found out that he owed more than he could pay. She was always saying she had no way to even the score between them.

Well, she'd figured out a way. Though that still didn't explain why she'd taken her sister.

He threw on a linen shirt, some gray breeches, an ivory waistcoat, and his dark blue frock coat. He had to look his best if he was going to show his face again still claiming authority as steward.

"Help me with this," he called to Jane.

She burst through his door and wrapped the starched white neckcloth around his collar. "Are you going to tell me why the great hurry?"

He didn't fully understand this feeling in his gut. It was that feeling Miss Darby had described about her doubts regarding her father. That sense of things being off balance, not wholly right.

"It doesn't make sense. I must go up to the house. Possibly on to London." He scooped up a shirtpin from his dressing table. "I believe Miss Darby has gone to town to pay the balance of our father's debt."

Jane faltered in her tying and had to start over. "Do you mean up to The Black Fox?"

He nodded. "Jane, those men will eat her alive."

She put the pin into his cravat. "Don't let them eat you alive either," she whispered.

"Don't worry, I'm not nearly as palatable as Miss Darby."

Jane pushed him away. "I know how you feel about her, Henry Morland. You can't hide it from me."

He waved her words away. "She is my employer. I feel for her as any steward feels for his master. And that is all it can ever be."

"Henry—"

"I must go."

With a hard jerk on the front door, he dashed away.

When he entered through the back of the house, the maid, Rachel, was there taking a load of rugs out for cleaning. She gave him a look to wither a plum. He could hardly blame her after he'd frightened her to death with his questioning only to be arrested himself for the crime. Still, if he was to retain any hope of authority with the staff, it had to start now.

He stopped her. "Just yesterday you were begging me to spare your job. Have you changed your mind?"

"No, sir."

"Then I recommend you keep yourself in check." He glared at her until she bobbed a curtsey and took her chore out the back door.

Henry grabbed the first footman he found. "Daniels. Where is Mrs. Tafford?

"I believe she's in her room, sir."

Henry went below stairs to the little office off the side of the servants' kitchen. She was there going over the grocer's list for the following day.

"Mr. Morland." She stood. "I didn't expect to see you back so soon."

He had no desire to recount his grievances against the constabulary efforts in Kippingham. He had more on his mind just now. "Mrs. Tafford. I'm going up to London. I have reason to believe Miss Darby might have taken on more than she's expecting with this trip."

Mrs. Tafford's note fluttered to the desk. "What on earth do you mean?"

Feet thundered down the servant's stairs, and a woman called, "Mrs. Tafford! Mrs. Tafford!" It sounded like Fanny's voice.

A moment later, Fanny burst into the room without even knocking. "Mrs. Tafford!" She came to an abrupt halt. "Mr. Morland. Thank goodness." She held out a small paper. "I found this under Susie's pillow when I was doing her sheets."

It was a note folded but not sealed. Henry opened it and read.

Miss Darby,

If you want your sister back alive, it will cost you £10,000. Follow the road to Chipstead; someone will meet you. You have until noon tomorrow.

Kidnapped?

Henry looked up at Fanny. "I thought you said Miss Darby took her sister with her to London."

"That's what I thought. With the mistress gone and the child nowhere to be seen." Fanny burst into sobs.

How could she not know where her only charge had gone? Henry turned to Mrs. Tafford. "When Miss Darby left, was Susie with them or not?"

She shook her head. "I didn't see anything of the girl. Just her, Mr. Tafford, and Jim, sir."

This could not get worse. He looked at the ransom note again. Ten thousand pounds. Whoever took her, the man was a fool. Willowkeep could easily pay twice that—and more.

However, he couldn't very well write a banknote payable to *The Abductor*. He needed ready money—which would require a trip to the bank. He checked his watch. Even if he left this very moment, the bank would be closed. It would be impossible to get to London, obtain the money when the bank opened, and be back by tomorrow noon. Whoever had taken Susie clearly had not thought things through.

Somehow they'd need to negotiate an extra day. He'd send a runner first thing in the morning toward Chipstead to barter more time. In the meanwhile, it seemed their best hope would be to find Susie and her abductor, even without the money.

Then there was the matter of Miss Darby. Henry had been on his way to ride up to London to save her from whatever her encounter with Fox might bring. If that was even where she'd gone.

He had to make a choice. Save Miss Darby or save her sister.

The thought of Miss Darby with the likes of Fox in that vile pigeon hole made his blood run cold. It was bad enough that he and Jane had to bear his father's burdens, but now Miss Darby was involved.

He couldn't help but compare his life to Sisyphus, condemned to haul a rock up the mountain for all eternity. Each time he neared the top, the rock slipped from his grasp and rolled back down, leaving him worse off than he was before.

If Miss Darby were here, he knew exactly what she'd say. She'd want her sister back, no matter the cost.

In truth, he couldn't get to London in time to offer any real help to Miss Darby. She would have likely arrived at The Black Fox by now. She had Jim and Old Tafford with her, so at least she wasn't alone. But Susie was. Alone with a stranger and likely crying her little heart out. Still unwell on top of it all. Not many men would tolerate her tears for long.

The child must be found. Miss Darby would never forgive him if he did not find her.

"Mrs. Tafford, assemble the staff. Again."

She nodded. "Yes, sir."

Something had happened between Miss Darby's visit to Kippingham early this morning and when she'd set off for London. "Fanny."

The girl jumped.

"You must think hard. What happened today that was different? Check the nursery inch by inch and look for anything that is out of place. Can you do that?" Fanny nodded and hurried away.

Henry climbed the two sets of stairs into the west wing. He pounded on Hardwick's door. Hopefully the man hadn't gone out for sport.

Hardwick opened the door, his hat in hand. "Thunder and turf, man. What is it?"

"Little Susan is missing." He handed Hardwick the ransom note.

Hardwick read it. "Taken? That much money can never be assembled so soon. Regardless, I don't think the child can last that long."

"My thoughts as well. I believe our best chance is to find her ourselves."

"Come. Mother is in the drawing room," Hardwick said. "What is your plan?"

"Inform the constable. Send the staff out to search the grounds and Kippingham, though I'm sure the blackguard would not be so foolish as to remain close."

Hardwick shrugged as they descended the main staircase. "He cannot be too cunning if he asks for so little."

They reached the main floor and turned down the hall. Jane was coming toward them, dressed for a walk.

"Jane?" Henry said.

"Henry!" Her eyes flicked to Hardwick and back. "I was just . . . heading out for a walk . . . and came up to see if Charlotte cared to join me."

Henry had already told Jane that Charlotte wasn't home. No matter. At the moment, Jane's reasons for being here were the least of his worries.

"You'd better come," Hardwick said.

Jane followed them into the drawing room and sat on the sofa, her eyes growing wider as Henry explained to her and Mrs. Kelton that while Miss Darby had gone up to London on an undisclosed task, Susie had been taken.

"But who? And why?" Jane asked.

"That's no mystery." Henry suddenly wished Willowkeep and all its riches had never come to Miss Darby. "Money, my dear sister. 'Tis the root of all evil." He handed over the ransom note for Jane and Mrs. Kelton to read.

Mrs. Kelton let out a huff. "Fool."

Hardwick nodded. "Everyone who's ever met Charlotte knows she'd do anything to protect her sister."

"Yes, Hardwick. Exactly," Henry said. "We need to figure out who knew about Susie and might have the competency to remove her from the nursery right under our noses."

Henry had no trouble coming up with the first name. "Robert Burton, Mr. Darby's old business partner, could have done this. He seemed keenly interested in Miss Darby's fortune when I collected her from Hull." Mr. Darby had even admitted that the scoundrel had read the letter.

"Is he here? All the way from Yorkshire?" Hardwick had stepped closer to Henry as they thought on the possibilities of who would have taken Susan. "What about Dr. Leigh? He was here. He would have known how to get his hands on the child."

"The doctor?" Mrs. Kelton said. "Leigh has served the family for decades. He is a respectable man. He's got little to gain and much to lose with such a scheme. What use could he have for that child?"

Hardwick snapped his fingers. "I heard that new asylum up in London is paying folks to bring them patients. To run tests with an electrostatic machine or something. It was in *The Times* only a week ago."

"Lud," Henry said. "In that case, anyone could have taken her. But Dr. Leigh? That cannot be right. If the child was only taken for the asylum money, why the ransom? No. That makes no sense. Who else do we know who needs funds?"

Hardwick let out a harsh laugh. "Everyone. Except, of course, Charlotte."

"Who did she talk to at the ball?" Jane asked.

Hardwick smiled at her. "Good question. There was the famous nephew, Mr. Farnham. I don't know anything about his situation, but he was very attentive. Charlotte danced with at least half the gentlemen there, but Farnham was the only man she spoke to alone."

"All right, then." Henry had had enough discussion. "Time for action."

"I'll ride over to the Westwood's and inquire about Farnham," Hardwick said. "Nothing overt, of course. I'll just see what I can uncover about his personal life and finances."

Henry nodded.

"I'll go to the doctor," Mrs. Kelton said.

Henry stared at her. They all did. He hadn't expected help from her direction. "That is very kind."

She did not smile. She rose in all her stately blackness. "Jane will accompany me. Send for the carriage."

"Of course." Jane eyed Henry as if he could somehow explain.

"Miss Darby has taken the coach up to London," Henry reminded Mrs. Kelton.

"I'm fully capable of driving the curricle." Mrs. Kelton left the room, Jane following behind her.

Henry glanced at Hardwick, and the man shrugged.

"Very well, then," Henry said. "I'm going to Kippingham for the constable and to ask about Burton."

"Burton?" Hardwick asked. "He's here?"

"I don't know." Henry gathered up his hat and headed out. "But I know someone who might." He broke into a run.

Henry instructed George Stayner to saddle up his and Hardwick's horses and have the curricle brought round for Mrs. Kelton. Then he had a thought. There was no telling where this hunt might take him. "I'll be right back," he said to Stayner.

Henry ran up to the house and lifted a box off the mantel in the library. Walter Kelton's dueling pistols. He loaded them both with powder and ball, packing the wadding carefully to keep the ball secure. By the time he returned to the stables, Hardwick had already left.

Henry tucked the pistols into a saddlebag and mounted up.

CHAPTER THIRTY-ONE

One of Fox's men grabbed Charlotte's arms and dragged her into a back room. He shoved her across the floor, then left her there. With Fox.

At one time, this must have been a sort of kitchen. A few rusted pots and pans teetered on a rickety shelf, and a bent cooking grate lay in the fireplace. A layer of grime covered the whole of it, but at least it wasn't thick with smoke and the other odors that made the gaming room rancid.

"I paid the debt. I demand you let me go." She took a step toward the door, but Fox blocked her.

He'd said Mr. Morland owed more than money. She wasn't so crack-brained that she hadn't figured out these were the curs who had attacked Mr. Morland back in Kippingham. So what more did he owe?

Perhaps this wasn't such a good idea after all. Charlotte took a step back. Fox's boots scraped on the bare wood as he came closer. He grinned, his teeth yellow and sharp like the animal he was named after.

"My man Rudge there"—he nodded to the door, where his ruffian undoubtedly stood guard—"he lost a tooth thanks to your Mr. Morland." He thumped his fist just like the sailors did right before someone got basted.

Fox wouldn't hit a woman, would he? What else might he do once he claimed his tooth? "Jim!" she cried out.

The sound of scuffling men came from the other side of the door. It ended with a thud.

She still had the stone wedged into her reticule. She could use it against Fox, but what about the other two? Mr. Tafford waited outside; perhaps he would come to her rescue. She'd been in here a long time. She put her hands behind her back and worked on wedging the stone out.

Fox drew closer. His breath hot on her neck. Seemed he was skipping the tooth collecting and going straight to the what else. She turned her head to the side, away from his reek.

On the mantel rested a vase filled with flowers, oddly bright and alive. Yellow cowslip. Blue Jacob's ladder. And a few stalks of foxglove towering over them all. A lovely arrangement. Mr. Morland had said blue was her color. If he was here, he would kill this man. She knew it in her heart and in her soul.

Fox's hand snaked round her waist. She shoved him. He stumbled back, his grin growing even wider. "I see ya got some spirit after all."

Charlotte hadn't grown up in the gentle gardens of Kent. Fox was not the first man to come too close. And she was not a helpless lass. "Stay away; I'm warning you."

He bared his teeth. "Or what?"

She hurled the rock with all her might. Fox was only a few paces away, and the stone smashed against his face with a crack. He flew backward, his arms flailing as he hit the ground. The vase of flowers crashed to the floor beside him. Pity.

A gash appeared across his cheek from nose to ear, and blood flowed freely onto his neckcloth. He moaned.

Charlotte bent over him and tugged the note of release from his waistcoat pocket. "I'll be taking this, thank you very much. A pleasure doing business with you." She turned and burst out the door.

Rudge and the other knave looked at her, stunned. That was all Jim needed. He pulled a hand free and floored one of them a smack on the nose and the other with a blow to the gut.

"Let's go, miss," Jim said, shooing her toward the entrance.

She needed no nudging; she already had her skirts hitched up and was bounding through the misty-eyed gamers.

Mr. Tafford was waiting for them out by the carriage. "'Bout time."

"Load up, sir," Jim called as he crossed the road. "We're off at once."

Mr. Tafford hoisted Charlotte into the carriage and scrambled in after her. Jim had the horses off at a trot before the door closed.

Charlotte leaned back in the seat, her heart clackety-clacking in rhythm with the wheels as they rattled along the cobbled road.

"Well, that was something," Charlotte said.

"What happened?" Mr. Tafford asked.

"He wanted more than money," Charlotte said, then burst out laughing. "So I gave it to him."

Mr. Tafford's face went from starched white to seaweed green to Turkish red.

"With a stone to his face. He were bleeding like an open sluice gate when I left."

Mr. Tafford put his hand over his heart. "Child, you just near gave me an attack of apoplexy."

She leaned forward and kissed Mr. Tafford on the cheek. She could get used to this. People caring about her. Folks what took an interest in what happened to her. It was nice not to be alone.

She would miss it. All of it. When she failed to marry and the estate fell into different hands.

She had one last errand. Her parting gift. She held out the paper of release.

Mr. Tafford grinned and leaned out the window. "To the Marshalsea, Jim."

CHAPTER THIRTY-TWO

Henry rode straight to the old parish hall. Mr. Poole sat behind his desk, shuffling papers. If it wasn't for the payroll of Willowkeep, Kippingham could never afford a constable.

Poole glanced up as Henry entered. "Back so soon?"

Yes, yes. It was all very comical. No doubt he'd be swallowing quips about his night in the jail for some time. "I need to speak with Thomas Darby."

"Why?"

"There's been a kidnapping up at Willowkeep."

Poole closed his notebook. "Who is missing?"

"Miss Darby's younger sister, Susan, has been taken. I believe he might have information."

Mr. Poole pushed his papers to the side and stood. "An abduction?" He took a ring of keys from a hook and started up the stairs. "And you think Mr. Darby is involved? It's his own daughter."

Henry followed him. "I think he might know something that could help. It's worth a try."

Poole unlocked the door to the room Henry had slept in last night. Darby was there, sitting on his cot, leaning back against the wall. Poole followed him in and locked the door.

"Missed me that much, eh?" Darby said.

They were all so clever. "Actually I've got a few questions for you. About Susan." Henry took a seat in the one wooden chair, keeping as far from the moldy mattress as possible. "She's been kidnapped. Taken by someone demanding a ten-thousand-pound ransom."

"My Susie?"

"Yes. I came for information." Henry looked over at Poole, who'd been following this whole conversation closely. Henry turned back to Darby. "What can you tell me about Robert Burton?"

"A chancer and a cheat," Mr. Darby said. "Make no mistake. Stole my business right out from under me. 'Course I were dead at the time, but that don't mean he could rook my daughter out of her fair share."

"That was years ago," Henry said. "What about now?"

Darby nodded. "I was in Hull a few weeks back. Burton weren't there. I found the letter Charlotte had left me, seal broken and read. Weren't hard to figure out where he'd gone. I followed him here, but afore I could find him, they locked me up."

"Does Burton have any connections in these parts?" Henry asked.

Darby shook his head. "None that I know of. His wife is passed. His son died in the war. Just him."

"What about this man you murdered?" Henry asked. "Could that have anything to do with Susie's abduction?"

Darby was shaking his head even before Henry finished his question. "No. That don't have nothin' to do with this. Nothin'."

Henry glanced at the constable. The man shrugged. "I don't know any particulars," Poole said.

Seemed Darby had nothing that would help Henry find Susie. "Right, then." He waited for Poole to unlock the door. "Guess we'll just have to keep looking."

Darby stood too.

"I'll call in the men to assist in the search," Poole said, slipping his key into the lock.

In one swift movement, Darby picked up the wooden chair and slammed it into Poole's back. The constable collapsed to the floor.

"What the devil!" Henry backed away, searching for any kind of weapon. Of course there was nothing. It was a jail.

"She's my daughter. I'm coming with you." Darby tossed what was left of the chair onto one of the empty cots.

Henry would certainly go to prison for this, and not just overnight. Facilitating the escape of a murderer. But if Darby had any information to aid in the recovery of Susie, he needed it.

They slipped quietly to the stables behind the hall. Henry mounted his horse, then turned to find Darby putting an ancient saddle on one of the constable's horses. "You will be hanged for that."

"Neck's already bound for the noose." Darby flung the girth strap around the horse's belly. "Besides, I'm just borrowing it. Mr. Poole won't be needing him anytime soon."

They could cover ground much faster if they both had a mount. Though Darby's beast was most certainly a carriage horse, it was better than nothing.

Only two days in the company of Miss Darby's father and Henry was turning criminal. Darby was already sentenced to death. He had nothing to lose. Henry had everything. Putting his fate in the hands of such a man may not have been the wisest move.

"Let's ride back to the house, organize a search party. We'll comb the countryside," Henry said.

"No. We ride south, toward Tunbridge." Darby tightened the girth.

"Why Tunbridge?" The letter had mentioned Chipstead, to the north.

"I know a place where we might find him."

"Why did you not say as much?" Henry trusted this man about as far as he trusted Burton.

"Not in front of the law. That's the last thing we'll need." Darby slipped an ill-fitting bridle into the horse's mouth and fastened it behind the ears. "If he's got the child, what do you think he'll do with her if he sees a regiment of men riding up, firearms at the ready?"

He had a point. Susie's safety was paramount. Burton might just as easily end the girl and flee back to Hull, none the loser.

Darby said he'd been in Kent *long enough*. Henry had supposed he'd meant long enough to know the whereabouts of Charlotte and glean something about Willowkeep. He must have meant long enough to crawl around the underbelly of this county to find the holes where people like Burton hid.

Henry had a powerful notion he would regret this. He nodded at Darby. "Lead on."

They set off at a gallop until they were under cover of the trees between Kippingham and Willowkeep. Darby slowed his horse, and Henry rode up beside him.

"This way," Darby said.

Weaving in and out of patches of forest, only using the road when necessary, they made their way south. Nothing like following a villain to the lair of a villain.

They reached the outskirts of Tunbridge, and Darby led him into a woodland. The sun dropped quickly, leaving them in the gloaming of twilight. Miss Darby would be home from London soon. He prayed he'd have her sister back for her by then.

Darby took his horse off toward a copse of trees. "We'll leave 'em here and finish on foot."

"Are you sure Burton is in these parts?" They'd wasted precious hours if this was a wild-goose chase.

"He were here a few days ago. Where else would be such a good place to go to ground?"

Plenty of trees for cover. Water from the river. Game from the woods. A very good place to lie low. If they found Burton without Susie, at least they could bring him in for poaching.

Henry dismounted and opened his saddlebags, lifting out the dueling pistols. Two shots. That was all he had.

Darby grinned at the pistols. "Good idea. I'll take one of those."

If things got precarious, it might be better to spread out the weaponry—one pistol each. Yet handing over a firearm to a man accused of murder seemed not the wisest choice.

Henry shook his head. "Before I give you a loaded weapon, I think it's time you tell me who it was you murdered. And why."

Darby eyed him, peering at Henry through slitted lids. Henry felt as though some kind of judgment was being laid upon him.

Finally the man said, "It were Otto Brand, captain of the fishing smack, the *Rising Sun*."

"Your own captain?"

"Aye." He pointed deeper into the woods and started walking. "When the *Rising Sun* came to port in Hull, it were right after my Louisa passed. I'd already failed my wife. I had nothing to lose. I left my business in the hands of Burton and went out. I meant only to be away a few weeks, clear my head, but things took a turn. See, we also took on a young lad of fourteen, William Papper."

So far, this seemed a fairly average circumstance.

"As it were, young William said something in jest but which angered the captain beyond reason. Afore we reached the mouth of the Humber, the captain started beating the poor lad."

Henry stopped walking, all his attention on Darby and his story.

"Every day the captain brought the boy closer and closer to death, inch by inch. He forced the lad to stand naked at the stem while he doused him with buckets of water. This were over Christmas, mind. Water colder than ice. Captain threatened us with a gun if any tried to interfere. The other three men seemed to take it in stride. And so it went, day by day. Captain starving him. Beating him. Freezing him. The poor lad died on New Year's Day."

Henry had heard about the cruelty of some captains toward the young indentured boys on their vessels, but this went far beyond.

Darby finished in a whisper. "Brand told us the lad had been swept overboard by the foresail, but we all knew the truth. I can't rightly say what happened next. Something inside me just broke. Next time the captain come up from the hold, I flung a rope round his neck and . . . Well, let's just say he found a grave at sea as well."

The boy had already died. He couldn't be saved. Darby should have waited till port and let the law take over.

"What about the rest of the men?" Henry asked. "Surely they cared that their captain had just been murdered."

"None were sorry to see him go. The lad William had suffered greatly. We'd been out nearly three weeks when we turned and made port in Grimsby."

"Did they accuse you?"

"They all agreed to say nothing of the matter—long as I disappeared. Fishermen die all the time on the North Sea. Second Hand Dench reported that Captain Brand had been swept overboard trying to save young Papper, and myself trying to save Brand. We were all three written up as lost at sea. And I fled. Had to. After Dench said I were lost, if anyone saw me, the truth about Captain Brand's fate would come out."

That explained why everyone thought he was dead—except Miss Darby. "Why does your daughter think you're still alive? There must be some reason, or she wouldn't have bothered to leave a letter at your warehouse."

Darby slipped under some low-hanging branches. It was fully dark now, and the going was slower. "As it happens, Second Hand Dench weren't so trustworthy as I thought. Not more than three months passed when he marched himself back in and told the law that I was the one what killed Otto Brand. When word of that spread, there weren't no going back. I was a wanted man.

"Still, I tried to help my Charlotte. Left her a bit of money now and then. I s'pose it were enough for her to question. Weren't no one else willing to help her."

He'd been on the run for six years. Someone must have seen him and reported it for him to end up in the Kippingham jail. Someone local.

"Who gave you up?" Henry asked.

"Who d'ya think?" Darby let out a mirthless laugh. "Burton must have caught sight of me and gone to the constable. Our friend Poole snatched me from the Grayling Arms the same day you come in." Darby stopped. He nodded his head to the left, and Henry peered off into the forest. An old cottage stood near the shore of a pond. The faint light of a fire flickered through a window.

"That's it," Darby whispered.

Henry pulled one of the pistols out of the back of his breeches. He considered it for a moment, then handed it over to Darby. The other man took it, inspected the flintlock and the trigger, then tucked it into his own breeches. Henry prayed he'd not just made the worst mistake of his life.

Darby grinned at him, then set off, moving quietly through the trees and bracken, closing in on the cottage.

Henry followed, crouching low, until a noise hit him that brought him up short. The wails of a child in distress. A cry Henry had heard many times. Seemed little Susie was giving her captors a run for their money.

CHAPTER THIRTY-THREE

Darby glanced over at Henry.

"Susan," Henry whispered. He started to run, but Darby grabbed him.

He put his fingers to his lips, silencing Henry. "Have a care," Darby whispered. "You can't help her if you're dead."

True, but it was unlikely Burton would actually kill him. Once discovered, it seemed he would simply turn over the child and give up the game.

Darby pointed deeper into the woods and whispered. "I'll go round this way. Surround 'em."

Henry nodded, though two men could hardly be considered a surrounding. He watched Darby until his figure vanished behind the trees. Susie's cries cut through the forest. Henry waited no longer. Branches scratched at his face and pulled at his legs as he pushed through.

At the edge of the clearing, he peered from behind a large tree trunk. The silhouette of one man was visible outside. He paced slowly back and forth, tossing something in the air and catching it. Not Burton—too short.

Susie's cries became muffled. They were trying to stifle her noise. The poor girl must be frightened to death.

Henry waited for the short man's back to turn, then approached the cottage from the rear, right where it met up with the water's edge. Crouching low, he sidled up to a window. Heavy curtains blocked the view inside. He tried another window, the glass cool on his forehead.

Through a small gap in the coverings, he made out a sliver of the scene inside. A man, Burton, from the looks of it, had a hand clamped over the child's face. Even through the filth coating the window, he could tell the child struggled to breathe.

With such a small field of vision, it was impossible to tell how many others were inside. He reached for the door and tried the latch. Unlocked.

"Enough," Henry said as he burst into the cottage.

Burton's hand slipped from Susie's mouth, and the girl filled the room with her sorrows. A few embers glowed in the fireplace, but the chimney wasn't drawing well, and the smoke had nowhere to go. Haze drifted in and out of the feeble light from the few candles on the table.

"The game is up, Burton," Henry said, yelling to be heard over Susie's cries. "Give over the child." Henry took two steps and reached for Susie.

Burton jerked her away, out of reach. His eyes narrowed at Henry. "Ain't you the man what come and took Charlotte away?"

"I'm the steward at Willowkeep. I've come to retrieve the child." Henry tried again to take Susie.

Burton turned and dropped her onto a threadbare chaise behind him. Stuffing popped from rips in the faded red fabric. When he turned back to face Henry, he had a knife in his hand. The gleam from the blade glinted through chimney fog.

Henry had hoped to avoid this, but if it was the only way to get Susie back, so be it. Miss Darby's life—or at least her happiness—depended on it.

Henry took a step back, drawing his pistol.

When he saw the bruises around Susie's mouth, the terror in her eyes, he understood in a small way how Darby had lost control and taken Captain Brand's life. It was all Henry could do not to send a ball flying into Burton's heart.

"Did you bring my money?" Burton asked. "I'm not giving her over until I have my money."

Henry pulled back on the flintlock. "I think you will."

The girl was thrashing on the chaise and fell onto the floor. He'd never seen her in a fit like this.

Burton grinned and shook his head. "I think not."

Strong arms grabbed at Henry, pinning his hands behind his back. He tried to fire the gun, but the man wrenched it out of his hand. Henry cursed when the pistol fell to the floor and fired. The ball shot out, tinging as it ricocheted off the iron grate in the fireplace.

There went his only advantage.

A cold, sharp blade pressed against his throat. Where the devil was Darby?

"We can get your money," Henry said. "Just give me the child." Henry again tested the strength of his captor, the muscles in his shoulders pulling tight as he strained.

"Didn't you get my note? Ten thousand for the girl. Not that she's worth more 'an a few shillings at best. Broke in the head, that one."

"Fine," Henry said. "But that sum will not be easy to assemble." No reason to let Burton know of his low demands. "It will take several days."

"What?" Burton said. He stepped closer to Henry to hear over the child's cries.

"I said it will take a few days to assemble the funds." Henry nodded in the direction of Susie. "The child will never last that long. Give her over now, and I'll get you your money."

Burton shook his head. "D'you take me for a fool? That's not how it works."

Indeed it was not. It seemed Darby had deserted him. Taken the dueling pistol and made a run for freedom. He should have been here long before now. He'd already abandoned his children once. Why not again? Would be better than the gallows.

Susie screamed and cried, making herself sick.

Henry may have lost the pistol, but he'd always been better with his hands. Whoever held him did not understand the finer points of the knife-to-neck threat. The blade pressed against his throat, but Henry's head was free to move. He threw it back, ramming into the man's face while at the same moment twisting out of his grip. The knife sliced along Henry's skin.

He spun and landed his fist right on the staggering man's jaw. For the first time, Henry got a look at him. He was tall but not so tall as Henry. His shoulders stretched wide under his shirt, and he wore no coat. The body of a sailor—probably from Hull.

If only Darby had some shred of integrity left.

Burton closed in. "Problem is, Steward, we're too far in now to quit. The halfwit's the only security we got. Not that we wouldn't be doing the world a service if she don't make it."

The sailor was making a recovery. Henry cursed when the door opened, and a third man appeared. He had a brace of quail slung over his shoulder.

"What's this?" he said, dropping the birds to the ground. He drew his musket up, lodging it against his shoulder, barrel pointed right at Henry. Even over Susie's cries, Henry heard the flintlock click.

He'd failed. He was no better than the rest of them—making promises he couldn't keep. Trying to play the hero when he wasn't more than a servant. Miss Darby continually upbraided the other Henry—Henry VIII—for all his promises and grand gestures only to leave poor Anne alone and headless.

Now Henry had done the same. Without her sister, Miss Darby would most certainly be lost.

Susie lay on the floor, coughing and screaming. She seemed oblivious to the struggle going on around her, lost in her fit.

The back door to the cottage opened, and Darby entered. At last.

He came to a dead stop as he saw his daughter thrashing on the floor. Her voice rough and spent but still crying. He bent over her. "Susan? My little Susie?"

Burton turned and stared at his old business partner.

Before Henry could stop him, Burton threw his knife, lodging it in Darby's side.

Darby looked down at it as if he'd no more than spilled a cup of tea on himself. He quietly raised his pistol and pulled the trigger.

The flintlock slammed like thunder. Smoke rose from the explosion of powder. Burton fell backward, a pool of blood forming in the center of his chest.

The sailor and the hunter fled the cottage, not even taking a backward glance at their fallen leader.

Darby pulled the knife from his side. He tossed it away and leaned over his daughter. "My dear," he said. "It's Papa. Remember me?" He took the child into his arms, stroking her matted hair.

Susie only cried harder, her worn voice rasping as she pounded against him. He rocked her and shushed her, uttering words of sorrow for his long absence, of his pride for her. How she'd grown. How beautiful she was.

Henry stepped over Burton's body.

After several minutes, he touched Darby's shoulder. "Give her to me."

Darby looked at Henry, then back at Susie.

Henry reached down and took the child, holding her close like he'd done so many times. In only a few moments, Susie's body stilled. Her cries died to whimpers. She sucked in ragged breaths as she clung to Henry's neck.

Silence landed hard after all her screaming.

Henry held her close. Until that moment, he hadn't realized how much he'd come to care for her. "There now," he said. "It's all over."

He had to get her home. She needed Charlotte. And perhaps the doctor.

Darby stared at him.

"Can you walk?" Henry asked.

Darby pulled himself to his feet, leaning heavily on the settee. "Yes. 'Tis only a small wound. I'm fine."

"Let's go." Henry opened the front door and stepped out.

Mr. Poole was running toward him, followed by four men. "Halt there, Mr. Morland."

Henry stepped aside, and Poole looked past him into the cottage at Darby stumbling forward. At Burton lying dead beside the glowing embers. At the dueling pistols spent and cast to the ground. Then back at the child in Henry's arms still shuddering with wild eyes.

"You found her." Poole had a small sticking plaster above his left eye.

Henry nodded. "That man there, the dead one, his name is Robert Burton. He's Darby's old business partner from Hull. He took her for money."

"And you shot him?"

"I shot him," Darby called from inside. He'd given up and sat down, holding his side.

"What happened to you?" Poole asked Darby.

"Knife," Darby said.

"Look, Constable," Henry said. "This child is ill. I must get her back. You know where to find me." He walked away, back through the woods, holding Susie close. He reached the horses and mounted up.

CHAPTER THIRTY-FOUR

It was quite late when Charlotte's carriage pulled up to the front of Willowkeep. It had been a long ride home with Mr. Morland's father. Even with both windows lowered, the smell was awful. She supposed that was to be expected after so long a time in one of the country's worst prisons. The filth he must have been living in.

He'd slept nigh the whole way home, and the times he'd woken, he'd seemed unsure of what was happening. He didn't stir when a footman opened the door and handed Charlotte out.

"See he gets home, Mr. Tafford."

"Yes, ma'am."

She looked up at Jim Coachman. "Thank you again, Jim."

He nodded at her. "My pleasure."

Mrs. Tafford came running out the front door, followed closely by Fanny. "Oh, miss. Thank all the saints you're back."

"What is it, Mrs. Tafford?"

Mrs. Tafford wiped her eyes with a damp handkerchief. "Susie's gone missing."

"Missing?" Last week Susie had ended up floating facedown in the river. That image would haunt Charlotte forever. If she'd gone to the river again . . . "We must find her! Organize a search party. Where is Mr. Morland?"

Mrs. Tafford shook her head. "She's been taken." She handed Charlotte a crumpled note.

Charlotte opened it and held it to the light of the carriage lamps. A ransom letter. Demanding ten thousand pounds. An impossible sum.

Charlotte looked up at Jim, perched on the driver's bench. Then over to Mr. Tafford, climbing out of the coach. She tilted her head back and gazed up. The night was clear, and the stars glimmered brightly. She couldn't live without her sister. Susie was all Charlotte had left.

"She's going to faint," Fanny said, her voice coming from far away.

So many stars. Her father had always told her how the sailors used the stars to find their way. He'd said night was the best time for navigating. The sun was brighter by far but didn't tell them nearly as much about where they were, where they were going, nor how far they'd come. A clear night was best, like this one. Cloudless. Soundless. And full of stars.

Was it stars that led her here, to Willowkeep? Was it stars that sent Mr. Morland to her doorstep all those months ago? Her life in Hull seemed like a dream, like looking out a window of warped glass.

Now Susie was gone. Weren't no stars in that. Only midnight and black far as the eye could see.

"Miss Darby?" Mrs. Tafford laid a hand on Charlotte's arm.

"Where is Mr. Morland?" Charlotte asked. He was the only star left.

"He's out looking, miss. And Mr. Hardwick. And most of the men. Even Mrs. Kelton went out, but she's back now."

The light coming from inside cast a dark relief round Aunt Nora's figure in the door. Charlotte would know that shape anywhere.

Out looking. They were still out looking. She may yet be found. Charlotte would be willing to sell her very soul to raise the money. A ransom note meant Susie was still alive, right? So that was something.

Another figure came out of the house and ran to her. "I'm so sorry, Miss Darby."

"Jane." Charlotte motioned to the carriage. "I've brought your father home. Jim will drive the carriage round and let you off by the Grange."

"You brought my father?" Jane peered into the coach.

"His debts are paid." Charlotte gave Jane a quick curtsey. "I think I must go in now." She did feel faint.

"Of course." Jane bobbed her head. "But are you sure you're quite well?"

Charlotte climbed the stone steps, stopping for a moment in front of her aunt.

"I'm very sorry," Aunt Nora said. "I'm sure they will find her."

Charlotte searched her aunt's face for her usual curled lip and barbed eyes. They were not there.

"Thank you, Aunt," Charlotte said. She crossed the hall and lifted her skirts, working her way up the grand staircase.

The emptiness of the nursery took her breath away. She entered Susie's room and sat on the edge of her bed. This never would have happened if she'd stayed in Hull. She'd had nothing there that would entice men to steal her sister.

Charlotte picked up Susie's pillow, pressing it against her body. It smelled of Susie. She buried her face in it, letting the down and the ticking absorb her tears. She'd thought money would save them, but it only brought a new set of troubles. First Susie nearly drown. Then Mr. Morland went to jail. Now this. Would there never be an end to sorrow? No. She already knew there was no end.

Ten thousand pounds. How could such a sum ever be got? How long would the men who took her be willing to put up with her sister? When they were tired of waiting . . .

Charlotte mustn't think like that. Despairing would not bring Susie back. Better to leave the nursery and put her mind to finding her sister. She set the pillow on the bed and dried her eyes. After one last glance round the empty nursery, she went down to the drawing room.

Aunt Nora sat by the fireplace in her windsor chair, reading. Her silk dress rustled as she shifted, watching Charlotte take a seat on the sofa.

"You've no idea where Mr. Morland and Mr. Hardwick went?"

Her aunt set her book aside. "Mr. Morland went to get the constable, I believe. And Hurst rode over to the Westwood's to see if they had any information that could help. He left on horseback hours ago."

"Who could have done such a thing?" Perhaps she should have Jim bring the carriage back. It wouldn't be impossible for Fox to be behind this. Even though she'd been with him in London, he had men who could have done it for him.

Jim would never drive to London this late at night, even with the moon near full.

Charlotte stood and walked over to the window. "I have to do something. I cannot sit idly while Susie is out there."

She looked over at Aunt Nora, but the lady only shook her head. "I'm afraid all we can do now is wait."

A footman entered carrying a tray. "Mrs. Tafford sent up some tea."

"Tea?" Charlotte said. "How can we be thinking of tea at a time like this? Like we're naught but barnacles clinging to the rocks, at the mercy of the tide for our very lives. We must *do* some—"

The sound of hooves pounding across the gravel drive drifted into the drawing room. Charlotte ran out and pulled open the front door.

Hurst climbed off his horse.

"What news?" Charlotte asked, rushing down the steps.

Hurst shook his head. "None, I'm afraid. At least not from my end."

Charlotte pressed a handkerchief to her face, no longer able to keep back the tears. Mr. Morland was her last hope. Hurst placed an arm round her.

She leaned in, laying her head on his shoulder.

"We'll find her," Hurst said. "She cannot be far. We will find her." He started toward the house. "Come inside. The night is cool, and you'll catch your death."

But she couldn't move. Hurst closed both arms round her.

She turned, hiding her face in his chest. "Without my sister, I cannot go on."

"My dear cousin." He tightened his hold, laying a kiss on the top of her head.

Another horse came clattering along the gravel drive. She peered over Hurst's shoulder.

Charlotte squinted into the night. A large figure came into view, tall and wide astride his mount. No. He wasn't wide. He was carrying something. It was Mr. Morland with a child across his chest.

Susie.

Charlotte bounded across the gravel, rushing at Mr. Morland. His horse shied, skittish as she dashed toward him.

"You found her!" she cried. Susie lay perfectly still, her arms falling limply to the sides. *Oh, please, God, no.* "Is she . . . ?"

Mr. Morland shook his head. "She sleeps. It has been a long day for her, and she's all worn out. Too tired even to enjoy a ride on the powpy."

"Give her to me." Charlotte needed her in her arms immediately.

Mr. Morland leaned forward and let Susie slip into Charlotte's reaching hands.

Susie mumbled something but didn't fully wake.

"Hush, hush, little one. You're safe now. Charlotte's here. You're home."

She looked up to find Mr. Morland and Hurst and all of them standing round her. Mrs. Tafford was crossing herself, muttering under her breath.

Charlotte felt like praying too and dancing and shouting to the heavens. If her sister hadn't been sleeping, she'd have spun her round and round in circles. Instead, she covered her face with kisses.

"Best get her up to bed," Mr. Morland said. He handed his horse over to a waiting groom.

He had saved her. Once again, Mr. Morland had been Charlotte's salvation. And her sister's. And everything. His eyes were dark and tired. Last time she'd seen him, he'd been locked up in prison. Which reminded her.

"Your father is here," Charlotte said. "I brought him home for you." She rubbed Susie's back as she spoke. How perfectly the child filled her arms.

Mr. Morland didn't seem wholly surprised. "Thank you."

"I went to London with Mr. Tafford and Coachman Jim and paid your father's debt, and now he is here."

"That must have been quite an undertaking. I'm very glad you made it safely out of the fox's den."

Charlotte laughed. Now that her sister was safe, all the world seemed merry.

He gave her a quick bow and said, "We are indebted to you for your kindness and courage."

"You have brought me my sister. We are even." Though she could never truly even the score betwixt Mr. Morland and her. He had done so much.

She hitched Susie up higher in her arms. Every day she grew heavier. Soon Charlotte would not be able to lift her at all.

"Do you want me to carry her up?" Mr. Morland asked.

"No." She pulled Susie closer. "I can't let go just yet." But she did need to get her sister inside and looked after. "I'll take her up."

"I'll have someone sound the horn and call the men in," Hurst said. "Morland, you'd better tend to your father." He strode off round the corner of the house.

Charlotte turned to mount the stairs to the front door.

Mr. Morland stopped her. "Miss Darby," he said. "I must speak with you."

His face was far too grim for her liking. "Can it wait till morning?"

"I'm afraid it cannot."

Must be serious for him to put it before going home and seeing his own father.

"All right, then. I s'pose you'd better come with us to the nursery."

Charlotte reached only the first landing in the middle of the staircase when her arms gave out. She was more tired than she'd thought.

"Here," she said. "I find I need help after all."

Mr. Morland shifted Susie into his arms.

Fanny burst into tears the moment they entered. "Oh, praise the heavens! You found her!"

"Yes," Charlotte said. "Mr. Morland found her, though he has yet to tell me where."

He gave her a dark look.

"I'll stay with her tonight." Charlotte had no intention of turning Susie over to another person.

Fanny lit some candles in Susie's room, then disappeared into her own quarters across the hall.

Mr. Morland laid Susie on the bed. Now that Charlotte had some light, she noticed the filth on Susie's clothing, her matted hair, bruising on her cheek and round her mouth.

Mr. Morland looked on. It occurred to her he hadn't smiled since he'd arrived. Not even after learning about his father.

"What has happened to her?"

CHAPTER THIRTY-FIVE

What was Henry to say to Miss Darby? Her father was alive, in jail for murdering a murderer; that he attacked the constable and escaped, then was stabbed by Mr. Burton—whom he then killed? Even now Darby might be dead. At the very least, he was back in the prison. Not to mention all her sister had suffered under the hands of Burton.

"Mr. Morland?"

He looked down at the child sleeping peacefully at last. She must have cried all day and half the night before Henry had rescued her.

"Tell me," Charlotte pleaded as she changed the sleeping child into a nightdress.

This tale would not be easy for her. "Mr. Burton took her."

"Robert Burton? From Hull?"

Henry nodded.

"The ungrateful worm. If it weren't for my father taking him on as a partner, that man would be nothing."

"He wanted money." Seemed to Henry everything was always about money. "He thought that by taking your sister, he could get a ransom from you."

"Yes." Miss Darby said. "Mrs. Tafford showed me a note demanding an impossible sum, but it didn't say who it were from."

She still did not have a full grasp on her wealth. Henry would need to turn that note over to Poole as evidence. "Do you still have it?"

"It's in the drawing room, I think. Or perhaps Aunt Nora has it now. I lost track when Hurst returned."

He hadn't missed Charlotte and Hardwick's embrace on the front steps. The way she leaned into him. Nor did he miss the kiss. Not to mention all this Hurst business instead of her usual Mr. Hardwick.

"But you are not answering my question, Mr. Morland. How did you find her?" Charlotte dipped a cloth into the washbasin, then wiped it gently across Susie's face. The child squirmed and pushed it away in her sleep.

Here was where the difficult part began. The truth seemed too much for her after all she'd been through. But if her father still lived, she would want to know. She might even wish to see him. He could not keep such information from her.

"Your father told me."

Miss Darby's hand paused. "My father?"

Henry sighed and sank into the rocking chair. "Remember when you came to me in the old parish hall?"

She nodded.

"The other man in the room—the other prisoner—he was your father."

She stared at him, appearing for all worth more shocked than when she'd seen Willowkeep for the first time. "Why did you not say so?"

"I did not know," Henry said. "It was not until after you left that I made the connection. Even then he didn't tell me; I recognized him from the portrait you showed me."

Miss Darby went back to work on her sister, brushing aside her tangled hair and pulling the blankets up tightly under her chin. At last she stood and asked, "Why was he in jail?"

This was the question he most dreaded. She'd already suffered quite enough because of her father. This had already been a trying day for everyone. Taking into account Susie's abduction and her trip to London, her meeting with Fox could not have been pleasant. And now he must tell her this.

"He is accused of murder," Henry whispered.

Her breathing paused for a moment, then she asked, "And who is it he's s'posed to have killed?"

"The captain of his fishing vessel."

She turned and gazed out the window, though with the night, little could be seen. "Where is he now?"

Henry scooted to the edge of his seat, expecting at any minute that she might faint. But of course she wouldn't. She was the strongest woman he'd ever met.

"He was injured trying to save Susie from Mr. Burton."

"Dead?" she asked, her voice utterly flat.

"I do not know. He saved my life and probably your sister's when he fired a pistol at Burton. Susie was in a bad way. I took her and left, leaving your father with Constable Poole and his men. They have most likely returned him to the jail."

"So he may yet be alive." She turned and looked at him. "Will you take me there?"

The life that danced in her eyes had vanished, replaced with the kind of emptiness that left a lasting mark. He would give anything to remove it if she would let him. He would take her broken heart and spend the rest of his life mending it if only she would give it to him.

But since it was not his, he gave what he could. "Of course."

Charlotte clung to the handrail as she followed Constable Poole up the stairs to the jail cell. The same room she'd entered when she'd come to visit Mr. Morland. 'Twas a dreadful place but nothing compared to the Marshalsea.

Mr. Morland had told her about her father's time on the smack on the way over. And about the poor lad who had died. About all the years spent in hiding because he'd had to appear dead. Perhaps it softened her heart a little. But no amount of softening could make better that he'd run out on them in the first place.

Her father lay on a cot, his breathing heavy.

"I tried to summon the doctor, but your father refused." Mr. Poole motioned her into the room. "Said why bother when he was consigned to the gallows anyway."

Mr. Morland had carried a chair up for Charlotte. He set it down near her father's cot.

She leaned over him. "Papa?"

His eyes opened. "My girl."

That was what he used to call her, her and her mother, when her mother was still alive. His girls. Then her mother had died, and he'd up and left. She used to be his girl. Not anymore.

"You're angry with me. You have every right. I deserve it." He took a few shallow breaths. "But I made it right for you in the end. Got you back what's rightfully yours, didn't I."

His mind must be off. He'd never made anything right for her since the moment he'd took to the sea.

"Came back, didn't I. Convinced old Walter to turn his place over to the rightful heir."

"You did what?"

That was why her uncle had changed his will at the last moment. How a vast fortune she'd never heard of fell into her lap. It must have taken more than persuasion to accomplish it. What on earth had her father done?

"And how did you convince him to do that?" she asked.

Mr. Poole and Mr. Morland both stood behind her. Maybe she shouldn't have asked. If her uncle had signed the will under threat of death, his confession might change her inheritance.

Her father shook his head. "It doesn't matter now." He closed his eyes, his face pained. "Walter always knew my Louisa had been wronged. Even told me right out that setting the will to rights brought him peace of mind. Like the Bard said, 'All's well that ends well.'" He reached for Charlotte's hand.

She took it, though it felt nothing like the hand she'd held as a child. She wasn't exactly sure why. His hands had always been rough from work. Maybe it was hers that had changed, soft now from her comfortable life at Willowkeep. Or perhaps the notion of holding a hand that had killed a man—two men—made her fingers twitch.

"Give my Susie a kiss from me," he whispered, his voice failing.

He was slipping away too fast. He should have made himself known to her. He shouldn't have kept himself hidden for so long. And yet, if he'd gotten himself caught before now, he'd have been hanged. He wouldn't have been here to save Susie. And Mr. Morland. Perhaps there was a touch of fate in all that had happened after all.

"I will, Papa." She kissed his cheek.

He lay silent for a while. The lines on his face were deeper, wider, and gray streaks spread from his temples. It had been six years since she'd last seen him.

"Go now," he said. "Go and live your life. Your mother is waiting for me. I can feel her already." He opened his eyes and looked past Charlotte.

Charlotte turned her head, half expecting to see the shadow of her mother standing there. But her father's eyes had gone to Mr. Morland. "Take her," he breathed.

Mr. Morland stepped forward. His touch on her elbow sent life through her veins. Life she'd felt draining away, sucked out by the cold grip of her father.

"Come away now, Miss Darby," Mr. Morland said. "He doesn't want you to watch."

No. He didn't. That was why he'd left. Because he hadn't wanted her to see him slipping down the slope that had brought him here.

She stood. "Good-bye, Father."

Mr. Morland led her from the cell. The constable stayed behind, closing the door behind them.

She would never see her father again. She'd already been dealt this blow, done her mourning, and come to terms with it. Now here she was all over again. Right back in the same sinking boat that had started it all—waiting for it to slip into the ocean.

"Miss Darby?" Mr. Morland said.

Her boat didn't slip. This time her father's death was certain, not simply presumed by the local magistrate. She should be wiping tears from her eyes. But all she could think about was losing Willowkeep. If it weren't rightly hers, what claim did she have to it?

"Are you unwell?"

Forced to sign a will while being threatened might void the agreement. She and Susie might be without a home sooner than she'd thought. Perhaps her aunt would give her some money to return to Kingston upon Hull. That would mean leaving Mr. Morland. Which was what she should probably do anyway. So it shouldn't matter one way or the other.

"Miss Darby?"

She looked over at him. Dark circles ringed his eyes. A cut stood stark red against his forehead. His collar and cravat were bloodied from a wound on his neck. He was tired. Probably worse than her, seeing as how he'd spent the night in that dreadful room. Still, the way he looked at her.

"Miss Darby?" His hand came up, grasping her arm as if she was about to fall down the stairs.

"What?"

"Are you all right? You look dazed."

"I am well." She started down the steps. She hadn't realized she'd been stuck on the upper landing. "Lost in my thoughts, I s'pose."

"I'm sorry about your father," he said.

He opened the door for her, and they left the old parish hall.

She stopped before climbing into the curricle. "Is it wrong for me to say that he was already dead to me? I already mourned him when I lost him as a father. I'm not sure I have it in me to do it all again."

Mr. Morland held out his arm to hand her in. "It's not wrong at all. He isn't the same man you knew as a child. That is something I can well understand."

CHAPTER THIRTY-SIX

After seeing Miss Darby back to the house, Henry made his way to the Grange. He'd been gone a good hour, taking Miss Darby to see her father, and now he wanted to see his.

He put his weight into it and pushed the front door open.

"Jane?" he called softly in case they were already asleep.

"In here." Her voice came from their father's room.

Henry hung his hat on the rack, his coat quickly following. His father lay in bed, propped up with pillows. A fire burned in the grate. His father's eyes were closed, but Jane was perched on the edge of his bed with a teacup in hand.

Jane smiled up at him. "Can you believe it?"

"I can't."

His father opened his eyes. "Henry. It is good to be home." His voice was weak and hollow, but a smile of true contentment lifted his face.

Miss Darby could not fully comprehend the gift she had given him. Both him and Jane. She thought she was bringing back his father, but she'd restored so much more. Freedom. A life without dragging the chains of debt. A chance to make something better of themselves. And most certainly she'd saved their father's life.

The old man shivered, and Henry added some coals to the fire. He pulled the blankets up to his father's shoulders, then sat across from Jane on the bed.

"How is he?"

"Ill. Nine months in that place has done him no favors. His spirits are much improved, however, even in the short time he's been home." Jane pressed the teacup to their father's mouth. His lips parted, and he sipped.

"Who did you borrow from?" his father asked, looking up at Henry.

Henry shook his head. "No one. Miss Darby paid your debts." He still couldn't believe she'd gone off to London by herself. And to Fox's den, no less! The things that man could have done to her.

"Miss Darby?"

"Yes, Father. Remember?" He'd just spent the better part of three hours in the carriage with her. "The young woman who came home with you from the Marshalsea."

This seemed to do little to enlighten him.

"Walter Kelton died these three months past. Do you recall?"

His father nodded. They had talked about this many times when Henry had visited.

"Now there is a new owner of Willowkeep. His niece, Miss Charlotte Darby. Daughter of Louisa Kelton and Thomas Darby. It was she who paid your debt."

His father seemed to consider that for a time. "I'm much obliged, I'm sure. But why would she do such a thing?"

That was the real question. What could've gotten into her bonnet that had made her decide to run off to the seediest parts of London, confront that blackguard Fox, and pay so many hundred pounds to free a man she'd never even met?

Henry leaned forward. "Because that is the kind of woman she is. She cares naught about herself. Only for the welfare of others." Most especially Susie. But himself, Jane, Hardwick, even her aunt. All those who came within her circle of reach mattered—she would see them looked after.

"I'm most grateful for her kindness and look forward to meeting her," Henry's father said.

Perhaps Henry should wait for him to recover his strength before pursuing this. A good night's rest in his own bed would do wonders for his mind as well as his body, Henry hoped.

His father lay back against the pillows and closed his eyes. How thin he'd become.

Henry took his hand.

"Thank you, son," his father said, his eyes still closed.

He could never repay Miss Darby for this. Never. She thought this made them even. She credited Henry for far more than he deserved. In truth, he'd done almost nothing for her save bring her down from Hull and comfort her sister now and then.

He'd worked his whole life to keep himself and his family independent and respectable. He'd failed. But now, thanks to Miss Darby, he had a chance to start over. To provide his father the care he needed and to give Jane the opportunity to have a life of her own.

"Where have you been?" Jane asked. "Mr. Hardwick stopped by and told me you'd found Susie. I've been expecting you any moment for over an hour."

"I took Miss Darby back to Kippingham to see her father."

That brought a shock to Jane's face. "He is alive?"

"He was." Henry yawned. "'Tis a long story, my dear sister. And I am in desperate need of a bed that is not bug infested. Suffice it to say that he helped me get little Susan back but was fatally injured in the process."

Jane scowled at him. "I suppose I can wait till morning for the details. You do look the picture of death."

"First thing we must do is hire a cook." Henry grinned. "I don't ever want you in the kitchen again."

She laughed, then slapped him on the shoulder. "Go to bed."

Charlotte woke late the next morning. Her head pounded, and her mouth was dry as driftwood. She had spent most the night with Susie. But between Susie's flopping limbs and Puppy's scratching claws, sleep eluded Charlotte. She'd crawled into her own bed shortly before sunrise.

She slipped into her dressing gown and went straight to the nursery.

"Is she awake?" Charlotte asked Fanny.

"Not yet. I just checked on her. Will came and took Puppy out, but she didn't stir."

She gently opened the door to Susie's room. Her sister's soft snores drifted over her like pillow down. She placed the backs of her fingers on Susie's cheek. No fever. The poor child was just done to a bone. Let her rest.

Charlotte went back to her room. She flopped onto her bed and gazed at the ceiling. Great conkers. What a day yesterday.

And now the sun was out, brightening the morning as if last night her world hadn't nearly ended. A new day. It seemed she had much to do, yet she had nothing to do. That fast, everything had gone back to its usual pace.

With a soft knock at her door, Mrs. Tafford entered. "There you are, my dear. It's nearly afternoon." She set a silver tray of food and a steaming teapot on her table. "I brought up some breakfast; you haven't eaten in a king's reign."

"Bless you, Mrs. Tafford." This would do wonders for her headache. "I'm starved."

Mrs. Tafford filled a teacup and added rich cream right to the brim. Charlotte closed her eyes and let the drink warm her soul.

"Shall I help you dress?" Mrs. Tafford asked.

Charlotte had dressed herself for nineteen years. As Mrs. Tafford cinched the back of her stays and tightened her frock, she wondered how she'd ever be able to do it on her own again. Somehow she would manage. Just as she always had.

Mrs. Tafford left, and Charlotte carried her breakfast over to the settee by the window. The grounds were lovely. Green trees and all the shrubs in flower. A row of lavender glowed in the sun, a world of delight for the bees that hovered over it.

If she lost the inheritance because of her father's interference, she would be forced to go. If that didn't work, there was the marriage stipulation from Sutton. That would surely mean her going. Everything pointed toward a departure from Willowkeep.

Mrs. Kelton didn't want her here. Hurst, for all his friendliness, would hardly complain if she vanished from his life. She was used to going it alone. Her and Susie.

It should not be so hard, save for this one thing.

Of all she'd hoped to find here, love was not one of them. It had found her anyway. And it was the one thing she could never have.

She sat at her desk and stared at the blank paper. She dipped the tip of her goose quill into the ink. She had one last letter to write.

Her Majesty Queen Anne Boleyn

CHAPTER THIRTY-SEVEN

THE KNOCK ON HIS DOOR snapped Henry out of his daze. Lud, he was tired. But, like always, he'd arrived at the great house exactly on time. He'd gotten no work done yesterday and had a whole page of expenditures that needed to be approved. If only he could stay awake to finish them.

"Enter," he said.

Miss Darby slipped through the door. She looked lovely as ever, her hair coming loose and falling over her soft yellow dress. He always preferred her in blue, but this creamy shade gave her skin a golden glow. In her hands, she clutched a bonnet. She must be on her way outside.

"Miss Darby. How is your sister? Recovering from her ordeal, I hope." He motioned for her to sit, and she did.

"She is. She woke for an hour or so, ate and played with Puppy, and has fallen asleep again." Miss Darby toyed with the strings of her bonnet.

Something was bothering her.

"She is not ill, I hope."

"No. She seems well."

Perhaps she wondered about her father. "The constable was here. I'm sorry to inform you that your father passed away shortly after we left."

She nodded, then lifted a fold of her dress. "I s'pose I should be wearing mourning. I'll have Mrs. Tafford order me something."

"I know it does not feel like it, but I believe he loved you and your sister. I think by coming to Walter, he tried to make things right. Or at least his idea of right."

"Thank you, sir."

"I took the liberty of arranging his remains to be buried in Hull beside your mother. I hope you do not mind."

"You take very good care of me, Mr. Morland." Still she did not look up.

"I could say the same about you." Henry shuffled his papers aside. "I have not had the opportunity to properly thank you for what you did to bring my father home. I am in your debt."

"'Twas nothing," she said, at last meeting his eyes.

"Nothing?" Henry leaned forward on his desk. "I have spoken with Mr. Tafford and Coachman Jim and heard the whole story. It took great courage. I should be angry at you for putting yourself at risk. Not one in a hundred women would have such mettle."

She shook her head.

"And lucky too that you are an ace at stone throwing."

The smallest of smiles crossed her lips. "He should've known better than to trifle with a girl from Hull."

"Indeed." Henry laughed softly. "I always maintain, Miss Darby, you are entirely anomalous."

She gave him a beautiful smile. Fleeting though. It came and went like a leaf on the wind.

"As it is, I am exceedingly grateful for what you've done."

Miss Darby went back to tugging on her bonnet. "I wanted to ask you something," she said.

"Anything."

"Last night, my father said he forced Mr. Kelton to change his will." She was going to ruin the ribbon the way she kept pulling on it. "Does that mean . . . Will that information affect the ownership of Willowkeep?"

Ah. She thought she was going to lose her inheritance. "No. Not at all. Walter Kelton's will was signed and sealed in the presence of Mr. Sutton and myself. Even Dr. Leigh was there. We all declared him of sound mind. We may never know what means of persuasion your father used. Nothing material points to threats or violence. Whatever prompted him to make the change does not affect the will. You are safe."

She relaxed a little, letting the strings fall to her lap. "Safe until my twentieth birthday."

Yes. There was that. "We won't know anything for certain until I get the records from Mr. Sutton. There are many aspects of this entail that give me grave doubts. I think we will find that this presumed heir of only fifteen years is actually the grandson of Edmund, thus lapsing the entail—if in fact it ever really existed in the first place."

"Yes, sir."

She was calling him sir again. She had no reason to worry. The law was on her side. Even Mrs. Kelton had not contested the will. Henry inched closer. "What is it that's really troubling you?"

Something weighed on her. He didn't like to see her so vexed. Especially now that her sister was home and everything seemed right.

She rose. "You look tired, Mr. Morland. I wish you would take the rest of the day off."

You look beautiful as ever. He didn't say it. He couldn't. It was wholly inappropriate for him to even think it.

"Go home and rest. I order it."

There were only a few hours left in the working day anyway. And he was very anxious to see how his father fared. Henry snuffed his desk candle and put on his hat.

They walked together for a ways on the path to the Grange. When the path split, Miss Darby paused. "Here is where I leave you." And she started off toward the willows.

She must have another letter. Perhaps she might reveal the source of her distress to Anne Boleyn. If she'd wanted Henry to know, she would have told him. It was private between her and Anne. Henry turned and headed home. He would take her advice and get some rest. Just as soon as he doubled back to the willows.

He waited out of sight until Miss Darby emerged from the bower of willows, cradling a small red flower of some kind in her hand. She hurried along the gravel walkway, back toward the house. The moment she rounded the bend, he made his way to the lion statue.

Another letter so soon. Miss Darby did have a lot on her mind.

He pulled it out from behind the teeth. With a quick snap, he broke the seal.

Her Majesty Queen Anne Boleyn
The Lion at Willowkeep, Kent
July 1810

Dear Anne,

I think at last I understand you. Who wouldn't want to marry a king? To live in the Tower. All the money in the world at your disposal. The envy of all your peers. All your problems would be solved. At least, that's what they want us to think.

But all that wealth and glory just brings a whole new set of troubles. A chopped head. A stolen child. A love that tears us apart.

Willowkeep is a beautiful place, I'll grant you. I don't blame you for haunting it. But I don't belong here. It's too much for me, and I cannot stay.

She was leaving? What was that woman thinking? He'd assured her at least a dozen times that the likelihood of the entail being valid was slim indeed. What about Susie? And Hardwick? This was her family home. What nonsense to say she didn't belong. She belonged here more than anyone.

My dear H is now more dear to me than ever.

Hardwick. The rake.

I thought I could repay his kindness by fetching his father for him, but I come home only to find I'm deeper in his debt than ever. He saved my sister from the hands of terrible men.

He read that last part again.

What the devil?

H for Henry. Not Hardwick.

He fell back onto the wicker bench. But all their secret looks. The embraces. Not to mention her many protestations that *H* was a gentleman far above her. By all the world's standards, Henry certainly did not qualify as a gentleman. Nor was he far above anyone, save perhaps the rat catcher. But Miss Darby had never quite embraced the world's standards.

There had been those few moments when she hadn't seemed completely indifferent toward Henry. Times when he'd caught a glimpse of something more.

He read on.

H has captured my heart completely. He has reeled me in, and I am a fish out of water. Heaven knows I'd choose to stay that way, but I could not live. And so I must leave. I will lose the estate when I fail to marry because marriage to any man is utterly impossible.

Perhaps both our happy endings were never meant to be.

Yours in shared disappointment,
~C

She loved him. Henry. All this time it had been him. *H* for Henry.

He had to know for certain what made marriage impossible to her. Surely she must know that he would never be intolerant of little Susie. The time had come to get to the bottom of this stone in Miss Darby's heart. And it was time to see if he had any chance at all.

He knew what he had to do. It was a great risk. It might cost him his job. His reputation would be mired. He would go down in legend as Kent's biggest fool.

If he had any chance at all with her, it would be worth the risk.

CHAPTER THIRTY-EIGHT

Charlotte parted the branches of the willow tree and halted. On the wicker bench, leaning back with his long legs sprawling, looking like the handsomest man in the county, sat Mr. Morland.

He smiled up at her. "I thought I might find you here."

Something was different about him this morning. He stood and took a step toward her.

"Good morning, Mr. Morland. Are you rested at last?" she said. He looked much better than yesterday when she'd sent him home.

"I had a very good night, thank you." He was so close now their toes were nearly touching. "How is your sister this morning?"

"Still tired but much improved. Thank you, sir." She used the formal title to remind herself that no matter how odd his behavior, she must keep her own heart closed. She should step back. Give herself some distance. Even the breeze whispering through the willow branches seemed to warn her. *Be careful*, it said. *Here is danger.*

"I'm glad to hear it." For the span of three heartbeats, he just watched her, his eyes roving her face.

She stared straight ahead at his neckcloth tied and pinned perfectly, as always. Leastways until Susie got to it. She lowered her gaze to his hands. Hands that had given her a new life. Hands that had brought back her sister. There was no part of him that didn't make her want him more.

"Is there something you need?" He must have been waiting here for a reason.

"Yes," he whispered. "Miss Darby, I wondered if you would allow me to . . ." He reached up, tilting her head back until his lips were on hers.

She pulled away and looked up into his face while the branches rustled. This was all wrong. So very wrong. She lifted her hands, curling her fingers into his hair.

Instantly his mouth was on hers again. How was it possible to want something so desperately she felt the pain and joy of it all the way to her toes? Toes that she now stood on to be closer.

Mr. Morland released her. With a few quick breaths, her head cleared. Great conkers. What had she done? Only the worst possible thing ever. And the best.

"Charlotte." His hands still pressed against her back. "We need to talk."

She nodded, her face too hot to speak.

He guided her to the bench and lowered her, then sat beside her. "What is it that is holding you back?"

She looked down at her hands, her fingers like spring buds compared to the long branches of his hands.

"Is it because I'm only a steward and you are—"

"No." How could he think such a thing? He who had seen where she'd come from. He could build all the mansions in the world round her and she'd still be Charlotte Darby from Hull. Shipping merchant's daughter. "'Course not. You know me better than that."

He nodded. "Do you think I'm interested only in your money?"

"No." She knew him better than that.

"Don't you want to stay here? Willowkeep is your home. You are happy here. Susie is happy here."

She wanted to stay more than anything. But people don't always get what they want. "I would stay if I could. But I cannot."

"Because you will not marry." He lifted her hand and kissed it. "I'm offering to help you with that. If you will have me."

She pulled her hand away. Where was Anne when she needed her? All Charlotte's efforts to avoid this moment had gone awry. Here she sat, sliced through, right down the middle, like a flounder being filleted. "I would if I could. You must believe me. But it is impossible."

"Why? Why is it impossible?"

Charlotte stood and paced away. "Because it would end in death and despair, and you would hate me by the end of it." She turned back in time to see the disbelief on his face.

He opened his mouth to speak, no doubt to tell her he would always love her. That nothing could change the way he felt at this very moment.

That was the problem. Everyone wanted roses as far as the eye could see. But the thorns were there too, hiding. And when the petals withered and fell, thorns were all what was left. Wasn't that what happened to Queen

Anne and her Henry? Sweet-smelling roses until the whole hedgerow lost its bloom. Then nothing but thorns.

So she stopped him. No matter how many declarations of love, they would not change the outcome. She'd already witnessed it once before. "Don't you see, Mr. Morland? Look at me. What is it that you want from me?"

He stood and took her hands. "I want you."

"And then what?"

He thought for a moment. "I . . . suppose a life together. Here—or Hull, if that's what you truly want. A family—"

"Aha! See the rub?" Gaw, she did not want to cry, but she could feel the tears brewing. "Do you see the problem now?"

He shook his head but then stopped. At last understanding of the horrible truth reached his eyes. He ran a hand across his face. He knew the history of her family. The babies lined up in the cemetery. Too many for her mother to endure. Charlotte would never inflict such pain on someone else.

"You think if you have children, they will be like your sister," he said. "That if you marry, you will be destined to repeat the misfortunes of your mother. That our lives will turn out like your parents'."

How could any man want a woman like her for a wife, knowing in advance the suffering that awaited? The thorns. The heartache.

"Even the doctor said it would be so."

"I heard enough from your father about what the doctors said." He shook his head. "I don't agree at all with their conjectures. They have no way of knowing. And what if we did have a child like Susie? Would that be so very bad? We've managed her well together, I think."

She needed him to understand. He had to see that saying things would all work out and actually having them all work out were two very different things. "I've been thinking a lot about Anne Boleyn," Charlotte said.

He seemed surprised by her sudden change of topic, but he didn't stop her.

"She married a man who divorced his first wife because he tired of her. Or she didn't give him the son he wanted. Who really knows his reasons. But Anne didn't see all that. She captured his attention, and he professed his love. But it weren't all happily ever after for them either. And look how that turned out."

"Charlotte Darby. That man was insane. If you are comparing me to a person who beheaded two of his own wives, I shall be very offended."

She couldn't help a laugh. "'Course not."

"Then perhaps you think I will follow in the footsteps of my own father. Do you see me visiting the gaming hells and running up debts such that you lose Willowkeep altogether?"

She shook her head. "No. You would never."

Mr. Morland pulled her close. "See there. We are neither of us our parents. Life will be hard whether or not we are married, so we might as well face it together. Doesn't that sound better than all alone?"

It sounded infinitely better. "But what if you live to regret me?"

He kissed her forehead. Then one cheek, then the other. She smiled as she remembered the time she'd done the same to him, even though he'd been fast asleep.

"If I ever come to regret you," he said, his lips brushing against her mouth as he spoke, "I give you leave to lay my neck on the chopping block." He took both of her hands in his. "Charlotte," he whispered.

She looked up at him. How she longed to say yes. How easy it would be to lean into his arms for the rest of her life. To let his strength be her strength, her troubles his. It was a dream that could not be. She stepped back. "I'm sorry. I cannot marry."

She pulled her hands away and pushed through the branches at a run.

Henry stood alone under the willow tree.

In the end, he was no different from his father. He'd taken a gamble and lost it all.

She would not have him. Her fear was stronger than her love.

Henry should have seen this earlier. Of course she would be worried about her own children. More than worried. Terrified.

She had already proven that she was not like her mother. When everyone had deserted Susie, Charlotte had stayed and cared for her. Charlotte had stood up to the scorn of the world to raise her sister. She had stood up to Fox.

Though she couldn't see it, she was stronger than all of them.

What was he to do now?

He'd known the risk. Now he must pay the price. Unlike his father, he would not leave the debt to be settled by someone else.

If it was too painful for her to be here with him, then he must be the one to leave.

He would stay long enough to settle the question of the entail. Once her future at Willowkeep was secure, he would tender his resignation.

Henry walked home slowly. He pushed the front door open with a slow grunt, his shoulder mark still rough and smudged in the center.

His father sat in his usual chair, reading—a chair that had stood empty for the past long while. Jane sat across from him, her sewing on her lap. A wonderful smell wafted out from the kitchen.

"Henry," his father said. "How are things up at the big house?"

Henry pinned on a smile. "They are fine, Father. How are you?"

"I'm feeling much improved." His voice did sound stronger, but he was still pale and gaunt.

"Jane." Henry gave his sister a nod.

"Henry, what is the matter?" she asked. She could always read him.

He fell into a chair. "Nothing. Nothing at all. Just tired still, I think."

She didn't appear convinced, but she let it go.

A woman entered the room from the kitchen, short and stout, hair threaded with gray. "Shall I bring the tea in now, Miss Morland?"

"Henry," Jane said. "May I introduce you to our new cook, Mrs. Hancock."

Henry stood. "Pleasure."

She gave him a short curtsey.

"Tea would be very nice, thank you," Jane said.

The woman bobbed her head and scuffled out.

Jane had a grin from ear to ear. "I saved you the trouble and went and got a cook myself. She's mother-in-law to one of the tenants. Her husband recently passed away, and she's only just moved here to live with her daughter."

That was all well and good, but Henry didn't know anything about her. What if she was a terrible cook? Though it would be hard to be worse than Jane.

"What do you know of her skills?"

Jane put her sewing aside. "Don't be so stubborn. You're not the only one who can do things for this family. She's already prepared Father a restorative draft that has done much to ease his coughing."

Mrs. Hancock returned with a tray of steaming tea, cakes, and toasted muffins, with a delicious-looking black butter. She set it on the side table, then bustled away.

Jane looked at him. "What do you say now?"

"I say you've done very well."

He hadn't seen his sister this happy in a long time. And all thanks to Charlotte.

It would pain Jane to leave Willowkeep. He wouldn't break the news to her until he had a new position secure and a place to live. It would take him a week. Maybe two. In the meantime, he must carry on as before.

Jane handed him a plate.

Henry shook his head. "I have no stomach."

In his room, he carefully tucked Charlotte's letters into the back of his drawer.

CHAPTER THIRTY-NINE

Charlotte sat in the nursery, gazing out the window in her drab, black mourning dress while Susie stacked colored blocks. Puppy lay beside her, wagging his tail. She hadn't gone down to dinner in nearly a fortnight, nor breakfast in the mornings. She didn't dare face Mr. Morland. Or anyone. Mrs. Tafford had brought up her meals, asking her if she was well.

Charlotte had told her she wanted to be with her sister. After Susie had been taken, it wasn't so far from the truth. And her father was dead. She had reason enough.

The sun beat down, casting long shadows across the lawn. A squirrel ran out of the hedgerow and scurried up the trunk of the oak tree. He didn't seem to mind the heat. The grecian maids in the fountain worked at their never-ending chore—pouring water day in and day out. Year after year.

She touched her lips where Mr. Morland had kissed her under the willow tree. For the hundredth time since then, she considered running down to his office and telling him she'd changed her mind. Perhaps it wasn't too late. He might take her back.

But it was better this way. In the end, she'd be saving them both a lifetime of disappointment. Better to do without roses than live forever among the thorns.

It happened just like she'd told Queen Anne: her heart had been torn open and blood leaked out. A steady stream that slowly drained her. She opened her history book to the pressed Tudor roses.

Why did Anne give her these? To let her know she was there? Or was there more?

Charlotte should forget about the queen's ghost. Anne Boleyn had done nothing to help her. She loved Mr. Morland now more than ever.

Susie tapped her on her knee.

"Yes, my dear?" Charlotte ran her hand along her sister's cheek. So soft and smooth.

Susie frowned.

"What is it?"

She pointed at the door.

She wanted to go out. To play in the sunshine. And probably with Mr. Morland. It had been some time since they'd gone with him to see the powpies or play fetch with Puppy.

"Not today, my love." She couldn't bring herself to ask him for his favors after she'd turned him down—not even for Susie. She'd have to face him eventually. But the mere sight of him and her resolve would melt like ice on this hot summer day.

Susie climbed up on Charlotte's lap, then pointed at the door again.

Charlotte shook her head. "Sorry, not today."

Fanny entered the nursery. "Mr. Morland wants to see you, miss. In his workroom. At your convenience."

"Mr. Morland?"

"Yes, miss."

"Wants to see me?"

"Yes, miss. Says to tell you it's Willowkeep business."

Business. Of course. He was still the steward, after all.

Perhaps she should take Susie with her. As reinforcement. But then she'd just want to go down to the stables. Susie wouldn't understand why they were there if they weren't going out.

She paced back and forth, biting her nails. Laws and gardens, she had to calm down. Otherwise he'd take one look at her and know she'd been pining for him this whole time.

"Is everything all right, miss?"

Now she was making a spectacle of herself in front of Fanny. "Perfectly fine, thank you."

Charlotte left Fanny in charge and made her way to his office. She smoothed out her black crepe frock, straightened her stays, and tried to tuck her hair back into its knot.

She stood outside his door, leaning close, listening. She couldn't hear anything, but he was in there. Somehow she just knew.

She tapped on the door with two soft knocks.

"Enter," came Mr. Morland's voice from inside.

She opened the door. Mr. Morland stood as she came in. He looked the same as he did every day. Perfect.

"Miss Darby. Please sit."

She did.

He held out a letter to her across the desk. "I've received news from Mr. Sutton regarding the entail."

She opened it. A large block of scrawl covered the entire page. She couldn't read it, not while her heart was leaking pools of blood right in front of Mr. Morland. "Can you not tell me what it says?"

He smiled, and she couldn't take her eyes off his lips.

"It says that the document claiming the entail has proved to be a forgery. An unknown individual paid the clerk in the law office to create the false document and to remove the true documents that would prove otherwise. There is no entail, and George Kelton does not even exist. You truly are the last remaining Kelton."

She looked down at the letter. The last Kelton. "So Willowkeep is mine?"

"Yes. Long as you remain here. You do recall that stipulation in the will?"

She had forgotten about that. If she moved out, she would lose the place—and the income it provided. But how could she remain here, with him? It would be like dying of thirst with a pitcher of water always in front of her but just out of reach.

He held out another letter. His face much less cheery than when he gave her the sheepdog's correspondence.

Her eyes went straight to the signature at the end. This letter was from Mr. Morland. She looked up, surprised.

He motioned for her to read.

Miss Charlotte Darby
Willowkeep, Kent
August 1810

Miss Darby,

I, Henry Morland Jr., do hereby tender my resignation as steward of Willowkeep Estate, beginning the fifth day of August, eighteen hundred ten. At such time, I shall no longer be working in this capacity and will vacate Willow Grange on said premises.

It has been a pleasure to serve you, and I am confident you will find a new steward who will fulfill all responsibilities admirably.

Respectfully,
Mr. Henry Morland Jr.

"You're leaving me?"

"I think it is for the best." He folded his hands together on his desk. "You are secure here; the estate is yours. You will be taken care of."

"Where will you go?" Now that it was upon her, she wasn't sure she could live without him.

"I have acquired a position at an estate near Canterbury. At Woolton Green."

So soon? "And Jane? And your father?"

"They will come with me, naturally."

Poor Jane. She will not be happy to be separated from Hurst. And Henry's poor father, only just home to be moved again.

"I'm sorry." She had brought this on him. "I can't help but feel this is my fault." If she hadn't rejected Mr. Morland, he might not feel this need to decamp.

"Please. Do not blame yourself. It was I who crossed the line." He looked at her like he was settling accounts with the thatcher. He must think she despised him.

"I do love you," she whispered.

Those words shattered his mask, and he lowered his head. The sinews in his hands strained as he clasped them together. When at last he looked up, he said, "And I you."

"But it's not enough, is it?" Perhaps she simply wanted him to say that he forgave her. That he understood. That he agreed marriage to her would never end well.

"What more is there?" He seemed genuinely surprised. "You are afraid of the dark, Charlotte Darby. You, who have lived so long in the shadows, should know by now that without darkness, there would be no light."

He was right. She feared the river and the sea and the little cemetery in Hull more than anything.

"How would I know the joy of freedom if I had not been bowed under by my father's debts?" He leaned closer. "Would Willowkeep be the haven it is had you not had to scratch and scrape for life in Hull? Is your sister not more infinitely precious to you because of five other graves? There will always be darkness—there must be—to illuminate the light."

He stood, his mask back in place. "I believe that concludes our business. It has been my greatest pleasure, Miss Darby."

She got to her feet, her head aswirl with his words.

He opened the door for her. Smiled. Bowed to her like she was the mistress and him the steward. A man of business.

"Thank you, Mr. Morland. For everything."

She took a few steps toward the door. Close enough that as she passed, his heat warmed her body. A keepsake to take with her, to remember him by.

Then he closed the door, and Charlotte braced herself against the wall.

So Willowkeep was hers. She was saved. Same as she'd been when the sheepdog from London had come up and told her the news. But this time she did not feel like spinning.

It wouldn't be Willowkeep without Mr. Morland. Perhaps she could beg him to stay. They could get past this, go back to where they were before.

Charlotte didn't return to the nursery. She turned and walked out the back door. For a moment, she considered a trip to the willows, the cool air, shade from the sun. But that would only make her want Mr. Morland even more.

She walked the lane toward the church. Usually she only took this route with Aunt Nora and Hurst on Sunday morning. The path led her along the border of a hops field. The vines had climbed all the way to the top of the framework, three times as tall as any man—even Mr. Morland.

A man on high stilts greeted her. "Good morning, miss," he called down.

She tipped her head to look up at him. "Good morning."

"Fine crop this year." The man plucked a small bud from the vines. "Take a look." He leaned to hand it to her, but his stilts were too high. He laughed and tossed it into her waiting hands.

Charlotte crushed the bud and brought it to her nose. It smelled like grass but sweeter.

"I'm glad to hear it." Lawfully, these were her hops. Mr. Morland was very proud of them. She'd barely given them any notice, yet they were the foundation of Willowkeep's wealth.

"Be careful up there," she said before continuing on.

He bowed to her from his great height.

When she reached the church, she went round the side toward the little churchyard.

A small family stood dressed in grays and blacks round a newly dug grave. The vicar must have just finished his words because two men came forward and lowered a coffin in. A wee coffin, just like those she'd helped her mother lay her brothers in. These people had lost a baby too. But her brothers weren't allowed to be buried on the church grounds.

The mother dabbed her eyes with a handkerchief. Her husband lifted her hand and kissed it. She smiled up at him.

Charlotte was an intruder in this family scene. She should leave, but the tiny coffin drew her in.

The woman noticed Charlotte tiptoeing across the grass.

She curtseyed as she approached. “Miss Darby. How good of you to come.”

They must be tenants. Charlotte should know them, but she'd still not ventured out that far. She'd need to, now that she was here to stay. Of course they recognized her; she sat in the Willowkeep box every Sunday for service.

The woman's clothes were outdated, like the ones Charlotte used to wear. Overly mended. Dyed to be mourning. Threadbare. Her husband joined them. His coat too was patched and missing a button. He put his arm round his wife, and she leaned heavily on him.

Charlotte looked over at the small grave. All of this was too close to home. If she even blinked, she'd be there again, at the little cemetery outside the city limits, where most of her family lay.

She should say something to this couple. Some sort of consolation or encouragement, but she had nothing. Yet they were waiting for her to speak.

“I've buried my family too,” she blurted. Gaw. Why would she say such a thing? She'd never spoken to anyone about that, 'cept to Mr. Morland. Not even Hurst or her aunt, though she figured they knew her whole story.

“I'm sorry to hear that, Miss Darby,” the woman said. She stepped forward and took Charlotte's hand. “Makes every moment we have with them more precious, don't you think?”

Charlotte nodded. She tried again to find words of comfort. She had nothing to offer. Not even a gift. Or perhaps she did. She was the mistress of Willowkeep, after all.

“That was a lovely service,” Charlotte said. “I know how costly a burial can be. Please let me help. Go to Mr. Morland and tell him I wish to compensate in full the cost of the funeral.”

“It shall be done,” Mr. Morland said.

Charlotte nearly screamed. She'd not heard him approach, and now he stood less than an arm's length from her.

The man took Mr. Morland's hand and pumped it like he was trying to get water from a well. “Thank you, thank you. You've no idea what a toll this last year has taken on us.” He bowed deeply to Charlotte.

“I'm sorry I'm late, Mr. Smith,” Mr. Morland said. “I was delayed with matters of business.” His eyes flashed to Charlotte. “Mrs. Smith. I'm very sorry for your loss.”

“Thank you, Mr. Morland. You're always so good to come.”

Mr. Smith gave another nod to Charlotte and Mr. Morland. He held out his arm. "Come along, then, my dear."

Mrs. Smith took her husband's arm, and they walked away. Two young boys followed them. They must be their sons.

Charlotte watched them until they disappeared round the corner of the church. How lovely they looked, even in their grief.

"That was very generous of you," Mr. Morland said.

Perhaps she should have consulted him first, before she went giving out estate money. "I hope I didn't do wrong."

"On the contrary. You are, as always, very kind."

She couldn't get used to the distance in his voice. To the way his words both pulled her in and pushed her away. She kept her sights on the ground, where her feet had flattened the grass as she'd watched the little casket go down. She couldn't bring herself to meet his eyes.

"The Smith's eldest son Albert was killed last fall when a cart full of hops collapsed on him." He was watching her, she could feel it, as he stood with both his hands clasped behind his back. "During the winter, their daughter Janette fell prey to an infection of the lungs."

She looked up.

"And, of course, you saw them laying to rest their infant daughter, Irene."

Three children in less than a year. She'd never have guessed it from her encounter with them just now.

"Why are you telling me this?"

He shrugged. "You are their landlord. I thought you'd want to know." He bowed to her. "I'd best get back to work. Lots to do before I leave." He turned and strode away. Charlotte took three steps after him, then stopped. There was no point in catching up to him. He'd turned off the lane anyway, taking another way home. Or perhaps off on another errand.

She'd best get back to Susie.

She retraced her steps, down the lane and past the ripening hops. The stilt-man was gone. The world seemed empty.

That poor Smith family, to endure so much loss. And yet, even while the dirt was being laid on Irene's grave, they seemed . . . happy. Not so much at the moment, but there was something about them that spoke of deep and lasting joy. Such a different view from the one she'd seen in Hull.

She wanted a life with happiness and love. According to Mr. Morland, that wouldn't come without the dark times too. If coming to Willowkeep had taught her anything, it was that bad things happened no matter where she lived.

Now Mr. Morland was leaving, taking the brightest light with him.

Maybe that was what Henry VIII hadn't understood. And poor Queen Anne had lost her head because of it. Maybe that was what she needed to understand too.

After the winter of thorns came spring. The roses would bloom again. But if she lost Mr. Morland, she'd be chopping down the whole bush. Killing the thorns, to be sure, but killing the beautiful roses too. Just because she couldn't always see the flowers didn't mean they were not still there.

Charlotte entered the house through the front door. She pulled herself up the stairs, hand over hand on the wooden rail.

In the nursery. Fanny sat on the floor, reading a book to Susie.

Susie looked up at Charlotte. She squirmed away from Fanny and ran at Charlotte as fast as her awkward legs could take her.

Charlotte fell to her knees, holding her sister.

Forget the roses. If she let Mr. Morland leave, she would be chopping off her own head. Maybe that was what Queen Anne was trying to tell her. Let go of her fears and cling to the light, light made all the brighter by the shadows of the night.

Queen Anne hadn't taken away Charlotte's hardships—gaw, Susie had nearly drowned. She'd been kidnapped. No. Anne hadn't removed the trials. Anne had given Charlotte a man who loved her through them, and that was something to hold on to.

"I've been so wrong, little sister. So wrong."

CHAPTER FORTY

HENRY HAD NOT EXPECTED TO see Miss Darby at the funeral. He'd had no idea she'd known about it. Every meeting with her taxed his restraint to the utmost. He'd taken the long way home, adding nearly half a mile to the trip.

Since arriving, he'd accomplished absolutely nothing. He'd paced his office a dozen times. He'd stared out the window. And he'd ruined another handful of goose quills. He might as well call it a day, save he still had an hour left.

Maybe he should ride out. A good long run on the gelding might clear his head. He could go inspect the new pig yard over at the Openshaw's.

There was a very soft, slow knock at his door. So soft he wasn't sure he'd actually heard it. But there it was again.

He opened the door, expecting to find a servant with a broken vase.

Instead, he found a pair of beautiful blue eyes smiling up at him.

He knelt. "Hello, little Susie. What are you doing here all alone?" He stuck his head out the door and checked both ways down the hall. No Charlotte.

Susie stretched out her little hand and held up a note. A letter, folded and sealed with the scrolled *W* of Willowkeep. Her face was alight with excitement for her clandestine mission.

Henry took it from her. "Thank you."

He leaned in, and Susie gave him a wet kiss on the cheek, then scuttled off down the hall and around the corner where, no doubt, Charlotte waited to collect her in her arms.

He cracked the seal and read.

Come to the willows at twilight.

What the devil was Charlotte up to?

Of course he would go, and he would spend the hours between now and then trying not to get his hopes up. But this seemed infinitely better than *no.*

After another delicious meal from Mrs. Hancock, Henry saw his father settled under a blanket with a cup of Mrs. Hancock's restorative and the *Times*. Jane had gone into Kippingham to dine with a friend.

Henry couldn't wait any longer. It wasn't yet dusk, but to sit doing nothing was torture. He paced the grounds behind the Grange until at last the sun hit the western horizon.

He set off at a run, then immediately slowed to a walk. *Don't get ahead of yourself, man.* There was no telling what Charlotte had asked him there for. It could be anything. Or nothing. For all he knew, she wanted the blasted lion removed from the premises.

Don't run, he told himself again.

At last he came to the willow bower. He slowed to a leisurely pace and, parting the branches, stepped in.

Charlotte was there, standing in the cool evening air. She'd changed out of her mourning frock into his favorite blue muslin. Her loose hair drifting across her neck. Eyes like the full moon. Beautiful.

"Miss Darby," he said.

"Mr. Morland." Her finger went to her mouth, but she quickly tucked it behind her back. "I wasn't sure you'd come."

Was she mad? She must know by now he'd go to the ends of the earth if she asked him to. "I will always come."

She smiled. A lovely, full smile, the likes of which he hadn't seen for some time. "Did you have something you wanted to ask me?"

Not that he could think of. Something about Susie, perhaps? Or the Smith family? She'd seemed quite interested in them.

"Ask me," she said again.

Could she possibly mean what he hoped she meant? There was a spark of something in her eyes, playful and merry. Henry tossed all caution overboard. He took both her hands in his. "Miss Darby of Willowkeep, my lovely and anomalous Charlotte from Hull, would you make me the happiest man in the entire kingdom and consent to be my wife?"

She brought his hand to her lips and kissed it. "Yes."

Henry put his arms around her, pulling her close until he thought he might break her. She tucked her head under his chin.

"There goes another perfectly good cravat," she said.

"May I never have another good one as long as I live." He lifted her chin to better see her. "What has changed you?"

"You have changed me. When I saw that letter saying you were off to Woolton Green, I knew I could not live without you."

"I would have resigned a month ago if I'd known it would have this effect."

She laughed. "When I stumbled upon poor Mr. and Mrs. Smith today, I finally understood what you've been trying to tell me. Whatever I must face in the future, it will only be bearable if I'm with you. You are the light that steals away the dark."

He brushed his fingers along her cheek, so soft and tinged with pink from her walk today in the sun. He leaned forward and kissed her. His whole world, right there in his hands.

"I believe I owe Walter Kelton a great debt of gratitude," Henry whispered into her ear.

She laughed softly, and her breath tickled his neck. So he kissed her again. Long and slow. No rush now that she was his forever.

At last he pulled away. He did have one final complication to work through. He had to come clean about the letters. "I have something to confess." He led her to the wicker bench, and they sat facing each other. "But you must promise you will not change your mind."

"What is it?"

"Promise."

"I promise I will not change my mind."

He reached into his coat pocket and withdrew a small bundle of letters.

She snatched them from his hand, jumping to her feet. "You? You took them?" Her face flushed deeper than it ever had before. Perhaps embarrassment that he'd read them, or, more likely, anger.

"I didn't want them to fall into the wrong hands."

"These were my private letters. What makes you so certain that yours are the right hands?" Definitely anger.

He shrugged. "One can never be too careful."

"Indeed," she said. "All this time I thought it was Anne Boleyn, that she was looking out for me. But it was you."

He had no excuse beyond what he'd already told her. He tried to look repentant, but she loved him; she'd agreed to marry him. He had no regrets. "Better me than someone else."

By her frown, she didn't seem to agree. "Did you read them? Of course you read them."

"I did try to resist."

She shook her fistful of crumpled and warped papers at him. "So you have known my feelings all along whilst I've been muddling round in the dark."

She had a right to be vexed, though he would not have done differently given the opportunity to go back. But they were on more equal footing than she supposed.

"On the contrary. These letters caused me quite a bit of agony." He pointed at them as she clutched them in her hands. "I thought your beloved *H* was Hardwick. You've no idea how I've been hating that man."

Charlotte laughed out loud, then slapped a hand over her mouth. "I'm surprised at you, Mr. Morland. For someone who seems to know everything about everyone in the entire parish, you really are blind. Mr. Hardwick is in love with Jane. And she with him, I daresay."

"Yes. That has not entirely escaped my notice. But whatever affection might be between them, it will not amount to anything. He must set his sights on more lucrative ground."

"Because I have taken all his money." Charlotte sat back on the bench with a sigh.

Even with his father's debts paid, Henry didn't have enough to set up a dowry for Jane. Not to the extent Hardwick would need.

"Mrs. Kelton will not condone it," Henry said. "Hardwick will have to marry for money, plain and simple."

"But," Charlotte said. "Once we are married, my money will be your money. And isn't it fitting for a wealthy man to bestow a generous dowry on his own sister?"

Henry chuckled. "You are wise beyond your years. Perhaps you should be the steward."

He reached out to take her hand, but she pulled it away and stood. "No. I'm still in dudgeon at you for reading my letters. Men who steal ladies' private correspondence do not get affection." She folded her arms and glared at him.

"That is fair."

She marched off, brushing past the hanging branches.

Seconds later the leaves parted again. "You will come for dinner though. Tomorrow evening. With Jane and your father. Yes?"

"Thank you for your kind invitation, Miss Darby," Henry said. "We are happy to accept."

"Half seven. Don't be late."

"I'm never late," Henry said.

"No, indeed." Charlotte trotted over and kissed him quickly on the cheek. With one last scowl, she disappeared behind the curtain of green.

Lud, how he loved that girl.

CHAPTER FORTY-ONE

Henry entered the drawing room with Jane on his arm. Charlotte was already there, along with Mrs. Kelton and Hardwick. His father had been too ill to come so they left him with Mrs. Hancock.

Henry gave Charlotte a nod and a bow like he'd always done. He hadn't even told his sister yet of their engagement.

Charlotte had knocked on his workroom door yesterday morning and announced that they should tell their news after dinner. They'd decided on a sum to give Jane. Henry thought it far too high, but Charlotte insisted and would not be moved. And now she seemed nearly out of her skin to tell Jane.

Henry didn't believe Hardwick deserved it, but Charlotte told him not to be resentful.

In any case, Henry had no guarantee Hardwick and Jane would end up together. With this much money to her name, she'd be the target of the Ton.

All their news would have to wait until after they'd eaten.

Henry worked hard to keep his demeanor the same as always. Charlotte failed miserably. She couldn't stop grinning. It was all Henry could do not to pull her from her seat and kiss her.

After dinner, when they were all seated in the drawing room and tea had been poured, Charlotte stood in front of the empty fireplace and cleared her throat. "My dear family, I have something I want to say."

Hardwick laughed. "Say it quick, before you burst."

Henry had been dreading this. He would be seen as the worst kind of social climber to ever walk the land. The scandal would rock the county, if not the whole country. Mrs. Kelton might faint, which, in all honesty, would probably be the best outcome of the whole night.

"Right." Charlotte clasped her hands behind her back. "Mr. Morland and I are going to marry."

Well, she'd made quick work of it.

Hardwick groaned and rubbed his temples.

Jane reached out and grasped Henry's hand. "How wonderful."

Mrs. Kelton gasped and rose to her feet. "The steward? You disgrace the name of Kelton."

Henry had warned Charlotte her aunt would take the news poorly.

"Yes, the steward," Charlotte said. "Now sit down. I'm not finished."

No wonder he loved her.

Mrs. Kelton sat.

Charlotte smoothed her dress and went on. "I know not all of you will rejoice at our news. When I lived in Hull, I thought I were the last of my family. Now look at us." She motioned around the room. "I have more family than ever."

She stopped and seemed lost in her thoughts. It wasn't hard to follow where her mind had wandered. When those blue eyes clouded over, it was her mother lost in the river. Or the brothers she'd never had. Henry wasn't sure she'd be able to keep going.

But she did. She choked out the words, "And family does not abandon family."

Henry stood up beside her, and she leaned into him.

"We are going to look out for each other," Charlotte said.

Hardwick looked up.

"Aunt Nora." Charlotte's voice was stronger now. "Losing two husbands must leave a deep wound. I understand what it's like to lose the ones we love. It would give me and Mr. Morland great pleasure if you would stay here at Willowkeep for as long as you like. Or forever. Whichever you choose." Charlotte nudged Henry with her elbow.

He nodded. "Indeed, it would give us great pleasure."

Mrs. Kelton gracefully dipped her head.

Charlotte turned to Hardwick. "Cousin Hurst. Mr. Morland and I hope you will also consider Willowkeep your home as long you wish."

He stood and bowed. "You are very kind."

"Jane," Charlotte said.

Jane's eyes flitted to Henry, then back to Charlotte.

"Your brother and I have decided to settle on you fifty thousand pounds."

Jane's head spun straight to Hardwick. His teacup fell from his hands, landing on the wooden floor. Tea splashed out, and the porcelain cup shattered.

It was enough to easily live on and to buy a modest estate. Charlotte had plied Henry with questions about how much this cost and how much that. She had very high hopes that Hardwick and Jane would come together.

All Hardwick would need was a good steward to grow his estate into something grand and lasting. The very thought made Henry chuckle.

"I'll fetch someone to clean that up," Hardwick said. He opened the door and mumbled to the footman.

"It is too generous," Jane said. "I cannot accept." She looked at Henry as if he could somehow change Charlotte's mind.

He shrugged. "She would not budge."

Mrs. Kelton stood. "How is it that all the Kelton money is going to the servants?"

"Mother," Hardwick said. "Sit down."

"No. I will not sit down."

One of the maids entered the room. Rachel, the impertinent one. She curtseyed and carried her cleaning box over to the spilled tea.

All talk in the room ceased. Mrs. Kelton would never dare air her personal grievances in front of the help. Except Henry.

The maid gathered up the broken pieces and set them in her box. She sopped up the spilled tea and hurried to the door. With her hands full of her work, she pushed it open with her shoulder.

Had she not done that, Henry would have never noticed the smudge of dark forest green on her dress when she turned and curtseyed. On the shoulder, in the spot she'd just now used to push the drawing room door open.

A smudge that looked remarkably like the one on his own shirt when he'd leaned against the wet paint on the front door of the Grange.

"Rachel Cowden."

She paused.

"What is on your sleeve?"

She spun around, her eyes suddenly wide.

"Where did this paint come from?"

"I don't know, sir."

She was lying. He could see it in her eyes. It was clear as day she'd taken the necklace and earrings and hidden them in his coat. Peters *had* repainted their door, but Rachel had spoiled it again.

Jane ran her fingers across the stain. "This is the paint from our front door. When and for what purpose were you at the Grange?"

Rachel scratched at her throat. "Uh. Mrs. Tafford sent me there."

That couldn't be true. Peters had painted the door quite late in the day, after her work at the house had ended.

"I know that you are lying," Henry said. "I'll ask you one more time before I summon Constable Poole." Henry might just summon him anyway, let her have a go at spending the night in that foul place.

Stealing the jewels and hiding them in his pocket could hardly be her own scheme. Someone must have put her up to it, and it was that person who needed to be ferreted out.

"Think carefully about what you say," Henry said. "I can tell you with certainty that the punishment for thieving is hanging. However, if you are forthright in exactly what happened, perhaps Miss Darby will be lenient."

Charlotte gave her an encouraging nod.

"So tell me," Henry said. "What business did you have at the Grange the night of the ball?"

She looked down at her feet, then toward the door. She couldn't be more than fifteen, and her family desperately needed the money she brought in.

"If I tell you, can I keep my post?"

Poor girl. Someone had used her ill to get at Henry. But still, she was in no position to bargain. "If you come clean, you will be saved from the noose."

Tears spilled from her eyes. She wiped her nose with her work apron. "Someone made me do it. Said I'd lose my job and my family would lose our parcel of land and we'd be evicted if I didn't. Gave me ten pounds."

More than she'd make in a year. "Who?"

The girl's mouth slammed shut. But her eyes darted to Mrs. Kelton.

The old harpy. Henry should have known. Who else was so conniving?

"Was it Mrs. Kelton?" Henry asked.

"How dare you," Mrs. Kelton said, but the guilt on her face was plain enough for everyone to see.

"Was it Mrs. Kelton?" Henry asked again.

The girl nodded.

"Go home," Henry said. "You are done here until further notice."

Rachel raced out the door, sobbing.

Henry turned to Mrs. Kelton. "You paid the girl to steal Miss Darby's jewels and pin it on me?" Henry thought even the old scarecrow wouldn't stoop that low.

Mrs. Kelton huffed. "Even I could see the girl fancied you. But Willowkeep was not meant to go to the steward. It should stay in the family. To Hurst."

"Miss Darby is the only one in this room with any Kelton blood in her veins. You are a self—"

Charlotte grabbed his arm. "No."

"And are you the author of the false entail as well?" Henry asked.

Mrs. Kelton turned her back on them.

Of course she was. An attempt to drive Charlotte into Hardwick's arms. She would have had to marry to keep the estate, and how convenient that Mrs. Kelton's son had been here, ready and waiting.

"Mother?" Hardwick seemed genuinely surprised. Whatever she'd devised, it appeared she'd acted without his knowing. "Don't you see what you've done? They'll never let you stay after this. You have nowhere else to go."

Mrs. Kelton looked at her son. She sank onto her hard Windsor chair. "I did it for you." She brought her handkerchief up to her face and wept, her whole body of black silk shaking.

All eyes went to Charlotte. She turned to Henry.

It wasn't hard to see what Charlotte wanted. The same thing she'd always wanted. A family, even though the pieces of that family were about as broken as Hardwick's tea cup.

Henry took Charlotte's hand. "The sapphires are back where they belong. It is forgotten."

Charlotte smiled up at him. She went over and knelt beside her aunt. "Please. Haven't we had enough? Let's just start over." She placed a hand on her aunt's.

Mrs. Kelton snatched it away.

"She'll be all right," Hardwick said. "Let me get her up to her rooms. It has been a very difficult few months, and she has not been herself for some time."

Hardwick helped his mother to her feet. "Cousin Charlotte. Though it has not always been easy for me, I would like to say, for myself, Willowkeep could not have gone to a more deserving person." He led his mother from the room.

"I should get back to father," Jane said. She clasped both of Charlotte's hands. "Your generosity has left me quite astonished. I don't know what to say. I think it will take some time to sink in."

"I know exactly how you feel," Charlotte said.

"Thank you, Miss Darby. Charlotte." Jane grinned. "Sister. And may I congratulate you both on this happiest of news." She kissed Henry on the cheek.

Henry and Charlotte were left alone in the drawing room.

"That didn't go so well," Charlotte said.

"Did you expect something better?"

She let out a huff. "No. I s'pose not. But I was hoping for the chance to pull out my smelling salts."

Henry laughed.

CHAPTER FORTY-TWO

CHARLOTTE SAT WITH MR. MORLAND on the lawn. Susie crawled through the grass, collecting dandelions. She blew the fuzz, and Puppy barked and chased the tiny seeds as they floated on the breeze.

Aunt Nora hadn't come down to breakfast. Hurst assured Charlotte his mother was having a change of heart but that the change was coming slowly. And not without pain.

Before they'd come outside with Susie, Mr. Morland had helped Charlotte pen a letter to Mr. Regis Farnham, cleric to the Archbishop of Canterbury, requesting a special license to marry without waiting for banns. That was the other thing she'd insisted on.

Why subject herself and Mr. Morland to a big public fuss when they could marry quickly and quietly?

Susie held up a dandelion top in front of Mr. Morland. He gave it a good blow, and Puppy and Susie chased after the fluff.

"What does that word mean?" Charlotte asked.

"What word?"

"That one you keep calling me. *Amamanous*."

"*Anomalous*?" Mr. Morland stood and offered Charlotte a hand.

"Yes."

She linked her arm through his as they followed Susie and Puppy across the garden.

"It means you are unique. There is no one else in the world quite like you."

Charlotte leaned her head against his shoulder. Well, close to his shoulder. He was so very tall. "But wouldn't that mean everyone is anomalous?" Seemed to her all people were different. Everyone had their own ways of doing things. Of thinking. "There's no one in the world quite like Aunt Nora."

Mr. Morland chuckled. "That is very true."

Charlotte reached for Susie's hand. They strolled along to her favorite place. Mr. Morland pulled back the branches for Charlotte and her sister. Charlotte crossed the first bower and went into the second.

She had never brought Susie here before. Her sister stared openmouthed at the lion statue. Mr. Morland picked her up so she could have a better view.

"Lion," Mr. Morland said. "Not real though, just a statue."

Susie ran her hands along the stony surface.

Charlotte tipped her head down and looked inside the mouth.

"Henry." She pulled out the little red rose.

He kissed the top of her head. "Have I told you how much I love it when you call me Henry instead of Mr. Morland, or worse, sir?"

She showed him the little Tudor rose. "Where do you find these?"

He took the flower and turned it over in his hand. "I've not seen one before. We don't have anything like this at Willowkeep. Looks like a Tudor rose. I didn't think such a flower actually existed."

He was teasing her again. It had been quite a disappointment to think that it wasn't Queen Anne taking and reading her notes. Charlotte had put a fair bit of faith in Anne Boleyn. She'd wanted to believe.

But it was Henry all along. Which made sense. Why would the ghost of a queen be loitering round a statue at Willowkeep caring one mite about Charlotte Darby from Hull?

"Be serious," Charlotte said. "If you took my letters, you must have put the roses in."

Henry shook his head. "I am completely in earnest. I've never seen them before."

Susie squealed and squirmed, and Henry put her down. Puppy circled her twice, then muzzled his way out of the bower. Susie went after him, and Henry after Susie.

Charlotte stood alone with the aging lion.

If Henry hadn't put the flowers in, who had? Perhaps Anne was here after all.

She slowly twirled the stem of the rose. It had not been an easy road, but at last she saw the hand of grace in all that had happened.

Whether the story was true or not, Charlotte had found peace here at Willowkeep. Home. A man who loved her. A family. She could never want for more.

"Thank you," she said. In case the queen was near.

A breeze picked up, blowing the cool air off the water. The willows rustled and swirled. Her stray hairs fluttered against her face and neck. As she reached for the curtain of green, she could have sworn she heard a whisper. A soft and gentle voice. *You are welcome, my lady.*

AUTHOR'S NOTE

In 1973, my mother gave birth to a boy with Down Syndrome. He is the youngest of five children.

As my mother lay in the hospital, my father at her side, they faced great uncertainty about caring for a special-needs child. As an infant, it was impossible to tell how functional he would be. Down Syndrome children often have congenital heart problems. They tend to be susceptible to respiratory infections, which quickly turn into serious cases of pneumonia.

Three different doctors offered their advice.

The first suggested that when he got his first cold, they simply not treat it, leaving him to die from the ensuing complications.

The second recommended he be institutionalized as quickly as possible. Forgotten.

The last doctor advised that they take the child home and love him as part of the family. This was the advice they listened to.

John has been the greatest blessing our family has ever received. I cannot imagine life without him. He teaches us unconditional love and the true meaning of family. He is an angel on earth.

When I discovered Jane Austen also had a mentally impaired brother, George Austen, I knew I had to write a story with a special-needs child.

George Austen, ten years older than Jane, was sent to live under the care of Francis Cullum in a nearby village. Very little is known about George, as he is mentioned only a few times in the histories and letters. It seems the Austens paid his room and board, visited him, and by most accounts, he lived a peaceful and pleasant life. It is believed he died in 1838 at the age of seventy-two.

Though some modern historians censure the Austen family for sending him away, given the fate of most disabled people at that time, the Austens behaved in quite a responsible way.

In Willowkeep, little Susan is not specifically intended to be a child with Down Syndrome. I have purposefully not given her a definite type of handicap. She could have any of a number of common mental disabilities. My heart aches for these beautiful children who suffered so unjustly during this and earlier times throughout history.

As to the fate of poor William Papper on the fishing smack *Rising Sun,* that is a story of true human depravity.

Although it occurred much later in the 1800s, most of his story is based on true events. Fifteen-year-old William was murdered in a horrifically slow and cruel way, but the captain responsible was not killed by another man on board—he was tried, convicted, and hanged afterward.

ACKNOWLEDGMENTS

Special thanks to the many people who helped me research this book. Specifically the BBC and all their fine Jane Austen adaptations, Colin Firth *and* Matthew Macfadyen (I like them both), and Pinterest.

My continued thanks to Samantha Millburn. Not only is she patient, but she's also very forgiving. One of these days I'll get the commas right. And a shout out to all the team at Covenant for taking such good care of my babies—I mean, books.

I would like to send a thank-you cupcake (you can pick the flavor) to my beta readers: Michelle, who actually liked all the names in this one. Taffy, who spent hours discussing with me how the story should end, only to have that discussion thrown out the window. Tiffany, she knows why, and I couldn't do it without her. And my writers group, Jaime, Yamile, and Scott.

This book did not come easily. It came with pain and suffering, mostly on the part of my family, as my children were orphans and my husband a widower for a good part of last year. If you see a starving family on the side of the road, feed them. They could be mine.

ABOUT THE AUTHOR

Julie Daines was born in Concord, Massachusetts, and was raised in Utah. She spent eighteen months living in London, where she studied and fell in love with English literature, sticky toffee pudding, and the mysterious guy who ran the kebab store around the corner.

She loves reading, writing, and watching movies—anything that transports her to another world. She picks Captain Wentworth over Mr. Darcy, firmly believes in second breakfast, and never leaves home without her verveine.

Connect on social media

Facebook: Julie Daines Author
Twitter: @juliedaines
Website: www.juliedaines.com
Pinterest: www.pinterest.com/juliedaines